DEATH, ISLAND STYLE

DEATH, ISLAND STYLE

MAGGIE TOUSSAINT

WHEELER PUBLISHING

A part of Gale, Cengage Learning

GALE
CENGAGE Learning·

Detroit • New York • San Francisco • New Haven, Conn • Waterville, Maine • London

GALE
CENGAGE Learning®

LIBRARY OF CONGRESS CATALOGING-IN-PUBLICATION DATA

Toussaint, Maggie.
    Death, island style / by Maggie Toussaint.
        pages ; cm. — (Wheeler Publishing large print cozy mystery)
    ISBN-13: 978-1-4104-4811-8 (softcover)
    ISBN-10: 1-4104-4811-8 (softcover)
    1. Large type books. I. Title.
PS3620.O89D43 2012b
813'.6—dc23   2012001532

Published in 2012 by arrangement with Tekno Books and Ed Gorman.

Printed in the United States of America
1 2 3 4 5   16 15 14 13 12

FD122

This book is dedicated to Craig
for indulging my bone-deep need for
beach vacations.

ACKNOWLEDGMENTS

Over the years I've been blessed with excellent critique partners. I'm grateful for their kind assistance and expert opinions. My pals JL Wilson, Judi Fennell, Lynne Connolly, Donna Caubarreaux, and Diana Cosby provided invaluable input on this book. Also, my longtime critique partner Marilyn Trent did a final read-through with a fresh set of eyes. My writer friends in First Coast Romance Writers and at the Book Spa helped me come up with the book's title. Like fine wine, good friends keep improving with age. Thanks also to two great editors, Deni Dietz and Alice Duncan.

CHAPTER 1

One of the perks of my new life is walking on the beach. I love to sink into the crisp morning sand, leaving behind perfect impressions of each plump toe, slender arch, and narrow heel. Those footprints proclaim to the world that MaryBeth Cashour lives here on Sandy Shores Island.

At least until the wind changes, the tide comes in, or someone else tramples my tracks. Oh, who was I kidding? My footprints were transitory, just like me. That's the worst part about starting over, figuring out who I am and what I'm doing.

I turn to face the wind, taste the salty spray on my face, and bask in the unfamiliar warmth of the October sun against my skin. Back in Maryland, a warm fall day like this was called Indian summer, but here in coastal Georgia, short-sleeved weather is standard fare. In time, I'd relinquish that northern concern that a howling snowstorm could hit at any minute, but for now, I was still stuck in that cold weather mindset of a nasty storm on my horizon.

After my husband of ten years drowned unexpectedly in April, I sold everything but one framed picture of the two of us and moved back home, only to discover that my mom had kept her terminal cancer a secret. I spent the next three months watching her die.

Two deaths in three months gave me the willies. Worse, it made me responsible for all their possessions. Grandmother Esther's gilt-edged porcelain lamp was a family heirloom, but I hated it. And Uncle Wallace's faded latch-hooked rug? It had clearly seen better days. The marble-topped buffets I listed on e-Bay, and I gave away Mom's junky old car, which was in worse shape than mine. The horrid checkered tile bathroom floor I left as was, and the house sold anyway, thank goodness.

By the time I'd finally gotten to the point of sorting through Mom's personal papers in August, I believed I could see daylight. I couldn't wait to finish this chore and do something, anything, else, but I learned a hard lesson. Be careful what you wish for. The information I discovered in her bank lock box knocked the wind out of me.

I'm adopted.

You would think that being thirty-five years old, I might have heard about this by that time, but my mom never mentioned it. Not once. I can't blame my dad for his silence, as he passed away two decades ago, but Mom had years upon years to tell me the truth.

She sewed my prom dress, mailed me crafty care packages all through college, and single-handedly created beautiful decorations for my wedding. No mention of my adoption. Not even a hint. And it wasn't like her death was unexpected. She knew the end was coming as surely as one ocean wave follows the next.

Secrets. I hate them. And yet the shores of my life were littered with them, much like the scattered shells dotting this deserted beach.

I stopped at another deposit of seashells and chucked them one at a time into my plastic pail. Justine Mossholder, the vibrant woman who'd sold me her gift shop named Christmas by the Sea, told me that part of owning the craft store was continually harvesting shells to make into Christmas ornaments. "Tourists love buying these local crafts as souvenirs," she'd said.

She'd left detailed instructions on how to

make oyster shell Santas, scallop shell angels, and sand dollar snowmen. "Paint the shell until the color suits your eye," she'd said. "Use a dollop of glue to hold the ornament together, and accent it with a clump of tulle."

Her instructions might as well have been in Greek. Turns out I had no eye for color, glue guns hated me, and I couldn't tell tulle from organza. So here I was, collecting shells as instructed, only I didn't want the nice big paintable shells.

I wanted the little itty bitty shells. I picked up one shell, then another, but that pace wasn't satisfying. I wanted great glopping handfuls of them. Something about these little shells felt urgently right.

I couldn't explain my sudden unfathomable craving for them, but I needed these tiny shells as much as I needed air. With increasing fervor, my fingers grabbed clumps of miniature colored shells and tossed them in my pail. It was as though I was in a timed contest, and I only got to keep as many shells as I could cram into my hot-pink pail in the next ten minutes.

Stupid, I know, but so was trying to start fresh when I'd lost myself along the way. I'd gone from functioning as a devoted wife and competent receptionist to a berserk seashell-grabber. What was I going to do?

I had no friends.

I had no family.

I had no roots.

All I had was a yellowed piece of paper that said I was adopted. How the hell was I supposed to deal with that? My whole life was a lie.

My throat tightened. I sat down and allowed the shells and dry sand to drizzle through my curled fingers. How could I figure out who I was? My past was a jumble of secrets, my lonely future too dismal to contemplate.

I touched my gold heart-shaped locket, a treasured gift from Bernie on our first anniversary. Engraved inside were the words, "All my love forever." Hollow words for a hollow life. I'm supposed to grieve and go on with my life, but the little kid in me wanted to stand up and shout, What happened to my Happily Ever After?

That sappy fairy tale sentiment wasn't real. It was fiction, and I'd best realize that MaryBeth Cashour was a ghost of a person.

The offshore wind whipped my hair under my glasses. I flicked the tangled locks away from my eyes and stared out at the sea buoys on the watery horizon. Sea gulls lazily rode on currents of air above the cresting surf. I huffed out my disgust at their free-wheeling lifestyle. Oh, to be so unencumbered. To let go and glide on the wind. If only I could be so free, so uninhibited.

After all the changes of late, I couldn't fathom living like that. I needed to know what was coming next. I needed structure and anchors to keep me grounded.

The tides were regular. I'd learned that in a few short weeks. Natives of McLinn County, Georgia, set their watches by tidal fluxes. High water meant big waves, depth in the winding creeks, and delightful on-shore breezes. Low water meant lots of beach sand, fish and crabs that could be caught moving with the tide, and offshore breezes. And nasty, biting flies.

I smacked one that was stupid enough to land on my ankle. *Take that you bloodsucking varmint.* I buried the insect carcass in the dry sand. My gaze drifted back to the hopeful blue sky above the cresting waves and noticed those sea gulls were still wheeling over the same part of the sea as before, just off the beach. That was unusual.

I caught sight of a dark shadow in the water. Something was out there beyond the breakers. Something big. Like a dolphin or a shark. Only it wasn't swimming. It was drifting with the current.

Curiosity had me rising to my feet. I brushed the sand and crushed shells from my Bermuda shorts and cupped my hands around my glasses. The dark shape appeared to be quite long, maybe six feet long was my guess. And it was definitely cylindrical, like a log.

The object approached the shore. It bobbed in the surf, slowly rolling over, a dark back, a light underbelly. That's when it hit me. My upside-down life wasn't completely ruined. Things could be a lot worse.

I could be the dead guy floating in the ocean.

CHAPTER 2

Eight hours later, I couldn't get the graphic image of the man out of my head. His faceless body played endlessly through my thoughts in my own private horror reel.

Thank God I hadn't known him.

For a moment, a teeny-tiny moment, when I'd realized a body was washing up on the shore, I'd worried it was my drowned husband whose body had never been recovered. Ridiculous, I know, as my husband drowned more than six hundred miles north of here.

Even so, shock and horror had grabbed hold of me and wouldn't let go. All day long in my Christmas store, I'd felt like I was viewing the world from beneath the water. I interacted with customers as needed, but my responses had been superficial.

This morning the police had asked me a zillion questions, and all I could tell them was I didn't know. I didn't have any male friends down here. I didn't know if anyone in the community was missing.

Some warped sense of ownership about finding the dead guy had kept me standing on the beach long after the police detectives had swarmed over him. I should have left well enough alone. I should have gone to work immediately instead of opening up two hours late.

Could be that's why they'd questioned me so extensively. But it wasn't like there were any other people around they could pester. Most of the houses at my low-rent end of the island were vacant summer rentals.

Children chattered happily around me, bringing me back to the reality of the moment. The cream-colored walls of my shop's back room amplified the noise until it seemed I had sixty kids in there instead of six.

I should have canceled the craft class I'd scheduled for six- to ten-year-olds this afternoon, but this was my first class. I didn't want to disappoint the kids or be labeled as unreliable. So here I was, standing in the middle of chaos and wishing I was home with a dozen chocolate donuts.

Eight-year-old John Curtis Washington was eating seashells. His impish smile showcased his missing teeth and his devil-may-care personality.

I battled through my mental slumber and leveled my glue gun at him. "Don't eat that! Spit it out."

"I'm not gonna eat these old seashells, Miz Cashour. I only wanna know how they taste." John Curtis spat the shells out of his mouth. Six plopped onto his paper plate of crafting supplies. Three shot over and glommed onto Claudia Barber's cute Christmas mouse.

"Oooh! Make him stop," Claudia yowled as she flicked the damp coquina shells off her decorated walnut. Her hip-length chestnut braids shivered with outrage. "Boys are so gross."

Across the table, Claudia's twelve-year-old brother, Steven, leered at the googly eyes he'd used for breasts on his X-rated Christmas mice. Privately, I agreed with Claudia about the antics of young boys, but someone had to act like an adult in this room. That someone was me. "Let's all settle down."

Daytona Washington hummed along with the Christmas music I was playing. "I'm ready for glue," she sang out in time with the chorus of "Gloria in Excelsis Deo."

At six, Daytona was the same age my oldest child would have been, if I hadn't miscarried. Her big brown eyes and curly black hair sliced into my heart in a would-have-been, should-have-been sort of way.

"That's lovely, dear." Did my voice sound as fake to her as it did to me? I lifted the felt triangles of her Christmas tree and glued them onto a cardboard form I'd pre-cut for this crafting class. Amazing how you could function and yet be haunted by a dead man rolling in the surf.

I summoned a compliment from my beleaguered brain. "I really like the way you used blue circles for your ornaments. And the gold glitter makes this extra special."

"It's fairy dust. For all the magic of Christmas," she said.

The gold glitter stuck to my glue gun and under my stubby fingernails. I'd be peeling it off for days to come. I surely could use a little magic in my life. "Steven, why don't you help Claudia measure that ribbon?"

Steven glared at me, but grudgingly got up to help his little sister. His yellow T-shirt read "Parents for sale, buy one get one free."

I should've insisted only one craft could be done per class. As it was, John Curtis was making jewelry from beads and shells, Claudia and Steven were doing the Christmas mice out of walnuts, Daytona was working with felt, and cute little Tyson, bless his heart, was making a mosaic picture frame using my itty-bitty shells and doing a fabulous job.

Jolene was making sparkly sequin sandwiches with white craft glue on her plate. My heart went out to poor little craft-challenged Jolene. I knew exactly how awful it felt to be surrounded by talented, creative people.

Trying to instruct six very different children simultaneously was impossible. I would have had more success trying to herd the lizards on the island.

My gaze rested on Jolene again. She wore a floppy faded cloth hat, the brim pinned up sailor style with diaper pins. Wisps of red hair straggled out from under the hat. With her fair skin, she'd probably been told to stay out of the sun her entire life. Hard to do on a southern island.

I should do something to engage her interest. My goal had been for my students to take home a completed craft after each class. Jolene's glue globs didn't fit that bill. I carried the basket of pre-cut felt over to her. "Would you like to make a Christmas tree?"

Jolene's upper lip curled into a sneer that would've done Elvis proud. "Felt is for babies."

"Is not." Daytona stuck out her tongue.

I tried again. "Maybe you'd like to try one of the other crafts? Beading? Shell mosaics? Christmas mice?"

"Nah. I like what I'm doing."

"Let me know if you change your mind." In frustration, I shoved my felt basket into a work counter cubbyhole. Why did Jolene come if she didn't want to make crafts? I didn't get it. I glanced at the clock over the sink. Only fifteen more minutes until I could go home and relax.

Without warning, the dead man rolled in my mental surf. Chills swept over me. My fingernails dug into my palms. I was just barely aware of the conversation going on around me in the room.

"Whatcha got there, Jolene, big green machine?" John Curtis asked.

Jolene's chin went out. "More than you. That's for sure. And I'm not a machine."

John Curtis's big brown eyes lit up. "Yes, you are. You're a globby gluing machine."

"Shut up," Jolene said.

"String bean, sewing machine, snarly queen, Jolene," John Curtis taunted.

"You moron." Jolene flung one of her sequin globs at John Curtis. He ducked, and it struck me solidly in the head. *Thwack.*

I jolted out of my mental fugue, but I was

too late. Jolene picked up another glob and flung it at John Curtis, who ducked under the table. I sustained another hit.

Daytona hummed and skipped about the room as if glue glob warfare were an everyday occurrence in her life. Steven moved closer to his sister and glared at Jolene, who made sure none of her sticky arsenal got anywhere near the Barbers.

John Curtis fired off a shower of little seashells at Jolene.

"That's enough." I stepped between them and got pelted with more seashells and another wad of sequined glue.

John Curtis smirked. "She started it."

"I'm finishing it." I snatched Jolene's soggy plate of glue bombs out of her hands and lifted it high over my head. "Time to clean up your stations and get ready for your parents to come pick you up."

"Those are mine. Give 'em back." Jolene shoved me, her pasty hands tearing at my bright green Christmas by the Sea craft apron.

At the sudden motion, the remaining glue globs rolled off the plate into my hair. If I'd carried any of my three babies to term, none of them would've been contrary and craft-challenged like Jolene, right? They would've all inherited my mother's crafty genes. I'd once heard that inherited traits could skip generations.

Oh wait. Mental head slap. I wasn't my crafty mother's biological offspring. My kids would've been fated to be just as craft-challenged as Jolene and me. Sobering thought.

I exhaled shakily. My eyes were not tearing up.

Jolene pointed at my hair and exploded with laughter. She laughed so hard I thought she would hurt herself. Self-consciously, I smoothed my hand through my war-zone hair, but the glue globs were stuck fast.

John Curtis tugged on my arm. "Can we make killer sharks next time?"

Next time. I shuddered involuntarily. I'd advertised this mayhem as a series of four weekly classes. I'd never make it through all four Wednesdays without killing at least one kid. But there was always the hope that Jolene would hate the experience so much she wouldn't return.

Thinking of sharks reminded me of the dead man. I shivered. "We'll see."

Jolene pranced in place by the glass-paned back door, like a dog that needed to go to the bathroom. If I let her out, would she run away and never come back? I could only hope.

"There's my dad." Jolene reached for the door handle.

"Thanks for coming. I hope you had fun." The words came out automatically, and I hated myself for sounding so accommodating. I had a conscious need to please everyone, even if they were evil and mean like Jolene the gluing machine.

"Tyler, time to stop for the day," I said as I policed wayward sequins from Jolene's area.

Tyler blinked in astonishment. "I'm not finished."

He'd glued one side of the frame, with all the shells equally spaced and of varying shades of white to off-white. After being raised by a perpetual crafter, I knew art when I saw it. His mosaic would be stunning. "Class is over for today. You can work on your frame next time."

His straight blond hair capped his round face like a cereal bowl. "You won't let anything happen to it?"

"Promise. I'll keep it safe for you."

The kids dribbled out, and I straightened my craft room. The loose seashells I dumped back in my colorful pails. The felt squares I jammed in a cubbyhole with the ribbon spools. The defective glue gun I threw in the trash.

Two months ago, buying this Christmas craft shop seemed a no-brainer. My mom, my adopted mom that is, always talked about owning a place like this. After my world imploded, I had no dreams, so I'd glommed onto hers. Except for the disastrous craft class, things seemed to be okay here at Christmas by the Sea.

Except *okay* was a relative term. I wasn't especially crafty. Craftiness wasn't an acquired skill, and I had the glue globs in my hair to prove it.

Finding the dead guy today wasn't okay either. According to the two cops who'd interviewed me, no one had drowned in McLinn County in three years. Though they weren't outright blaming me, once they knew about my death magnet past, I felt sure they'd blame me for the man's death.

Then where would I be?

In jail?

The door opened. Daisy Pearl Washington swooped in, all two hundred plus pounds of her, with her son John Curtis in tow. "Miz Cashour?"

"Please, call me MaryBeth." I untied the strings to my craft apron and hung it up on a peg inside the craft cabinet. "What can I do for you?"

"John Curtis has something he wants to

say to you," Daisy Pearl said.

I noticed she had her small son by the ear. My back ached, my stomach growled, and I thought longingly of those chocolate donuts I deserved to eat for supper. "Let's hear it."

"I apologize for my behavior," John Curtis said to his shoes. "I'm sorry for acting out. I'll be better next time."

Oh dear, I'd never been especially good with apologies. They made me want to apologize, too. Only I hadn't done anything wrong. Taking a deep breath to collect my thoughts, I ran my fingers through my hair and got tangled up in a glue gob. My new hair ornaments. How could I have forgotten about them?

"Apology accepted," I finally managed.

"Dear Lord, what's that stuck on your head?" Daisy Pearl twisted John Curtis's ear. "You do that?"

"No, ma'am."

Daisy Pearl let John Curtis go. "Since she's already cleaned up over here, you go on back over to the bakery and tell Peachy you earned an hour in the kitchen washing dishes."

His lower lip jutted out. "An hour? That's not fair."

"It's fair, all right. You mess up, you gotta pay the piper, and boy, did you mess up.

Now scoot on over there while I take care of Miz Cashour's hair."

"Yes, ma'am."

I wrung my hands together as he left. I knew a little about the formidable Daisy Pearl. She and her husband Peachy Washington owned Sweet Things, the bakery and ice cream shop next door to Christmas by the Sea. So far I'd met ten of her children. Rumor was there were twenty-three Washington siblings out there. From my childless perspective, she seemed especially blessed, but then I'd barely survived today's class.

How had she raised so many children and not gone stir crazy? Or killed a couple of them? You'd think with twenty-three kids that at least one of them would be contrary like Jolene.

Yet Daisy Pearl retained an ageless grace and a full head of dark hair. Since adoption was on my mind these days, I'd been meaning to ask Daisy Pearl if any of her kids were adopted. Except we weren't close enough friends for me to ask such a personal question like that.

After today's eye-opening experience, I had second thoughts about motherhood. I'd only had six kids for an hour, and they'd wrecked my workroom and trashed my hair. I already dreaded next week's craft session.

Maybe I'd be blessed with appendicitis and have to cancel.

"Sit down in that chair, child," Daisy Pearl said in a no-nonsense tone. "So I can take a look at that hair."

I pushed my glasses up my nose, hoping to preserve what little dignity I had left. "I'll be fine. I'm sure everything will wash right out."

"We'll just see about that." Daisy dampened a sponge and dabbed at a glue glob in my hair. With work-thickened fingers, she tugged and tugged.

"Ouch." I batted her hand away, pressing my fingers into my scalp to ease the smarting sensation. "That hurts."

"Uh-hmmm. It's a rat's nest all right. We better get you next door to Mr. Russ."

"The pharmacist? Why?"

Russ Marchone had growled at me on both previous occasions when I'd entered his pharmacy. I wasn't sure who'd wronged him, but his perpetually grumpy mood left me cold. I'd rather have yucky hair than throw myself on his mercy.

Daisy Pearl ignored my questions and guided me out the back door. She outweighed me two pounds to my one, and I didn't have any choice once she latched onto my arm. No wonder John Curtis had come over and apologized once she had hold of his ear. Thank God my ears were safely glued to my hair.

I got the feeling that Daisy Pearl didn't have any problem with self-confidence or courage. I was on shaky ground in both of those areas when it came to looking out for myself.

Once upon a time, I'd had no trouble lighting into the dry cleaners when they'd missed a stain on Bernie's suit, but when they'd melted buttons on my one silk shirt, I hadn't complained. Stupid, I know, but that's how my brain worked. Bernie's work clothes were important. Mine weren't.

The Island Pharmacy held the usual beach essentials of sunscreen, candy, and toiletries. Daisy Pearl marched me down the personal hygiene aisle past rows of tampons, menstrual pads, and condoms to the high counter in the back of the store. "Mr. Russ, we got us an emergency," Daisy Pearl said.

Russ Marchone peered down from his high seat as if in judgment, his customary scowl firmly in place. I cringed at his sweeping perusal. He wasn't much older than me, but he had a way of looking right through a person that set my teeth on edge.

Under the fluorescent lights, his white lab

coat gleamed as brightly as the toothy Halloween display by the cash register. Those intense brown eyes of his swept my length and came back to rest on my hair. His eyebrows beetled together.

Heat rose up my neck to my already steaming face. He had to be thinking I was utterly incompetent. Not a strand of his hair was out of place, and I knew for a fact he'd worked a ten-hour shift. I steeled myself for his nasty comment, and he didn't disappoint.

"What the hell happened to you?" he asked.

"Now you know I don't tolerate swear words." Daisy Pearl waggled her finger at him. "Uncork one of those fancy potions you keep back there and fix this Christmas lady's hair."

Surely he would refuse. As I interpreted the body language of his tightened jaw, he was on the verge of tossing us out of his store. I desperately wanted to run out of there, but his perverse mood made me mouthy. I turned to Daisy Pearl. "I knew this was a bad idea."

Russ sighed in defeat. "Come on back here so I can diagnose the problem."

Crap. He'd tricked me by agreeing to help. And I'd sounded so bitchy. My feet stuck fast to the gleaming tile floor. Did I really want the Grim Pharmacist touching my hair?

Nope.

Time to backpedal and go with my first instinct — run home and jump in the shower. I started backing up. "I can get the tangles out myself."

"Go on. Git up there." Daisy Pearl pushed me forward and blocked my escape with her considerable bulk. "Let the man put his edumacated brain on this problem, and you'll be good as new."

Russ stood. "You might as well do as she says. Daisy Pearl is a veritable force of nature."

"I can see that." I knew she meant well, but her take-charge attitude had me feeling like I was a screwed-up kid who didn't know any better. Honest to God, how many thirty-five-year-olds got glue globs stuck in their hair?

The same number of them that found dead bodies on the beach. The sound of rolling surf filled my thoughts. Once again the dead man stared at me with his sightless eyes. I blinked to clear my head. I couldn't do anything about the dead guy tonight, but I could try to salvage my hair.

I took a centering breath and joined the

pharmacist behind the counter. I'd never stood this close to Russ Marchone before. He wasn't as tall as I thought, and he smelled as briskly clean as an ocean breeze. His ever-present scowl didn't dim. No smiling for this man.

If Bernie had been the pharmacist, he would've smiled at everyone and welcomed them to his store. But my late husband was long gone, and I was at the mercy of a scowling stranger, trying to forget about the events of this lousy day.

I sighed out another big breath as I slid onto the warm padded stool he'd vacated. My face heated more at the thought of our bodies sharing heat. Lord. How could I get through this if I got flustered over being so close to a man?

Testosterone swirled around me like a numbing fog. My brain, so long attuned to the steady reliability of my husband, wanted to let someone else take charge. I'd been muddling along for a few months, making one bad decision after another. Allowing someone else to make decisions for me would be a gift from heaven. Oh, that I could drift through life again.

I shook my head to clear it. I must be going insane. That was the only explanation for my response to the pharmacist. After all,

I was a capable woman. I didn't need a man to fix my life.

He reached in front of me to close the file displayed on his computer. "To protect the privacy of my customers," he explained.

"I'm sorry to put you to so much trouble," I stammered.

Russ Marchone's deep-set brown eyes could double as an X-ray machine. His full head of dirty blond hair was beginning to gray at the temples. Though his blade of a nose was a veritable ski slope, his olive skin tone gave him a healthy glow. He had what might be politely termed a burly physique, but I didn't hold that against him.

If I'd been a man, I'd be called burly, too. According to the insurance industry standards, at five foot four, I was a bit short for my one hundred forty pounds. I swallowed thickly. What must he think of the numerous sparkly sequined globs lodged in my hair?

"What did you try on this?" he asked.

"Elbow grease," Daisy Pearl eased down on the padded wicker sofa in front of the pharmacy counter. "That stuff didn't budge. It's stuck fast."

"What kind of glue is it?" Russ added.

Hating that they were talking over me, I found my voice. "Craft glue."

His hands felt whisper soft in my hair. No tugging at all. A shiver of awareness zipped down my spine. I'd never thought to feel a man's hands in my hair again. A pang of loneliness assailed me, opening the internal wounds that grief hadn't healed, supercharging my senses.

His scent penetrated the testosterone fog. Sorta citrusy, sorta manly, sorta, well, yummy. That stopped me. What was the matter with me? I'd never acted this way around a man before. The overwhelming events of the day must have eroded my self-control.

With concerted effort, I put my libido in neutral, kept my gaze on Daisy Pearl, and knotted my hands in my lap.

He dabbed at my hair a bit longer. It was hard to tell if he was having any success with that dour face. I didn't want to waste his time or mine. "Well? How bad is it?"

His grunted reply struck me as funny. I bit my lip to keep from laughing. Then I heard him rummaging through his cabinets. Another wisecrack boiled out of my mouth before I could stop it. "Sending out for reinforcements?"

Yikes. I should've clamped my hand over my mouth. I couldn't believe I was joking around with this man I barely knew. A man who gave off "I'm not interested in being friendly" vibes to everyone within a fifty-mile radius.

Perhaps that's why I felt comfortable with him. Because I wasn't interested in a romantic involvement either. It hurt too much when someone you loved died. I wasn't ready to go through that ever again.

My teeth gritted at the distinctive snip, snip of scissors. In the back of my mind, I'd been holding out for a pharmaceutical miracle. Silly me. The cold hard reality of my hair disaster washed over me once again.

"Good as new." Russ tossed the hairy globs in a shiny metal trash can.

With caution, I patted my tangle-free head. What I wouldn't give for a mirror right now. "Can you tell where you cut?"

"Looks fine to me," he growled.

His gruff tone alarmed me. The sooner I left here, the better. I slid off his stool and edged away. "Thanks. I appreciate your help. Let me know if I can return the favor."

A corner of his mouth quirked up momentarily. Maybe that was as close to a smile as he ever got. Wasn't much when you considered the full range of facial expression, but Russ wasn't exactly a member of the happy club.

Guess he never stood between kids throwing glue globs. Well, I hadn't planned this disaster. It had just happened.

"You come on over to Sweet Things when you close up, Mr. Russ." Wicker creaked as Daisy Pearl lumbered to her feet. "I'll buy you an ice cream cone."

Russ grunted in reply. He slid back onto his stool and plugged himself back into his computer. The strong silent type made me nervous. I'd always gone for a man who was comfortable in his own skin, a man who was true blue, like my late husband. A shaft of fresh pain pinged my heart as I left.

Outside, I thanked Daisy Pearl for her help, fumbled in my purse for my keys, hopped in my dark green Jeep, and drove home. It wasn't until I turned off the car that I chanced to look in the rearview mirror at my haircut. Six large holes were gouged out of my straight, shoulder-length hair. It looked like the cookie monster had taken big chomps out of my head.

The dead guy had better hair than me. A wail rose from my throat, and I let it come. Trouble was, once I started crying, I couldn't stop. I wanted my old life back. I didn't want to have anything to do with dead guys on the beach, wild kids, or grumpy pharmacists.

CHAPTER 3

Business was brisk on Thursday. Out-of-towners oohed and aahed over my red and green displays. A balding man in a tropical shirt asked, "Don't you ever get tired of listening to Christmas music?" A woman with a strong Jersey accent asked me if I made the ornaments, and I told her the truth: all the items for sale in the shop are hand-painted.

But not by me. I'd tried. Lord knows I'd tried. Only my results weren't commercial like Justine Mossholder's, the former shop owner. Mine were laughable, and I'd hidden them away underneath my beading supplies.

What the heck would I do when I ran through Justine's hand-painted stock? Last I heard, she was living large in Vegas. Painting seashells and plastic sharks probably never crossed her mind these days.

I glanced at my watch. One more hour to

go, and I could close up for the day. Under twinkling white lights, I perused the musical library Justine had amassed during the ten years she'd owned the shop. The collection ranged from ethereal children's choirs with orchestral accompaniment to caroling house pets.

It was the latter that held my attention now. I quickly queued up the *Christmas Pets* CD and was treated to animals singing, howling, and panting in time with holiday music. Cute. Not something I could take all day, but it definitely put zip in my flagging step.

My head itched. I removed the bright red baseball cap I'd been wearing. This morning I'd glanced in the mirror, cried over the checkerboard gaps in my hair, and donned a hat.

This latest disaster didn't prove that I couldn't take care of myself. It had been an accident, one that could've happened to anyone. I was as competent as the next woman.

I ran my fingers through my seriously flattened hat hair but that didn't perk it up any. I bent over and fluffed it. Just then the door played the first seven notes of "The First Noel."

I had another customer. Straightening, I

observed a vaguely familiar couple entering the shop. He was a brawny white man. She was a whipcord-thin black woman. Both wore linen blazers, black T-shirts, pressed jeans, and dark reflective sunglasses. They scanned the shop then honed in on me behind the sales counter.

Dogs barked, and cats meowed in an almost melody. Hat in hand, I froze in recognition. These were the detectives working the dead man's case. They'd grilled me at length yesterday.

My first impressions of the pair remained true. Muscle-bound Kent Schorr looked like he'd be more at home in a weightlifting competition. Trim Shanelle Monroe walked like she had chips on both shoulders. Their unsmiling faces had me worrying they'd learned something unsavory about my character. Was there an unpaid parking ticket in my past?

I gulped and tried to hide my nervousness. "Detectives. What can I do for you?"

Detective Schorr thrust a clear plastic bag at me. "Do you recognize this?"

As I stared at the bag in his hands, dogs yipped out the notes to "Jingle Bells." I wanted to yip too. The Christmas scents of evergreen and cinnamon surrounded me, but the normally soothing aromas grated on my ragged nerves. I had a very bad mental equation going through my head. Cops plus a dead body equals MaryBeth in trouble.

Inside the bag was a touristy Christmas ornament. The grinning plastic shark with bloody teeth adorned with a cheesy seashell necklace proclaiming the current year was a staple in my shop. A hot seller, too, although I didn't get the connection between bloody sharks and Christmas ornaments.

"This is one of our Christmas sharks. I've got a bin full of them for sale over there." I pointed out the container in case they couldn't make out the cheerful green shark hopper through their dark glasses.

"Do you remember selling a shark to a man in his late fifties recently?" Detective Monroe asked.

My stomach sank down to my toenails. The barking dogs faded from my hearing as my gaze narrowed to their alert cop faces. The one-two punch of dismay and fear sent me reeling. I clutched the edge of the counter for balance. "This is about the dead guy? He had one of my sharks?"

Detective Schorr nodded tersely. His head barely bobbled on that strongly corded neck.

"I don't remember seeing any tall men in the shop recently. Most of my customers are women or young families." I stepped back from the counter, fingering the brim of my hat in my hands. "Do you know who the dead guy was?"

"Not yet," Detective Monroe replied. "The medical examiner hopes to make a positive identification soon."

The terrible image of the corpse rolling in the foaming surf came back to me. Black suit. White shirt. Missing eyes. Red bullet hole in his white shirt. I shuddered. "How?"

"The usual ways. Fingerprints. Dental records. Tattoos. In the meanwhile, we're following up on the shark. Are these items exclusive to your shop?"

I glanced at the bagged shark again. Sharks belonged in scary movies and nightmares and the shadowy depths of the ocean. "The former owner of Christmas by the Sea added the bloody teeth and the shell necklace to the plastic shark. I've got boxes of them yet to be painted."

Violins swelled from the shop speakers as the "Nutcracker March" began. "Arf yip-yip-yip-yip woof arf yip-meow," the animals sang. The zany combination of sounds added to the unreal sensation of this interview. I was past ready for this interview to be over.

"The former owner, that would be —"

41

Detective Shanelle Monroe checked a previous page of her pocket-sized notepad. "Justine Mossholder. Do you know if Miz Mossholder had any enemies?"

I eased in a shaky breath. They weren't after me. "Justine is the sweetest old lady I ever met."

Detective Schorr's cheek muscle twitched. "Justine is my third cousin. Trust me, she's not sweet. We think the John Doe on the beach was here checking this place out. We suspect he was interested in either my cousin or you."

"Me?" I squeaked. "Why would anyone check me out?"

"You tell us," Detective Monroe said.

My heart pounded in my throat. They weren't going to pin this man's death on me. They couldn't, could they? The basis of our legal system was innocent until proven guilty. And I was oh-so-innocent. I gestured with my hands, accidentally knocking my baseball cap off. "I'm boring. I'm dull. I can't imagine why anyone would check out a widow like me."

"For someone who's boring and dull, you sure have an unusual hairstyle." Detective Monroe's locks were neatly sleeked back in a clubbed ponytail. "What happened to you?"

Heat steamed up my neck, my face, and off the tips of my ears. I crammed my baseball cap on my head to hide my icky hair. "I had a crafting accident last night. Glue ended up in the wrong place and had to be cut out. That's all. I guarantee you I'm boring and dull."

"We checked you out, Miz Cashour," Detective Monroe stated matter-of-factly. "Your husband was declared dead last spring in Maryland. Would you care to elaborate on his demise?"

Oh, Lordy, they knew about Bernie. Probably about Mom, too. I was doomed to be a harbinger of death. Would they arrest me? I worked to unclench my jaw. "Bernie? What does his passing have to do with anything?"

"Walk us through his death," Monroe insisted.

I momentarily closed my eyes against the searing flash of loss. It hurt to think about that painful time. "I'd rather not."

Detective Monroe leaned close, too close. "We'd rather you did."

Just like that, I was awash in a flood of memories from that fateful night. The smell of brownies filled the house. Fresh carnations adorned our dining room table. When the doorbell rang, I'd been annoyed at the interruption because I'd been in the middle of making meatloaf, Bernie's favorite dish, for his homecoming dinner.

Two uniformed police officers stood at my door. They informed me of Bernie's certain death. I'd dropped the egg carton I was holding and spent the next week holding my breath, hoping against hope Bernie would miraculously materialize in the flesh on my doorstep.

Though six months had gone by, that breathless agony of waiting seemed like yesterday.

With effort, I pulled myself together. These detectives didn't need to witness my emotional meltdown. I gave them the dry facts. "Bernie was coming home from a business trip. While crossing a bridge, he had an accident. Witnesses claimed his car plunged into the storm-swollen river."

"His body wasn't recovered?" Detective Schorr prompted.

I didn't care for the sharp edge to his voice. It was the same one I'd gotten from insurance agents, bankers, and my mortgage company. I still felt sick about those people thinking I was trying to scam them. I'd left Maryland to get away from that gnawing suspicion. Now the lingering sense of guilt had followed me here.

My shoulders slumped. I rubbed my stiff

neck and wished the cops would leave. I stared down at my sturdy brown clogs. "No, but the police said it wasn't unusual for his body to be missing. In the past, when cars went off this particular bridge, the bodies never surfaced."

"What can you tell us about Mr. Cashour's work?"

Detective Schorr wasn't letting this drop. I hated thinking about Bernie. He'd been such a control freak, he'd turned me into an automaton. I hadn't realized how controlling he was until he was dead, and I had to start making decisions. I loved him, and I hated him.

I grabbed a duster and flitted among the twinkling artificial Christmas trees. "He analyzed energy sources and power plants throughout the country. It wasn't unusual for him to travel for one or two weeks at a time." Another memory surfaced. My chin quivered. "He called me every night on his cell phone."

"His body never turned up?"

Irritation surged through my veins. Was he hoping I'd give him a different answer this time? "No. One minute I had a husband, the next he was gone."

"What about his cell phone?"

I glared at him. "What about it?"

"Was it recovered?"

"No. I cancelled the number the next month so that no one else could run up calls on it."

The two detectives looked at each other for a long moment, white twinkle lights bouncing randomly off their reflector sunglasses. Detective Monroe pocketed her slim notepad. "We'll be back as soon as we have a working ID of the John Doe."

I paused, duster in midair over an elaborate seashell wreath threaded with red and green ribbons. "I thought you didn't know who he was."

"Don't. But this guy has done time behind bars." Detective Schorr rolled his thick shoulders back, flexing and stretching those massive bodybuilder muscles of his. "I recognized one of his tattoos."

The gruesome image of the bloated dead man rolling in the surf replayed in my mind. I grimaced. "You think he's connected to a prison gang?"

"Or something. Don't leave town," Detective Monroe said as they exited my shop.

Leave town?

Anger unfurled like a flag in a storm, snapping and popping. Did she think I was holding out on them? I'd told them everything I knew. I didn't kill him. Heck. I didn't even know his name.

I wished I had somewhere else to go, but this craft shop and my tiny beach cottage were all the family I had left in the world. My bank account wasn't flush with cash either. That's the real reason I had to make this shop work.

After ten years of marriage, I'd been shocked to discover I was flat broke. Both our checking and savings accounts were empty. We were behind on our mortgage payments, too.

I'd sold our house to pay Bernie's memorial expenses and our stack of pending bills. Deep shame had me hiding my dire financial circumstances from my mother when I'd moved back home. I hadn't wanted to burden her with my financial woes.

Bernie had seemed so competent, so successful, but his death revealed we'd lived way beyond our means. My hands tightened into fists. He'd kept our financial situation hidden from me. He'd treated me as if I were a child and couldn't comprehend the complex details of our finances.

Damn him and his secrets.

Secrets made me feel tiny and insignificant and stupidly naive. I'd trusted Bernie with my heart and our checkbook. He'd taken both and wrung them dry.

His glossy exterior image of competence had been fake. A fictional image, not the real thing. I'd been a fool to trust him, but I'd learned my lesson. I might not know who I was or what I was doing, but I'd never be so gullible again.

CHAPTER 4

Daytona Washington's girlish voice drifted over to my back door as I locked up for the night. "There she is, Mom. The Mary Christmas lady is locking up."

The young girl bounced over to me, her loose black curls springing with every pogo-like stride she took. What I wouldn't give to have her energy. "Hey, Daytona. Hey there, Daisy Pearl."

"Saw you got a visit from the Captain and Tennille this afternoon." Daisy Pearl wiped her glistening brow as she lumbered closer. Though it was early October, the temperature was still in the mid-seventies.

"What's that?" I'd had several groups of folks come through Christmas by the Sea this afternoon, and I had no idea who she was talking about.

"The Captain and Tennille." Daytona latched onto my hand and tugged me in the opposite direction of my Jeep. "Don't you know nuttin'? The cops. He's strong and silent. She's hot and vocal."

I had no choice but to fall into stride with them. "Oh. I get it." Though I wondered how Daytona knew about the aging pop star duo. As much as I enjoyed this vibrant little girl, I wanted to go home and put my feet up and think about something other than tattooed dead bodies. "Yeah, they came to see me."

"About the dead guy?"

Inwardly, I sighed. In small towns like this, gossip spread fast. Would the locals avoid me once they knew I was a death magnet? That would be very bad for my bottom line. "Yep. I'm the one who found him."

Daytona's eyes went as round as saucers. "Was that scary?"

"Sure was. I'm trying not to think about it." I looked over my shoulder at my distant Jeep. "Where are you taking me?"

"It's a surprise," Daisy Pearl huffed. Palm trees rustled in the breeze above us, the ocean shimmered mirror bright all the way to the horizon.

"I was planning on going straight home," I said. "It's been a long day."

My protest had no effect on these two determined females. We passed the bright lights of the Island Pharmacy and continued down the empty sidewalk toward another cluster of shops. What was going on? Couldn't they see that I was exhausted? I had a frozen dinner at home just begging to be nuked.

But I didn't want to hurt their feelings. Daisy Pearl had helped me get the glue removed from my hair yesterday. I could wait a few more minutes to prop my feet up.

Daytona kept a tight grip on my hand as she bounced beside me on the sidewalk. "Did you know my birthday is next month? I'll be seven years old then. Seven and in the second grade."

"That's a milestone all right," Daisy Pearl said. "Here we are."

I glanced at the slowly turning red and white pole with mounting apprehension. My hand went self-consciously to the strands of my butchered hair drifting out from under my red ball cap. "I don't understand."

"Mr. Russ meant well but he don't know nuttin' about a woman's hair," Daisy Pearl said. "Now Gabby, he's your man for hair. He'll fix you right up." She gestured to the bald gentleman brandishing a broom inside the barber shop.

I chewed on my bottom lip. What would that older gentleman know of current women's hairstyles, much less how I liked my hair? "I appreciate your offer of help. Truth is, I'm uncomfortable about this. How can he fix the holes in my hair?"

Daisy Pearl gave me a gentle push. "You're asking the wrong person. Go on in there and let Gabby work his magic."

There was that word again. *Magic.* Did I have enough imagination to believe in something I couldn't see? Against my will, my eyes teared up. I wanted to believe in something more than my uncanny ability to attract death. I really did.

I sifted through the facts. I didn't want to wear this ball cap everyday for the next six months while my hair grew out. Gabby was a hair professional. Anything would be an improvement over the gaping potholes currently adorning my head.

Belief warred with logic, but I was so tired logic didn't stand a chance. I wanted to believe. I exhaled slowly. "Okay. Let's do it."

Daytona dragged me into the shop. "Here she is, Uncle Gabby. This is Mary Christmas, and she needs a special haircut."

I waved in greeting at the grinning barber who was two inches shorter than me. He wore a blue and white flowery shirt, baggy tan shorts, and thick-soled flip flops. The overhead fluorescent lights gleamed on his mahogany head. I removed my hat. "Hi, I'm MaryBeth Cashour, and I have a hair disaster."

Gabby wiped off the barber chair with a small white towel and gestured me into it. "That you do, Mary Christmas. That you do."

"I'm not sure what can be done to fix this mess."

"You let me be the judge of that. Why don't you take off those glasses and let me listen to your hair?"

Another twinge of logic assailed my shaky belief in magic. If I took my glasses off, I couldn't see what he was doing. It all came down to trust. Did I trust this stranger? He had such a nice, earnest smile. It would be hard not to trust him, and in truth, I needed to look like a business professional.

So, I stowed my glasses and my red cap in my large purse. The world went out of focus. All that remained were blurs of color and light. Much easier to believe in magic in an out-of-focus frame of mind. I allowed myself to breathe again.

Gabby ran a comb through my hair and scrunched it in a practiced manner between his skilled fingers. "Hmm," he said. "I can feel how this needs to go. Tell me this. How wedded are you to this cut?"

I squinted at the mirror to see if he was teasing me, but being nearsighted, I couldn't make out his expression. "I'm not wedded to anything. This style is who I am. Mary-Beth Cashour wears a shoulder-length bob."

I heard the creak of wood nearby as Daisy Pearl sat down in a vacant chair along the wall. Daytona skipped around the small shop humming an upbeat tune I didn't recognize. "Come over here and sit down, Daytona," Daisy Pearl grumbled. "I can't hear myself think for all your commotion."

"I see things in your hair," Gabby began.

My hand darted up to my head. I envisioned miniature dead bodies, monster-sized sharks, poisonous snakes, and those huge cockroaches so prevalent on the island all skittering along my scalp. "You do? What kinds of things? Bugs?"

"No. Nothing like that. I see you've made some changes in your life recently. Your hair wants to reflect the new you."

I turned around to glare at him. He didn't need to know that I couldn't see beyond the tip of my nose. "Don't do anything too drastic or trendy. I'm a very conservative person."

Gabby covered me from the neck down with a black plastic cape. "I'll take care of your hair. Don't you worry about a thing. Tell me about your people."

"My people?" A surge of fresh alarm shot through me. Would I be rendered an outcast at the barber shop due to my lack of relatives? From what I'd gathered, Southerners recited ancestry by chapter and verse.

"Your family, child. Where you from?"

"Oh." I grimaced. Might as well get this over with. "I don't have any people."

He pinned up some of my hair and started snipping in the back. "No people? Everybody's got people."

I closed my eyes in preparation for his disappointment. "My father died when I was a kid. My mother raised me, but she died of cancer a few months ago. My husband died in a car accident in April of this year."

"What about brothers or sisters?"

I sighed at the pleasure of his gentle touch. His fingers massaged the nape of my neck between snips, and the tension streamed out of me. I was so relaxed that the next words out of my mouth startled me. "I don't know."

Gabby paused and leaned in close by my right ear. "How's that?"

I hadn't thought to tell anyone about my adopted status. My secret was too new, too raw, but now I'd all but blurted it out to a near stranger. I took another blind step into uncharted waters. "I thought I was an only child. But in my late mother's files I found papers that said I'm adopted."

Gabby went to work on the side of my head. "Adopted, eh? Whatcha gonna do about that?"

"I'm not doing anything. My birth parents didn't want me. My adopted parents lied to me about my origin. To answer your original question, I got no people. My family starts and ends with MaryBeth Cashour."

"Child, you always got people. You wait and see."

"I'm adopted." Daytona piped up from my elbow, her black curls softly framing her animated face. "Daddy Peachy found me in Daytona and brought me home to Mama Daisy Pearl. I'm glad I'm adopted cuz I have lots of brothers and sisters now."

"What about your husband's family?" Gabby asked. "Where are they?"

"Bernie didn't have any living relatives. His parents died before I married him. He was an only child. That was one of the things we had in common."

"You can be part of my family," Daytona said. "Mama, can we adopt Mary Christmas?"

"I'm too old to be adopted, but thank you for asking." I had to stop this awkward conversation before it went any further.

Gabby snipped around my face. My breath hitched in my throat as shortened hair drifted down on my forehead. I hadn't had bangs since elementary school. Too late now. The damage was done. Next, he gooped coconut-scented gel in my hair and fluffed it briefly with a blow drier. He removed the vinyl cape with a flourish. "Okey-dokey, Mary Christmas, put your eyes on and take a gander at the new you."

I groped in my purse for my glasses. My head seemed light and airy. I knew he'd parted my hair on the left and swept the long bangs to the side. Even so, knowing it was going to look different didn't prepare me for the radical change.

Instead of a very conservative style with all the ends tucking under, my chin-length ends were layered and flipped out so that the overall effect was windswept and tousled. Sexy, even. "Wow."

Furrows lined his forehead. "Is that a good wow or a bad wow?"

"It's a different wow." I studied the stranger in the mirror. Would Bernie have liked this new style? Heck, who cared what Bernie thought? My opinion was what counted now. "Very different, but I like it. I want to buy that gel you put on my hair. I like the way it smells. A lot."

He pressed the tube in my hand. "Here you go."

Daytona bounced beside my chair. "I like your hair, Mary Christmas. It's all flippy and fun."

Daisy Pearl planted a beefy palm on my shoulder and squeezed reassuringly. "You done good, Gabby."

I stood. Magic and energy hummed through me. Thank goodness I hadn't let logic win my mental argument outside the barber shop. I pulled out my slim billfold. "How much do I owe you?"

With a damp cloth, Gabby wiped the rest of my shorn hair from his barber chair. "First cut is on the house, lady bug."

"At least let me pay you for the styling gel."

He shook his head, the overhead lights glinting in his kindly brown eyes. "Your money's no good today, Mary Christmas."

Words stuck in my throat. No one had ever given me a free service like this. As I tucked my billfold back in my purse, I made a mental note to thank him with a gift bag of Christmas things from my shop. "Thanks. I can hardly believe this is me. I look, well, a lot less boring."

Gabby nodded sagely. "You look like a smart lady who's on her own and loving life."

Heat rushed to my face. I wasn't used to compliments or kindness from strangers. "Thank you, Gabby. This is the best haircut I ever had."

He winked at me. "We have our own ways down here. You'll see."

All the way home I kept glancing in my rearview mirror, trying to get used to the woman who stared back at me. Was what Gabby said about the new me true?

I was definitely on my own. I moved to this island on a whim. I bought a craft shop even though I wasn't crafty. For someone who was all alone in the world, I didn't feel so lonely anymore. I was loving life, making my own choices.

So what if I found a body on the beach yesterday? It didn't mean anything. It couldn't. There was no way I knew the dead guy. No way could his death be laid at my feet.

CHAPTER 5

Two days later, the twinkling Christmas trees and scowling detectives faded from view as I stared at the stark mug shot. Recognition flared through me in a mouth drying, white-hot gut punch.

I knew the dead man from the beach.

My heart and lungs froze. I couldn't stop blinking at the picture.

I should say something. Anything. But all I could do was stare hopelessly at the vaguely familiar face. Who was he?

I didn't remember.

Oh, God. Oh, God. Oh, God.

I drew in a ragged breath, and my thoughts jump-started. No wonder I hadn't recognized the dead man. The body on the beach looked nothing like the thug in this photo.

The cops watched me with their all-seeing eyes. My delayed reaction had probably already condemned me to a prison cell for the rest of my life. The urge to lie thrummed through my veins. Knowing him might incriminate me.

I was an outsider. An outsider who recognized the murdered man. They would toss me in the lock-up and throw away the key.

Don't lie. Lying is wrong. Lying will only get you in more trouble.

Ring, ring-a-ling, ring, ring-a-ling the woodwinds lilted from my shop's speakers. Strings and horns echoed the melody of the "Carol of the Bells." Then the bass notes joined the fray. As the beautiful instrumental music flowed around me, my brain added words to the song. *I'm going to jail. I'm going to jail. I'm going to jail.*

Christmas tree lights flashed around me like a horde of photographers at a press conference. White lights, colored lights, bubble lights, lighthouse lights, seashell lights. All of them signaling their warning of imminent danger.

I could see my new life crumbling away. My beautiful shop. My lovely seaside cottage. All would be lost to me if I couldn't snap out of this mental funk.

"Death magnet," an insidious voice whispered in my head. A feverish chill shot down my spine. Sweat broke out on my brow.

I clung to the knowledge that I was innocent. I hadn't done anything wrong. That truth was my lifeline on this overcast Friday morning.

"Miz Cashour? Do you know this man?" Detective Shanelle Monroe's voice was green apple crisp, her gaze German shepherd intense.

I glanced up at her unsmiling, rounded face. Both blazer-clad detectives had removed their sunglasses today upon entering my shop. Now I wished they'd left them on. Those piercing cop eyes saw everything.

I summoned my courage as I drew in a shallow breath. I was innocent. They couldn't arrest me without due cause. "He looks familiar, but I don't know why. So many people come through the shop each day, I don't remember when I saw him."

"What about the Christmas shark he had on him?" Detective Monroe scribbled a few notes as she spoke. "Are there any distinguishing batch marks on the ornaments that might help us pinpoint his visit to the shop?"

Hope flared. They wouldn't condemn me out of hand. "Do you have it with you?"

Detective Kent Schorr handed the plastic-bagged item to me. I hurried over and compared it to the others in the bright green shark bin. I kept repeating to myself that I was innocent. Just because I was a death magnet didn't mean I was guilty of murder.

I didn't even own a gun. Why didn't they ask me about that? I could tell them. No. No. I shouldn't volunteer anything.

Calm down. No one's accused you of anything yet. This is an informational visit. Yeah, right.

I pushed my glasses back up my nose and focused on the Christmas sharks. There were no dates on the sharks. No obvious batch variations. Dang. "I don't see anything different about this one. I really don't know how to help you."

"Is there anyone else who staffs the shop for you? Someone else who might have been here when the shark was purchased?" This from Detective Monroe again. With her taking the initiative in speaking for the pair, I could see why the Washingtons had nicknamed her for an outspoken vocalist.

I shrugged and faked a smile. "Nope. Just me."

My hopes teetered on a piano wire. Would they believe me? The shark in his pocket was bad for me, but it was circumstantial evidence. That's all they had to go on.

People had been convicted on circumstantial evidence. My breath came in shallow pants. My heart pounded in my ears. Would they arrest me?

Detective Monroe caught my eye. "We'll leave the photo with you. Try to remember how you know him."

My fingers sought the comfort of my gold locket. "That's just it. I don't know him personally. All I can tell you is he looks familiar."

Her gaze intensified. "Is he someone from your life in Maryland?"

I studied the photo on the sales counter again, certain that I'd seen those close-set brown eyes, the large hooked nose, the sunken cheeks before. It frightened me that I drew a blank as to his identity. Had I committed a terrible crime and purposefully erased it from my memory? Doubt swirled through my head like a free-wheeling water-spout.

No. I was raised better than that. I wouldn't hurt anyone. That much was certain. Time to quit stalling and lay the truth out there. "He didn't work at my place of employment. I don't remember meeting him, but there's something about his face I recognize. I've seen him before."

Detective Monroe handed me another one of her business cards. "Call me if you remember anything."

I placed the card near my cash register.

That was it? They were going to walk out of here?

It seemed anticlimactic for them to leave when I'd been half-expecting to be hand-cuffed and *Mirand*ized. "Wait. What's his name? If you have a mug shot, he must be in the system."

"Macklin Rudd. He went by Mac." Detective Monroe leaned on the sales counter in a casual way but darned if I didn't feel her eyes peering deep into my soul. "Does his name ring a bell?"

A bell? All I could think of was the "Carol of the Bells" and me going to jail. But I gave it my best effort, rolling his name around on my tongue. I drew a blank. My fists knotted in frustration. "Sorry. Nothing."

"One more thing." This from the mostly silent Detective Schorr. "What was the insurance payout for your husband's death?"

"What?" I staggered back into the wall, clutching my chest. My earlier fears of incarceration roared back full force. My eyes darted from the front door to the back craft room. Did I have a chance to make a run for it?

I wanted out of here, fast. For them to assume I had anything to do with Bernie's death was ludicrous. The music changed to "Christmas in Killarney." Anne Murray joyously sang of all of the folks back home, where all the doors were open.

I didn't have any folks back home, and I sure as heck didn't murder anyone. Did they think everything I told them was blarney?

I'd assumed Detective Monroe was doing the bad cop routine. Now I knew she'd been softening me up for Detective Schorr's bad cop role. My spine stiffened. They weren't going to get away with casting me in the role of the villain. "I didn't get any insurance money. No body meant no pay-out. Why do you ask?"

"Money. It's the oldest motive in the world. Where did you get the money to buy this shop?"

His amber-hued eyes drilled into me, pinning me in place. My collar seemed to tighten until it choked me. Gulping, I sorted through my chaotic thoughts for a response, clinging to the rock of truth. I wasn't to blame for Bernie's death or anyone else's. Outrage shot up from my core, threatening to blow my brains from my head.

I should have kept my old job, kept Mama's house, and stayed in Maryland where folks knew I wasn't a rampaging murderess. My heart raced under Detective Schorr's unrelenting gaze. I sensed he hoped I'd trip myself up and say I was a murderer.

After what seemed like an unending, brittle silence, I composed myself enough to turn the question back on him. "Are you suggesting I had something to do with my husband's death?"

"The circumstances aren't straight-forward. View them from our perspective. You're new in the area. Your husband's alleged death raised red flags with his life insurance company. You quit your job, left your hometown, and moved seven hundred miles away."

I banged my fisted hand on the counter, sending the photo of Mac Rudd spinning down to the floor. "You left out the bank foreclosing on my home of ten years, creditors descending on me like a flock of vultures, and having to move in with my mother so I'd have a roof over my head and food to eat."

Detective Schorr didn't bat an eye at my fireworks. "That insurance money would come in handy, wouldn't it?"

I pried my back teeth apart. "I didn't kill my husband. I would rather have Bernie alive than receive a single dime from the insurance company."

"But you don't have either one. No money. No husband. Then you're at the scene of two more deaths, your mother's and Macklin Rudd's. You are the single connection in all three events. In police work, we deal in the realm of connections."

That was the most he'd ever said in my presence, and his accusations probably represented his entire word budget for the month. I wished he'd stored up his words for some other guilty schmuck.

I thought about what Gabby said about my new hairdo. He'd created it because I had changed. I was standing on my own two feet. I was innocent. The new me didn't meekly go along with the program. The new me spoke up for herself.

"Those connections are the wrong ones." My eye twitched under my glasses, making Detective Schorr appear to be in several places at once. The pressure inside my head and chest mounted. God. Was I having a heart attack? I clutched my chest, just in case. "My mother died from cancer. Check with her doctors. Read her autopsy report. I didn't kill anyone. And I most certainly didn't kill the guy on the beach, Mac whatever-his-name was. All I did was find him."

"But you do recognize him?"

I tried to control the twitching by closing my eye for a moment, then I stared directly into Detective Schorr's laser-sharp amber eyes. "I said I did. I just don't remember how I know him."

"You wouldn't be lying to me, would ya?"

"Why would I lie? I'm exactly what I appear to be, a widow trying to make a go of her life. Why can't you accept that and leave me alone? Is that too much to ask?"

Both detectives stared at me in grim silence. Emboldened by their lack of response, I pounded my fist in my hand. "It's not my fault Bernie died or that I had to sell everything I owned. Bernie paid the bills in our household. I clipped coupons and lived on a tight budget for my entire marriage. I didn't learn the truth about our finances until he was gone. I don't know where our money went. His death and our lack of funds blindsided me."

Their continued silence was unnerving. More facts from my life tumbled out of my mouth. "The money for this shop came from my mother's estate. I paid cash for this place and for my cottage on the north end of the island."

Detective Monroe spoke up. "Are you absolutely certain your husband is dead, Miz Cashour?"

My heart twisted at the thought of poor Bernie, crunched up and sightless underwater. Would some woman walking along the river suddenly find him the way I'd stumbled onto Mac Rudd? "Of course I'm certain. The Maryland cops said he had to be dead. His car crashed in the river. He hasn't called me. If he isn't dead, where would he be?"

"Good question," Detective Monroe said as she shoved her sunglasses on.

"Don't leave town," Detective Schorr said, his sunglasses firmly in place. He pressed his business card into my hand. Surprise, surprise, it didn't burn a hole in my hand. I added it to my collection of police cards on the cash register.

They left, but the pounding in my head intensified. I didn't like the way this was shaping up. I wasn't directly responsible for any of the deaths. No way. If only my brain would work, I could figure this out. How did I know Mac Rudd?

I massaged my throbbing temples. Why couldn't I remember? It was maddening that his scowling image danced through the shadows in my mind. Old timer's disease. That's what they called it when folks couldn't remember well anymore. If they didn't lock me up in jail, they'd throw me in the nut house for sure.

My phone rang. I reached for it. "Christmas by the Sea, how may I help you?"

There was no response. Perhaps I'd spoken too fast. I tried again. "Hello? Anyone there?"

Nothing. I hung up. Must have been a wrong number.

I stared at the phone for a few seconds. My memory wasn't what it used to be, but it dawned on me that this was a common occurrence. I'd received multiple hang-ups in the last two weeks.

Did the Sandy Shores phone service have a lot of crossed phone wires? Or was there a reason someone kept calling and hanging up? The hairs on the back of my neck snapped to attention.

Cut that out. You're overreacting. A phantom caller, that's what this had to be. But why would anyone call me and remain silent? It didn't make any sense.

Were Detectives Schorr and Monroe onto something in their investigation of Rudd's death? Was it possible Bernie was alive? I couldn't deny the tiny spark of hope that flickered in my heart. I anxiously fingered my gold locket.

Bernie. Alive. Was he out there somewhere?

Nah. He loved me.

He would've called me if he'd survived

the crash.
    Wouldn't he?

CHAPTER 6

The phone rang first thing on Saturday morning.

I tensed over my whole grain cereal then I reached across the counter to pick up the phone, expecting to hear the creepy silence of my phantom caller. "Hello?"

"Miz Cashour? Cindy Grayson from the *Island Gazette.* I'm calling about that body you found on the beach."

Her piercing voice blared in my ears, causing me to nearly drop the phone. Great. The high-strung reporter from the weekly newspaper.

I'd run into her once over at Sweet Things, and she'd talked nonstop. Cindy was a bit much to deal with at the best of times, and early morning wasn't my best time. "What about him?"

"How did you happen to find him?"

She was interviewing me? No one had ever thought I was newsworthy before. I leaned into the phone. "I wasn't doing anything special. I happened to be shell collecting that morning."

"You stumbled over the body?"

"I guess you could say that."

"You were collecting shells, and you saw a dead man on the beach. Is that right?"

I shifted uneasily in my chair. Answering her questions probably wasn't a good idea. She might take what I said out of context. Or she might write the story whether she talked to me or not. This was my chance to make sure she got it right. "No. That's not how it happened. I saw him in the surf first. I didn't realize it was a person right away. I thought it was a shark or a log."

"He was bobbing in the surf? Like a fishing cork?"

"Not bobbing." Cindy's insistent probing brought to mind the gruesome shadow lurking just below the breakers. I shuddered. "More like rolling under the surface."

"What was your reaction to finding the body? Were you shocked?"

In my mind, I saw it happen again. The dark cylinder shape slowly rotated, only this time, Mac Rudd's close-set brown eyes followed me from under the water. My breath hitched in my throat. The eerie image wasn't photo clear; it was as if a strip of gauze were over his face. A waterfall of white gems sparkled on his left earlobe just before his face rolled underwater again.

God. Where did that come from? That wasn't how it happened. There'd been no earrings on the dead guy I found. And his eyes had definitely been sightless. My blood chilled in remembrance.

On a shaky breath, I answered her question. "I was shocked." The morning sunshine pouring through my kitchen window didn't touch the bone-deep numbness I felt. I pressed the phone tightly to my ear. "It was horrible."

"Did it stink?"

"I didn't get that close. Once I realized it was a body, I ran home and called the cops."

"So you didn't try to perform CPR?"

I shuddered. "He didn't need CPR by that point. He'd been underwater for a very long time."

"So you ran from the body?"

The way she said it sounded like I was a little kid afraid of the dark. I didn't want to sound like a huge coward in the paper. "My late husband died when his car plunged into a river this past spring. His body was never recovered. For me to discover a body in the water was very unsettling."

"I see." Cindy paused for a moment.

"Would you meet me on the beach and show me the exact spot where you spotted the body? I'd like to get a picture of you for our newspaper."

I recoiled as if she'd thrown cold water in my face. Having my photo in the paper and being linked through the media to a murder would be bad for my fledgling business. "Sorry. No pictures."

I hung up. Thank God she hadn't asked me if I knew Mac Rudd. That admission would've been worse than having a photo of MaryBeth the Death Magnet in the paper.

She might call back. If she did, I wanted to avoid her call. Good thing I had a job to go to. And I should collect more shells on the way.

But that meant walking on the beach. I grimaced. I hadn't been down there since Wednesday. It would be impossible to walk on the beach and not hear the ocean waves or see the water kiss the sand.

I shook my head. This is crazy. I live on an island. It's surrounded by water. Shells are part of my livelihood. If I started making excuses about walking on the beach, I might as well pack up and move elsewhere.

And I wasn't doing that. I squared my shoulders. I wouldn't let my fears win.

Shelling pail in hand, I crossed the dunes

to the beach, the sand cool on my bare feet. To bolster my courage, I said a quick prayer. Please God, don't let any more dead bodies wash up today. I scanned the empty beach in both directions. All clear. I sighed audibly. I could do this.

On my back was a book bag containing my purse and shoes. The new MaryBeth wasn't locked into the same old daily grind. She occasionally walked to work.

The tide had brought in a patch of miniature sand dollars and a few big conch shells, all of which I collected and lugged down the beach to Christmas by the Sea. It felt good to know I was behaving like a responsible adult. I wasn't a 'fraidy cat little kid. I'd faced my watery demons and won.

As I set the pail on my craft room counter, the shop phone rang. I glanced down at my watch. I didn't open until ten, and it was barely nine-thirty. After the answering machine beep, I listened to see who might be calling, but all I heard was silence.

My phantom caller again. The police suggested Bernie might be alive. Was it possible he was calling me?

Acting on impulse, I snatched up the phone. "Bernie? Is that you?"

Cold silence pulsed through the line. I

hurriedly hung up, rubbing the chill from my ear. God. Why did I do that? Bernie was dead.

Ghosts didn't use the telephone. Whoever called was a real person. Only how did he or she know I was in the shop? Was someone following me around? From a strategic hiding place behind a tree decked out in bubble lights, I peered out my storefront window.

My pulse raced as I scanned the street. Two empty cars were parked in front of the pharmacy, which opened at nine. A ponytailed young man with a bag of donuts exited the bakery next door. A brightly dressed woman with a leashed dog walked on the beach. A few grizzled men fished from the pier.

Everyday sights. Not one person was looking in my direction. I was jumping to conclusions.

There was nothing to worry about.

I took a deep breath, but I didn't flip my sign over to Open. Something was going on here that I didn't understand.

I needed advice. And breakfast. I went next door to Sweet Things for my coffee and molten chocolate cupcake. The mingled smells of brewed coffee, chocolate, and cinnamon welcomed me. "You having any trouble with your phone?" I asked.

Daisy Pearl rang me up and took my money. "Nope. My phone doesn't ring often enough to suit me. I'd like to hear from my children at least once a week, but they're too busy with their lives to stop and call their mama. Why? Is your phone busted?"

"I wish. My phone rings at the oddest times, but there's nobody on the line. It's like a phantom is calling me."

Daisy Pearl came around the counter with her own chocolate cupcake and sat with me at the corner café table. Sunlight flooded the shop, making it cozy and warm.

"Phantom?" Daisy Pearl dragged her finger through chocolate icing and licked it thoughtfully. "Like a ghost?"

"Yeah. It's ghostly all right. The phone rings. I pick it up, but the caller is silent."

"Sounds like a kid prank. What kid has it in for you?"

I removed the wrapper from my cupcake, savoring the mouth-watering aroma of just-baked chocolate before I took a big bite. The chocolate hummed down my throat and into my stomach, infusing me with courage.

"The only kids I know are the ones in my craft class. Your kids wouldn't do it. I don't see either of the Barbers doing it. Cute little Tyson Price wouldn't do it. Jolene Thompson might have it in for me. I can't figure out why she's in my class. She seems completely uninterested in crafts."

Daisy Pearl cocked her head in interest. "After raising twenty-three kids, I know a thing or two about how children think. If she's not in it for the crafts, then she must have a crush on one of the boys."

I took another bite of the molten chocolate cupcake. My eyes rolled with bliss. "These are so good. I'm going to weigh three hundred pounds if I eat these every day. But back to Jolene. She's eight years old. Isn't that a bit young for adolescent crushes?"

"Nope. Everything happens fast these days."

"If that's so, she wouldn't be calling me. Wouldn't she call the boy instead?"

Daisy Pearl nodded. "Didn't think of that."

Steam from my coffee tickled my nose and fogged my glasses as I sipped from the paper cup. "So, I'm back to where I started. Someone is calling me who won't identify himself. Do you think he or she is looking for Justine Mossholder?"

"Nope. Everybody knows Justine flew the coop. Whoever is calling you is up to no good. You better tell the Captain and Tennille. They'll take care of it for you."

"I'm not on their favorite persons list." Daisy Pearl raised her dark eyebrows at me, giving me the maternal version of the truth glare. I had no choice but to explain myself. "They came by again yesterday. They think I had something to do with the dead guy who washed up on the beach."

Daisy Pearl leaned forward, her short stubby fingers splayed flat on the round table. "Do tell."

I didn't feel nearly so alone now, nor as scared as I had felt yesterday when the cops questioned me. Daisy Pearl was my friend. She deserved to know about my death-inducing personality.

"The cops dug into my past. They know my husband died in a car accident last spring and his body wasn't recovered. They know my mom died a few months later. That's why they keep bugging me about the dead guy. Death follows me around. So you might want to rethink your friendship with me."

Daisy Pearl snatched up my hand and squeezed it in the tight vise of her fingers. Now I knew exactly how John Curtis felt when she'd had him by the ear. I would say or do anything to get her to let go of me.

She fixed me with stern eyes. "Did you

kill those people?"

My other hand closed around my gold locket. No wonder I was a bundle of nerves. These constant accusations were shredding my veneer of self-confidence.

I broke and began babbling. "Heck, no. I didn't kill anyone. There's a spider living in my side view mirror of my Jeep. I can't bring myself to kill him, even though he builds a new web on my door each time I park my car. I loved my husband, in spite of his mismanagement of our finances. And my mom was all the family I had. She died of breast cancer. I wasn't responsible for either of their deaths. And I didn't kill the guy on the beach either." I topped off my emotional outburst by bursting into tears.

Daisy Pearl released my hand, and feeling slowly crept back into my fingers. I was reacting all out of proportion to her question, but I couldn't help myself. Self-loathing welled up in me.

I ripped off my glasses and swiped the moisture from my cheeks. Good thing I didn't put on mascara for everyday wear, or I'd have raccoon eyes by now. "I'm sorry. I don't know what came over me."

"There, there." Daisy Pearl patted my shoulder. "You got the weight of the world resting on your shoulders, child. I believe you didn't kill anyone, but you better learn to start killing spiders or they will take over your car, your house, and your shop. Spider bites are wicked. You see a spider you want dead, you just call Daisy Pearl and I'll squash it flat."

I glanced up and saw two of her older kids, John Henry and Tamiqua, had ventured out of the kitchen and witnessed my meltdown. I winced at the concern in their eyes. "Sorry I was so loud. I never used to feel so out of control. I knew who I was and what my daily routine would be. I've got a new life now, but I'm hollow inside. I don't know how to fix myself."

Daisy Pearl patted my arm. "Looks like you're doing the right thing to me. Get up each day and keep going. Before you know it, your new life will fit like an old shoe. You can't hide from your past. It always catches up with you and bites you in the butt. Ain't that right, John Henry?"

"Yes ma'am," he muttered, turning to go back in the kitchen.

Daisy Pearl beckoned her daughter over. "Tamiqua, come here and tell Mary Christmas your story."

Flour coated Tamiqua's arms from fingertips to elbow. When she took a deep breath, I saw that her front two teeth were missing.

"Eight years ago my birth father kidnapped me after I got adopted. Daisy Pearl and Peachy catched him and made him go to jail for being so mean."

Her missing teeth tugged at my heart. Here was someone with very real problems. "Your father was mean to you?"

She nodded. "Every chance he got. He beat me and my sister Ronelle and then he'd go out and get real drunk and forget to come home. We begged food from our neighbors to stay alive. Lot of times we ate garbage cuz we had nothing else."

God. I'd never had to eat garbage. The thought of having to do so made me shudder violently. And no one had ever beaten me or knocked my teeth out. Suddenly, my troubles weren't quite so overwhelming. "But you're safe now," I said.

Tamiqua broke into a beautiful, gap-toothed smile. "Yep. I'm safe. Ronelle's safe too. We're proud to be Washingtons. We ain't going back to that other life, but it's part of how we got here."

Daisy Pearl patted Tamiqua's floured hand. "Thank you, dear. Go on and finish up with the baking. I'll be back there to help directly."

Impulsively, I reached out and squeezed Daisy Pearl's work-thickened hand. "Thank you. I appreciate what you did for Tamiqua and Ronelle, and I appreciate what you just did for me."

Daisy Pearl rose. "Well, we cain't have the Christmas lady being sad, now can we?"

"Nope. I'll put my jolly face on and get to work."

I felt good about myself. So what if the police knew about my past? Worry wouldn't change my lack of family or my lack of direction in life. Instead of worrying, I hummed Christmas carols and sold lots of hand-painted Christmas treasures to tourists.

I even went so far as to glue my newly collected sand dollars into petite snowmen. They looked distinctly grayer than Justine's snowmen. She must have painted hers white to get the purer color. Well, I liked the gray. I snipped red satin ribbons and glued loops of them on each snowman for hangers. MaryBeth Cashour, master of the glue gun.

I surveyed my finished products with pride. I'd finally done a craft that resembled the original. For once it didn't look like a preschooler had done it.

Though dark clouds filled the sky, I whistled my way home that evening. What was a little rain when you knew blue skies followed? The new me could handle a shower now and again. Or so I thought.

CHAPTER 7

After a guilty pleasure dinner of yogurt and cheese curls, I carried my glass of wine out on the screen porch and sat down in a plastic chair. I pulled Mac Rudd's picture out of my pocket and studied it. Where did I know him from? Here? Maryland?

My life in Maryland had been so regimented. Go to work each weekday. Do the laundry and ironing on Monday evening. On Tuesday, I cleaned the bathrooms and kitchen. Wednesday was for dusting and vacuuming. Grocery shopping happened on Thursday on the way home from work. Friday night was hamburgers on the grill. Saturday was for yard work and home repairs. Sundays I hung out with Bernie.

There hadn't been time for friends or acquaintances. Between my home, my marriage, and my career, I'd been busy nonstop. And I'd loved the security of my routine.

Things were sure different in Georgia.

I walked to work if I wanted the exercise. I opened and closed my store on my own schedule. I didn't do housework every night. Wonder of wonders, Daisy Pearl Washington had befriended me.

My craft class reflected the new me that gave back to the community. The old me wouldn't have been so free with my time because Bernie had been dead set against volunteerism. Each time I'd wanted to help out in our local soup kitchen, or go on a mission to Central America with our church, or raise money for breast cancer, Bernie had said it would take time away from us. I'd relented, letting him have the final say. Now, with the clarity of hindsight, I saw my volunteerism would have taken time away from him.

My lips pursed with distaste. Though I was lonely, I was better off without him. If I could just figure out how I knew Mac Rudd and get rid of my irritating phantom caller, I'd be in good shape.

What had Daisy Pearl said about my silent caller? Oh, yeah. Someone was up to no good. I rested my chin on my knees and stared blankly ahead in the dusky twilight. Her words echoed through my head.

No good.

I yawned.

Someone was up to no good.

A scene from the past came to me in a blinding flash. Bernie had been yelling, "You're no good!" at a man on our Maryland patio in late March. A man with a waterfall of sparkly stones on his left earlobe. I'd seen him through our sheer living room curtains when I came home early from work that day. The two of them were outside arguing.

I remembered that day because I'd miscarried again. I'd been spotting throughout the day when the cramps had started full force, and I knew I was losing my third baby. Just thinking of that day made me sad all over again. If I'd carried that baby to term, I wouldn't be alone now.

At the time, all I wanted to do was to crawl in bed and shut out the world. That's why I hadn't paid much attention to Bernie and his angry friend. Because I had serious problems of my own.

At least now I knew where I'd seen Mac Rudd. In my back yard. That wasn't good news. I would have much rather remembered him as a tourist I'd met down here. I gulped in a breath of air.

Of all the people I knew in Maryland, why did Mac Rudd follow me to Sandy Shores? His visit couldn't have been social since we'd never officially met.

If Mac Rudd had been an associate of Bernie's, what did he want with me? Was it a coincidence he came here?

I didn't believe in coincidences.

The cops didn't either.

Which meant I'd better figure out what Mac Rudd had been doing on Sandy Shores, or I might land in jail.

Bernie and Mac Rudd. Why hadn't I asked Bernie about Rudd later? I didn't like having a tie to this murdered man. It wasn't such a stretch to think the cops would make a mountain out of this molehill.

And then where would I be?

I took a sip of my wine. I had to be proactive on this. I wasn't a killer. I was a widow trying to build a new life.

If the cops were right, Bernie might still be alive. The possibility sent my blood pressure soaring. If Bernie was alive, I'd kill him with my bare hands. I just couldn't wrap my mind around the possibility of his survival.

He was gone.

I was alone.

Those were the sure facts.

But what if I suspended disbelief and accepted the possibility Bernie was still alive? Where would he be? Who would he have contacted?

A name sprang to mind immediately. Shawn Ellis. He'd been Bernie's roommate in college, and he'd been a frequent Sunday night dinner guest at our Maryland home. He always brought a twelve-pack of beer when he came, beer that he and Bernie consumed while I served them dinner. My fingers tightened around my wine glass.

Excessive drinking wasn't all that irritated me about Bernie's friend. At Bernie's memorial service, Shawn had oozed charm and clung to me. In a drunken haze he'd promised to do anything he could to help me. At the time, I'd discounted his offer because he'd been drinking, but it gave me a reason to call him.

I dashed into the kitchen and whipped out my address book. Minutes later I had Shawn on the phone. Loud music blared in the background around Shawn's slurred voice. My heart sank as I realized he'd been drinking heavily.

Some things never changed. My hopes plummeted, but I forged ahead anyway. I'd made the call. Might as well follow through. "Shawn. This is MaryBeth Cashour."

"Hey, cutie pie. I've been hoping you'd call me. Did you know your phone number doesn't work?"

I rolled my eyes. "That's because I moved, Shawn."

"You did?" He hiccupped. "Where'd you go?"

"To an island in Georgia."

"An island? Cool. So it's like vacation all the time?"

Did he think I'd won the lottery? "I have a job. I'm not on vacation." I tried to quell my irritation. "Look, I need your help. Did Bernie ever mention a man named Macklin Rudd?"

Shawn's breath caught in his throat, and then he hiccupped. "Macklin Rudd? Who's he?"

I'd heard that sharp intake of breath. Trouble was, I didn't know what it meant. Was he lying to me? Or just drunk? I wished I could see him to read his body language. "He's a dead man. The Georgia cops say he was murdered. Do you know anything about that?"

"No. Why would I?"

Asking Shawn about Rudd had been a long shot. Time to get down to business. "Shawn, have you heard from Bernie lately?"

"You're weirding me out, MaryBeth. Bernie is dead. I sat with you at his memorial service."

Shawn had slung his arm across my shoulder and tried to hold my hand during the ceremony. His alcohol breath had soured my stomach. His physical closeness repelled me, and I'd been relieved when we went our separate ways.

I couldn't let my unease over his previous inappropriate behavior hinder my information gathering. "I know he's supposed to be dead. The cops down here are asking me a lot of questions about Bernie. They say it's suspicious his body never turned up."

After a moment, Shawn belched. "That was a good one. Those Georgia cops are dumb-asses. Bernie's dead, and he's going to stay dead."

My internal radar kicked up to high gear. "What do you mean by that?"

"I don't want to talk about Bernie. He's yesterday's news. What I want to talk about is us."

I held the phone out and stared at it. "Us? There is no us. You're Bernie's friend."

"I'm gonna be your friend too, MaryBeth. I figure we'll have the same deal you had with Bernie. You do the cooking and the cleaning. I'll provide unlimited stud services. I guarantee you'll be pregnant before the end of the month."

I shuddered at the thought of sleeping

with Shawn the sperminator. I wouldn't sleep with him for all the yen in China. Not now. Not ever. I'd rather rot in jail for a murder I didn't commit. "Forget it. How much have you had to drink?"

"The O's lost in the play-offs. I'm drowning my sorrows with a twelve-pack of brew."

The O's. I drew a blank, then my brain clicked in. The Baltimore Orioles. He was talking about the baseball playoffs for the World Series. "Shawn, I'm not interested in the O's."

"I don't hold that against you, darlin'." He belched again. "Whatcha say to me coming down to your island next week? We could do a trial cohabitation to test the waters."

Ack. I jumped out of my chair and writhed in revulsion. "Forget it. I will never sleep with you. Tell me how Bernie knew Rudd."

"He didn't tell me about his work. We talked about the beaver we'd bagged."

My teeth ground together. I couldn't stand Shawn's juvenile ways. Or much else about him. "That's exactly why I won't sleep with you, Shawn. You brag about your multiple conquests."

"It wasn't just me bag-bag-bagging beaver."

His stumbling declaration waved a bright

red flag in front of me. I snorted in a breath. "What? Bernie was sleeping with other women?"

"Shit. You didn't hear it from me." He slammed down the phone.

White-hot thoughts fired through my brain at nauseating speeds. Could Shawn's slip of the tongue be correct? Had Bernie been cheating on me?

He'd been so attentive. I would've known if he was with another woman. Wouldn't I?

I rubbed my pounding head. I didn't know anything anymore. Shawn had it right for once with his swearing response. Only one shit wasn't nearly enough. Shit. Shit. Shit.

I didn't want to know that my husband had been unfaithful to me. That's what happened when you started flipping over rocks. Dangerous critters crawled out that you weren't expecting.

CHAPTER 8

Shawn's allegations of Bernie's unfaithfulness kept me tossing and turning all night. I lay there thinking of all the private moments I'd shared with Bernie. They'd meant the world to me. Had Bernie told Shawn everything?

I shivered with cold and heartache. By God, he better be dead. It wasn't fair he could still hurt me. Not fair at all.

I squished my extra pillow against my hollow middle and held on till dawn. I'd just closed my eyes when a mockingbird started singing outside my window. Great. Another day. I stumbled out of bed and drank my coffee on my sunny porch.

Boughs on the old oaks lining my property swayed in the morning breeze. Tufts of Spanish moss waved like flowing beards as squirrels darted playfully along the oak's bent limbs. Everything looked oh-so-normal, but the perfect day was at odds with my sour mood. I hadn't gotten far in my pursuit of learning who Mac Rudd was.

That was still my top priority. Knowledge was power, and I needed empowerment if I was going to come out of this unscathed. Since Shawn denied knowing Rudd, I should call Bernie's old boss, Frankie Valerio, at Jesseman and Associates.

Though it was the weekend, I dialed Bernie's old work number from memory and left his boss a message. "Mr. Valerio. Hello. This is MaryBeth Cashour. Bernie Cashour's widow. I'm trying to track down a work associate of Bernie's. Would you please call me at your earliest convenience?" I recited my home phone number and hung up.

Now what?

It was too early to walk to work. And I was spending so much time at the shop these days. I should do something else around here, something to help make this place feel more like my home instead of an impersonal motel room.

I glanced around at my bare walls. I'd been meaning to hang that trio of prints I'd bought at the mainland craft store last weekend. The artwork had been an impulse buy. Mama would've been horrified that the black frames were so plain, but she wasn't here to doctor them up for me. Besides, minimalist frames suited my budget.

I bopped out to my Jeep to get the pictures and frames, but the bag wasn't in plain sight. A nasty black fly bit my ankle, and I smacked him. Then I looked under the back seat for my purchases. Nothing.

Funny. I didn't remember taking my purchases in. I'd done grocery shopping that evening as well, so I'd carried in the food, thinking it wouldn't hurt to leave my decorative purchases in the Jeep. Only now they weren't there. How odd.

Was this early onset of dementia? If so, I'd already retrieved the prints and frames and forgotten where I'd stashed them. Curious, I searched the house again. A check of the kitchen, the pantry, the laundry room, the porch, the den, my bathroom, and my two bedrooms revealed no shopping bag with prints or frames.

I did buy them, right? I pawed through my purse until I found the dated sales receipt. Yep, I'd bought them all right. Where were they?

I shivered, and the brightness went out of the sunny day. What else was missing? In a frenzy, I went through every drawer, every cupboard, every closet, inventorying my meager possessions. My wardrobe of beige-toned sensible clothes was intact. As was my stock of peanut butter, tomato soup, and macaroni noodles.

Twenty minutes later, I concluded my search. None of my drawers had been rifled, not until I went through them just now. Nothing else was missing. Just the framed prints. Chances were good that my home hadn't been violated, just my vehicle.

Someone uninvited had been in my Jeep. They'd violated my privacy and stolen from me. My skin crawled.

I hadn't been vigilant about keeping my house and Jeep locked. I'd certainly double-check their status each time I entered or left from now on. The theft unnerved me. I'd moved down here to get away from urban hustle-bustle and crime.

I'd been fooling myself. People were the same no matter where you went. Suddenly I wanted very much to be around other people. I needed the comfort of my shop and my customers. I locked every window and exterior door and sped down Ocean Drive to work.

A horrible stench rolled out of my shop when I unlocked the back door of Christmas by the Sea. It took my breath away. My eyes watered and my throat constricted. I covered my nose and mouth with my hand and back-pedaled. The foul odor followed me, clinging to my clothes like warm fog hugging the marsh.

I coughed to clear my lungs. What was that noxious odor? How could I even go in there and see what the problem was without passing out? Cold fingers of dread brushed the back of my neck, and my heart stilled as I took another shallow breath, considering, comparing.

Awful as it seemed, the smell was familiar. A newly acquired recognition, unfortunately. Briny. Putrid. Nauseating even. My gut knotted in recognition. It smelled like the dead guy on the beach.

My stomach sank. Oh, no. Not another one. I sagged against my Jeep, eyeing my shop door like it was the gateway to Hades itself. The heat from the engine warmed my clammy skin.

I hugged my arms to my chest, but the chill in my bones intensified. Finding a dead man once was unlucky, but finding a second one would seal my fate. The police would lock me up and throw away the key.

I needed help. Fast.

Daisy Pearl and Peachy were next door in Sweet Things. They probably could identify a million reeking odors after raising twenty-three children. But if my problem was another dead body, I didn't want to involve them.

That left Gabby the friendly barber or Russ the grimacing pharmacist. Russ was geographically closest, so I ran to the drug store. With a death grip on my purse, I peered over the pharmacy counter and beckoned him over. "Russ, you got a minute?"

His perceptive brown eyes widened then narrowed as the customary scowl slid into place. Could he smell me from over there? The vile scent clung to my clothing and hair. I tried not to breathe too deeply.

As usual, he looked professional in his crisp white lab coat. "What can I do for you?"

I fingered my gold locket as I stared at the word "Pharmacist" embroidered in red thread prominently on his coat pocket. Now that I was here, I couldn't help feeling foolish. I should've called the cops right away. "I've got a problem next door. Something is amiss in my shop."

"Amiss? Is the power out?"

"No, I have electricity." There were customers in the drug store, so I waved him closer. "It smells bad, like something died," I whispered. "I'm a little weirded out from finding the dead guy on the beach. What

101

should I do?"

His features hardened, like a seasoned soldier looking down the barrel of an opponent's gun. "Were things out of place? Is anything missing?"

I shrugged. "I didn't get that close of a look, to tell you the truth. The smell almost knocked me down. Should I call the cops?"

Russ turned to the pharmacy technician. "I'll be right back." He shucked off his lab coat and hurried around the end of the counter. "Let's take a look-see first. Was the door locked when you arrived?"

Because I'd been focused on locks this morning, I was certain of my answer. "Yes." I hurried to keep up with his long, prowling strides. "The door was locked, but I left it unlocked when I came over here. Trust me. No one will accidentally wander in there. It reeks, big time."

Moments later, we stood in the back doorway of Christmas by the Sea. The rotting stench hadn't lessened. My eyes watered. Russ leaned in and looked around. "You're right. There's no sign of forced entry or foul play. No dead bodies in sight either. Wait here while I check the rest of the shop."

I didn't like being left behind, but I didn't care to immerse myself in that vile scent either. It was bad enough out here. I clutched my hands together. "Be careful."

What a horrible day this was turning out to be. First my art prints had gone missing, and now something was dead in my shop. How could Russ stand it in there? The hairs inside his nose must be burnt out by the smell.

Russ reappeared in the craft room, closing the door to the shop behind him. He inspected my craft sink and then darted back outside to fresh air.

"Oh, my God," I said. "How did you stay in there so long?"

He took a deep breath before he answered. "Military training. I can hold my breath for a long time."

"Is there —" I couldn't bring myself to ask the question. If there was a dead person in there, I might as well turn myself in right now. Where were the get-out-of-jail-free cards when you needed them? "What did you see?" I finally got out.

"Nothing. The problem is localized in your back room. Have you been collecting seashells lately?"

No dead bodies.

What a relief.

I took a deep breath and promptly gagged on the pervasive stench rolling off Russ.

Would we have to bathe in tomato juice to smell normal again? "Yes."

"That's your problem, Little Miss Christmas. Your shells need to cure before you paint them."

"Cure? Like tobacco leaves?"

"Same concept. You need a protected outdoor location for the sand dollars to dry out. Did you notice if anything was in those conch shells before you collected them?"

"No. I just dumped them in my bucket. Justine told me to pick up the big shells, but I've been obsessing over the little shells ever since I got here. When I saw big shells yesterday, I grabbed everything in sight."

"Where are your garbage sacks?"

"Under the sink. Why?"

"I'll help you out this time, but next time you're on your own. I'm going back in."

Minutes later he tossed a black garbage bag at my feet. My beautiful sand dollar snowmen were in there. So were the large conchs I'd wanted to group and decorate with twinkling bubble lights. My face fell. As did my confidence.

"They're not salvageable?"

"You need to boil the conchs to remove the dead hermit crabs. I don't recommend using your indoor stove to do it. Do you have an outside grill or fire pit?"

"No. Couldn't I keep them in my back yard?"

"Be my guest. But that smell won't diminish for a long time."

"What about my sand dollars?"

"Put them on your roof. It's hotter up there."

"Justine didn't say anything about putting seashells outside."

"Everyone down here knows to leave their shells outside. That course of action is automatic for locals."

My cheeks flamed. Anyone with half a brain knew how to collect shells. Anyone but a craft-impaired mainlander. If the ground opened up and swallowed me, I'd be eternally grateful. "How can I thank you? Can I give you a lift home so you can change your clothes?"

"Nah. We carry good odor-reduction products in the pharmacy. I'll be glad to sell you some."

I swung the sealed bag of smelly shells up on the roof of my Jeep. No way was I putting that reeking bundle in my vehicle. The shells clattered together as the bag landed inside the luggage rack supports. Too late I remembered the fragile sand dollars. I'd be lucky if any of them remained intact after all this. "Deal, and I'll cook you dinner tonight."

"Deal." Heat briefly flared from his eyes. If I hadn't been studying him closely, I would have missed it. In spite of my determination not to cater to any man, I found myself standing taller, sucking in both my butt and my stomach.

I bought two of every odor product he carried, including a small oscillating fan. Nothing like stimulating the local economy. I'd better sell lots of seashell Santas and Christmas sharks to cover this expensive goof, or I'd be eating mac and cheese for the foreseeable future.

On the bright side, I hadn't discovered another dead body, and I wasn't on my way to jail.

CHAPTER 9

My roasted chicken was nearly done, my fresh vegetables already sautéed. I foil-wrapped the Italian bread and tossed it in the oven. An apple-scented candle flickered on my coffee table, spilling its golden warmth over the room.

Russ would be here any minute. Despite my best intentions to remain calm, I was on pins and needles. A man was coming to dinner.

Music selection for this meal stumped me. Were Norah Jones and Sarah McLachlan too girly? Did Russ prefer Jimmy Buffet or Ray Charles? Would my instrumental harp CD put him to sleep? I was deep in contemplation when the low-throated rumble of his diesel pickup caused my shelved wine glasses to shudder.

I peered through the open window over my sink, enjoying the pleasant onshore breeze and the mouthwatering sight of Russ

Marchone. He'd changed clothes. Shaved, too. His snug jeans accentuated his muscular legs, his white polo shirt molded to his sculpted biceps. Leather sandals encased his tanned feet. He carried a bottle of white wine.

Bernie hadn't been a slouch in the looks department, but he'd been safe with his ordinary brown hair, glasses, and modest build. Russ wasn't safe. Russ was a high-performance military tank, armed and dangerous. I swallowed around the thick lump in my throat.

This wasn't a date. This was two neighboring shop owners becoming better acquainted. This was a friendly dinner where we might discuss marketing strategies, building rents, and the annoyance of filing quarterly tax returns. There would be no heart palpitations, no hand holding. No kissing.

Especially no kissing.

Where were these unwarranted romantic thoughts coming from? Romance wasn't on tonight's agenda. I opened the screen door for him. "Come on in."

"Thanks." Russ handed me a bottle of Chardonnay and inhaled deeply. The corners of his mouth waggled. "It smells great in here."

His compliment warmed my heart. Heat rose to my face. "This isn't a date," I repeated silently as I set the wine on the counter. "I hope you like chicken. Would you select a CD while I open the wine? I wasn't sure what style of music you preferred."

He stopped short. "I've got just the right CD in my truck. I'll be right back."

"Okay." My fingers tightened around the corkscrew. His rejection of my music challenged my newfound freedom. My irritation ramped up a few notches.

There were thirty-two CDs in my living room. That wasn't good enough for him? The voice of reason snuck into the brew. Why was I upset over his musical preference? It wasn't like I cared which style of music we listened to.

Ten minutes remained on the oven timer for dessert. I poured two glasses of wine and carried them to the living room. The ocean breeze ruffled the airy white café curtains, their freshness a stark contrast to the distressed wicker furniture I'd purchased from the thrift shop. I'd covered the thick cushions with abstract fabric in splashy shades of red, blue, yellow, and green. My bare walls were painted the same bright yellow as the cushions. Those missing art prints would've looked great in here.

Russ returned and handed me his CD. "Here, try this."

My fingers tingled when his brushed against mine. It was as if I'd been transported back to high school, and the football quarterback had accidentally wandered across my path. Anticipation flared, embarrassing me.

Geez. I was responding to Russ like a school girl with a crush. My body didn't believe this was a casual dinner. My body believed this was a date. I gulped.

His music was an intricate instrumental guitar set. Just the sort of thing casual acquaintances might enjoy. I kept that thought in mind as I handed him a glass of wine.

My body tightened at his nearness. Oh dear. This evening would be rough if I couldn't get past this man–woman thing.

Think business acquaintance.

He gestured to the furnishings. "This is nice."

My face warmed again at his comment. If I did nothing else right tonight, I needed to keep the topic of conversation on matters of mutual interest. "Thanks. Please make yourself comfortable. Say, I can't thank you enough for helping me with my odor problem today."

He shrugged easily and sat down on the sofa. "Not a problem."

I sat in the opposing chair. "And those odor elimination products you sold me worked great. Customers didn't run away holding their noses."

Russ smiled. Or maybe it was a grimace; I couldn't quite tell. We sipped our wine. As the music swelled around us, the white curtains breezed away from the open windows on the ocean side of my house.

Okay. This silence was awkward.

Almost as awkward as finding a dead body on the beach or having stuff stolen out of my Jeep. Because I'd been living and breathing cops lately, I looked for a connection between the two events. Both involved a bad person, someone who stole what wasn't theirs.

Huh?

Could my minor theft be related to the murder? It didn't seem possible that thirty dollars of missing folk art had anything to do with a homicide.

Nah. They couldn't possibly be related.

I blinked. I'd certainly let the conversation lapse. What should we talk about next? Did I know him well enough to ask who did his taxes? Should I ask him what rent deal he had with the landlord, Island Properties?

He gave me the look again, that slow perusal of male appreciation that made me glow. "Even though we're work neighbors," he said, "I don't know very much about you. How did you end up in Sandy Shores?"

I could lie to him. Make something up about how much I loved crafting or Christmas, but I wasn't a liar. Unless I mismanaged my shop, we'd be neighbors for a long time.

I swallowed a slug of wine. "Have you ever felt like you were marking time, only you didn't know what you were waiting for?"

He hesitated and then nodded.

My fingers circled the rim of my glass as I searched for the right words. "That was my life in Maryland. I was happily married. I had a good job. My mother lived an hour away. I wasn't setting the world on fire with my career, but my routine filled my life. Then my husband died on a business trip, and I learned our finances were a huge black hole. I moved home to be with my mom as she recovered from surgery, only to find out the cancer was too far gone and she was dying. In three months, I lost my husband, my security, my home, and my mother. It hurt to stay there. So I hopped in my car and drove until I got here."

He whistled softly. "That's quite a story."

"No kidding." My glasses slipped down my nose. I pushed them back in place. "There are mornings when I wake up, and I can't figure out where I am or even who I am. The old MaryBeth Cashour stayed within a twenty-mile radius of her home."

"Why Sandy Shores? Why not Savannah or Hilton Head or Amelia Island?"

"You probably think I have a systematic, logical answer. Well, I don't." He sure had a lot of questions. Looking back at my life with the benefit of hindsight, so did I.

"This was how far I got in a day as I drove south. I spent the night on Hotel Row, then the next morning I wandered through the various shops. Justine and I struck up a conversation and before I knew it, I owned her shop."

"I didn't know Justine's business was for sale."

His pointed glance had me squirming in my seat. Did he doubt my story? "I wasn't looking to buy a craft shop either, but as I stood in Christmas by the Sea, I had an epiphany about owning a small business. Justine apparently had one about selling her shop. The rest is history."

"You'd never visited here before?"

I smiled. "Nope. Crazy, isn't it?" I wasn't

doing such a good job of keeping the conversation on neutral topics. Time to turn the tables on him. "How about you? How'd you end up in Sandy Shores?"

His foot tapped in time to the music. "I was raised here. Went in the army right after high school. Didn't like fighting, didn't like taking orders. So I went to pharmacy school. That's pretty much it."

I absently toyed with my locket. His summation sounded overly simplistic. What wasn't he telling me? "You have family in the area?"

"My sister and two brothers live near my mother over in Brunswick."

"Do you see them often?"

He flashed a brief wolfish grin that curled my toes. "Often enough that I've dreamed of getting in my truck and driving until I am somewhere else, but I never lived that particular fantasy."

He admired my new beginning? How odd that he thought I was brave. "Starting over isn't as easy as you think. There's no safety net of friends or co-workers. You have to learn where all the shops are located, find the cheapest place to buy gas. That sort of thing." I probably should have put out cheese and crackers to soak up all the alcohol in my empty stomach. Too late now.

"I've noticed Schorr and Monroe are keeping a close eye on you."

I drained my wine glass. "Yep. They think I'm a serious criminal. They believe I killed Macklin Rudd."

His gaze intensified. "Did you?"

Whoa. I didn't expect such a direct question. Zinged by the pharmacist. Or maybe by the wine. "Heck, no."

Russ extended one arm over the empty section of the wicker sofa and examined his bluntly cut fingernails. "You want me to take them out for you?"

The danger laced through his words stopped my heart momentarily. Was he serious? Earlier today he'd mentioned military training. He might very well have lethal skills. I sighed inwardly. Had the world fallen off its orbit? How did a dinner between two business professionals veer so sharply off course? Murder wasn't on my menu.

Best to treat his offer with humor.

I laughed weakly as I got up to fetch the wine bottle. "Would ya?" My voice sounded lighthearted. "I'm tired of being their chief suspect. They even think I had something to do with Bernie's death."

His penetrating gaze speared me again. "Bernie?"

I refilled our glasses. This music had a weird rhythm that energized me. I needed to get the name of this CD before he took it home. "My late husband. He didn't survive his car plunging off a bridge into a river."

He seemed to consider that for a moment. "You're a black widow? Roving the country, marrying wealthy men, then killing them for their bank accounts?"

Genuine laughter bubbled out at his absurd remark. "I wish. I'm flat broke. I financed my new start here with my mother's life savings. All I want is to find a new rut and crawl into it."

Russ quirked up an eyebrow. "Be careful what you wish for. Wishes have a way of coming true."

"In your world, maybe. My wishes never come true."

He was silent for a long time. "Perhaps they weren't your wishes after all."

Well, dang. Who was Russ Marchone? Was he an Army-trained killing machine? Or was he an amateur philosopher? "What do you mean by that?"

"It's my observation you've been many things to many people. I'm willing to bet you've never just been yourself before."

My fingers tightened around my gold locket. His off-the-cuff appraisal was way too close for comfort. "Have you been talk-ing to Daisy Pearl?"

"Nope. I'm good at reading people."

My chin went up in the air. "Did you ever consider some folks might not like being read?"

He waved off my protest with a fierce smile. "I also know when to shut up."

"Good. Because we need to talk about something else." The oven timer went off and I exhaled audibly as I stood.

Russ grinned up at me. "Saved by the bell."

As we ate dinner at the table, I wondered about his accurate assessment of my situa-tion. Was Russ as discerning as he claimed to be?

Had his army training honed his ability to detect the truth? A terrifying thought struck me out of the blue. What if Russ was con-nected to the murdered man on the beach?

CHAPTER 10

The phone rang as I was almost ready to leave for work on Monday morning. I froze in the doorway. Was this another call from my phantom caller? I decided not to answer it and wished I had a phone with caller ID. I lingered to hear the voice mail message as it was recorded on my machine.

"Mrs. Cashour? Frankie Valerio returning your call."

At the sound of that familiar gravelly voice, relief swept through me. Progress. Finally. I lunged for the phone. "Mr. Valerio? Thanks for calling me back."

"What can I do for you?"

Straight to the point. That was Mr. Valerio all right. I'd be just as matter-of-fact. "I'm seeking information about a business associate of Bernie's. A Mr. Macklin Rudd. Do you know him?"

"He doesn't work for Jesseman and Associates. What's this about?"

His dismissive tone aggravated me. "He doesn't work for anyone. He was murdered five days ago. Here in Georgia."

"Georgia?" Frankie Valerio barked into the phone. "What the hell was he doing down there?"

Curious. It sounded like he knew Rudd after all. "That's what I'm trying to find out. Was he one of Bernie's clients?"

Valerio swore. "I'm on the road. I'll look into it when I return to the office. Give me your contact info again so that I can write it in my planner."

I hesitated. If he was somehow involved, should I give him more info about me? Should I hang up instead?

"I'm waiting, Mrs. Cashour."

Bernie never kept Mr. Valerio waiting. Off-balance, I rattled off my home and work phone numbers and hung up.

The conversation left me feeling disjointed. Bernie's boss claimed Macklin Rudd didn't work for him, but reading between the lines, it sounded like he knew Rudd. Were Rudd's and Bernie's deaths related? This wasn't helping. I had more questions than when I started. More and more I had the sensation of being outside the circle of knowledge.

Secrets.

That's what this was about.

Because if it wasn't about secrets, Mr. Valerio would have come right out and told me the truth about Rudd. Who else was in on the secret? Probably Rudd. And maybe Bernie too. His car accident could have resulted from a highly skilled driver tapping his car at the opportune time.

Wait.

My imagination was running amuck. There was no evidence Bernie's death was murder. The eyewitness reports on the bridge didn't mention his car being tapped. I'd definitely watched too many cop shows. I was seeing conspiracies where there were none.

Mac Rudd had been shot in the chest. Bernie was supposed to be dead, but his body was missing. Bernie knew Mac Rudd. Beyond that, I had nothing tying them together.

Nothing but questions I couldn't answer. I shivered, suddenly wanting to climb back in bed and pull the covers over my head until my troubles went away. I wanted my old life, where everything progressed on an orderly schedule.

Things weren't as they seemed on this idyllic island. I'd stumbled across a dead man. Someone stole framed art prints from my Jeep. Someone kept calling me and not speaking. And an ex-army guy had offered to kill someone for me. My nerves were set to a hair trigger. One more thing and I'd snap for sure.

Worrying wouldn't solve anything. What I needed was to busy my hands and my head with work so I'd quit thinking about my troubles. I secured the deadbolt on the house then unlocked my Jeep, navigating around the latest spider web in my side view mirror. I drove straight to Christmas by the Sea.

I held my breath as I slid my key into the lock of my shop back door. I half expected to find another bucket of putrid sea life inside.

I jiggled the key in the lock. This stupid door was so hard to open. I should see about getting someone in here to fix it. Finally, a distinctive snick sounded, and the door opened.

With trepidation, I surveyed the craft room. It looked okay. I took a cautious breath. No stink bombs today. So far, so good.

I stashed my purse in a file cabinet drawer, locked the cabinet, and secured the key around my wrist. I perused the Christmas CDs to select the morning's music. Something about the sales counter seemed off. It seemed emptier. Why?

When I left yesterday, I'd stacked the seashell-rimmed picture frames on the sales counter because I meant to vacuum the dust from them this morning. They were gone.

I frowned. What did I do with them? Had I returned them to the display cabinet? I walked over and peered at the montage of seashell art. Nope. Not there either.

I rubbed my forehead. I must be losing my mind. What could I have done with a stack of picture frames?

They had to be around somewhere. It wasn't like they could walk out of here. I plugged in the tree lights, checked that all was in order for the day. A sneeze welled up in my nose. I grabbed a tissue just in time. When I tried to discard the used tissue, that's when I made my second discovery.

No trash can.

The hairs on the back of my neck stood on end. The only time I ever moved the trash can was when I emptied it at the end of each work day. I'd done that last night, and I distinctly remembered putting it back under the counter afterward.

I took a closer look around the shop. Things were tidy, but there were subtle differences. The bin of Christmas sharks was all jumbled up. I always aligned the sharks on top with the heads closest to the front door.

My oyster shell Santas weren't quite right either. It looked like a kid had pawed through the display in a hurry. I fingered the tangled ribbon hangers. It'd take me a good hour to straighten them out.

My Christmas by the Sea coffee mugs had been moved, too. From my customary position behind the sales counter I could normally see the letters "rist" in succession on each mug. Now I saw random parts of every word.

Someone had been in my shop.

Both doors had been locked when I came in just now. Who could walk through locked doors?

Not even the bright fluorescent shop lights dispelled the chill in my bones. It seemed as if someone were hiding behind each shadowy Christmas tree, waiting to pounce on me. Fear pounded through my veins, urging me to run far away.

This was way more than I could deal with. Time to call the cops. I snatched up their business cards from my cash register. Detectives Monroe and Schorr would know what to do.

I reached for the phone, then stopped.

What if I destroyed fingerprint evidence by using the phone? I couldn't take that chance. I ran next door to Sweet Things and borrowed their phone.

"What's going on?" Daisy Pearl wanted to know after I placed the call.

"Someone was in my shop last night," I said.

Worry crowded her brow. "Oh, dear. Was the place vandalized?"

"No. Things are jumbled up. A few items are missing. It doesn't make any sense." I looked around the bustling bakery. "Was anything out of place in here this morning?"

"Nope. Everything was as it should be."

"I don't understand why these odd things keep happening to me. All I want is to live a quiet, uneventful life. Is that too much for a law-abiding shopkeeper to ask?"

Daisy Pearl handed me a cup of steaming coffee and a molten chocolate cupcake. "Here. You need fortification."

"Thanks. But I can't eat a thing. My stomach is too jittery."

"Give it a try." Daisy Pearl urged. She ushered me to a table. "How'd the big date go last night?"

My ears flamed with heat as I remembered my schoolgirl reaction to Russ being in my house. "Big date?"

Daisy Pearl nodded toward my shop, her jumbo silver hoop earrings swinging wildly with the abrupt movement. "You know. You and Mr. Pharmacist."

I blinked rapidly. "How'd you know about that?"

"Ain't nothing on this island goes on that I don't know about it."

My indignation at being the source of island gossip fueled my tongue. "If that's true, who broke into my shop?"

"You got me there. Someone's up to no good. He had to come in late last night. People come and go down here until about ten, when the restaurant closes. Peachy comes in at four to get started on the baking."

A dark sedan pulled up to the curb. Detectives Schorr and Monroe saw me in the bakery and came in. I lurched to my feet, cupcake in hand. "For once, I'm glad to see the two of you."

"You reported a break-in?" Detective Monroe said. First thing in the morning must be too early for her terminator sunglasses. Without protective covering, her dark brown eyes drilled into me.

"Someone was in my shop last night." I told them what I'd observed.

"The locks weren't jimmied?" Detective

125

Monroe asked. "What about the window in the back room?"

"It was locked. I always leave everything locked up tight."

"Did any of the other shop owners experience break-ins?"

"Nobody came in here." Daisy Pearl gestured toward the door. "Y'all go on over to her shop and figure out who's hounding Mary Christmas here. Someone on this island is stirring up trouble. We can't have that."

The detectives dutifully inspected everything in my shop. Cupcake in hand, I stood in the doorway and pointed out items that were out of order. It seemed deathly quiet in the shop without the music on.

Detective Schorr stopped beside me. "The only things missing are your trash can and the seashell picture frames?"

"Yes, although I can't imagine what anyone would want with my trash can. It was empty. There wasn't anything special about it."

"Have you had any other problems here?"

"Not really."

His eyebrow quirked up.

The gesture reminded me of my father. I guess it was male-speak for "Yes?" I didn't want to mention my odor problem, but it

126

would look bad if I stopped now that I'd started down that road. "I had a minor problem here, but I caused it."

The eyebrow didn't lower.

I swallowed thickly and relayed the incident to him. By the time I finished, it was clear he was trying hard not to smile. My pulse ramped up. This wasn't funny.

I wanted to cosh him on the head with something, but that would probably get me arrested.

My phone rang. Thank God. "Can I answer it?"

"It's your phone. Go ahead."

"What about fingerprints?"

Detective Monroe pointed to a box of tissues next to the register. "Use one of those."

I picked up the receiver as instructed and gave my standard shop greeting. Nothing. The line stayed silent, but I sensed the person there, waiting on the other end of the line, and the pregnant silence annoyed the crap out of me. "Who is this? Why do you keep calling me?"

After hanging up, I turned around and ran smack into Detective Schorr. It was like hitting a brick wall. The air huffed out of my lungs. "Oomph."

"Crank call?" he asked.

I nodded. "I've been getting a lot of them,

both here and at home."

"Do you have caller ID?"

"Nope. I have the basic phone service."

Detective Schorr hit a series of buttons on the phone and listened. After a moment he hung up.

"What did you do?"

"I called the number back. No one answered. We could put a tracer on your line."

"I hate this. I can sense the person waiting there in the silence. It creeps me out."

"Did you have this problem in Maryland?"

I shook my head. "No, the calls started down here." I hugged my arms to my middle. "Now that I think about it, the crank calls started the day before I found the guy on the beach. A couple of ghost calls at the shop that afternoon. A few at home that evening. A call before I left for work the next morning. Do you think this is connected to Mac Rudd's death?"

"It's too soon to tell. Let's place that tap on your phones, then we can figure out what we're dealing with."

"Tap all you like. My caller never says anything." I needed to tell them that my memory had started working again. Admitting anything about the dead man to the cops was probably a mistake. But they already thought I was a murderess. I couldn't get in much more trouble.

I took a deep breath. "About Mac Rudd, I remembered how I know him. He was a work associate of Bernie's. I saw them arguing on our patio one afternoon."

Both detectives stared intently at me. "But you never met him?" Detective Monroe asked.

"No. I never saw him down here either. Not until he washed up on the beach, that is. It's a coincidence that both of us were here and in Maryland."

"I don't believe in coincidences." Detective Monroe's lips pressed tightly together.

"Looks to me like the connection may be your husband," Detective Schorr said.

"Bernie's dead." He had to be mistaken. My insides chilled to subzero. I clung to the sales counter. "There's no connection."

"People disappear for all kinds of reasons, Miz Cashour. Oftentimes they go to great lengths to hide their problems," Detective Schorr drawled. "We've sent an inquiry up to Maryland to find out more about your husband's job and any problems he might have had there."

"Bernie didn't have work problems. He loved his job. This doesn't make any sense."

"That's because we don't have all the puzzle pieces yet," Schorr continued. "Once we do, everything will fall in place."

"I talked to Bernie's boss this morning. Mac Rudd didn't work for Bernie's company."

Detective Monroe's spine went ramrod straight. "Miz Cashour, keep your nose out of our business. You stick to running your shop, we'll catch the murderer. No more calls to Maryland. You got it?"

"Yeah. I got it."

"Okay. You need to make a signed statement and then we'll be on our way."

I filled out their form and handed it to them. After they left, I picked at my cupcake. I didn't have all the puzzle pieces. I had a silent stalker, a thief, and a dead or missing husband. My husband knew the murdered man I'd found on the beach. The cops said these weren't coincidences.

Did that mean Bernie's death wasn't an accident? Had he been getting calls from my phantom caller too? I wished he'd confided in me. A shiver tripped down my spine. Had Bernie been murdered? If so, would his murderer come after me?

One thing I knew for certain. I sucked at puzzles. I couldn't solve a crossword puzzle to save my life, and jigsaw puzzles were only good for one thing: kindling to start a fire. Unless the answer to this murder puzzle reared up and bit me on the butt, I was in deep trouble.

CHAPTER 11

As soon as the weekly *Island Gazette* hit my shop door on Monday afternoon, I took one glance at the screaming headlines and realized I needed chocolate. I hung a "Back in Five Minutes" sign on my door and hurried next door to Sweet Things.

The sun's rays slanted over my corner table, illuminating my bowl of chocolate chip mint ice cream. After four spoons of courage, I was brave enough to face the paper again. Two bolded headlines crowned the front page. On the left was a photo of Christmas by the Sea. On the right was Mac Rudd's unsmiling mug shot. The top headline read: "Widow runs from rolling body." Underneath in slightly smaller font I saw "Murder on our fair shores."

I groaned. Anyone picking up the paper would assume I had something to do with the murder. And my store photo. Why on earth was that in the paper? My shop had nothing to do with the dead man.

Why had I even talked to that newspaper reporter? If I'd known she was going to do me wrong, I'd have hung up on her right away. The edge of the paper crumpled in my fisted hand, and I had to work to smooth it out. Taking a deep breath, I read the article sandwiched between the two photos.

Christmas by the Sea's new owner, Mary-Beth Cashour, made a shocking discovery last Wednesday morning. This former Maryland resident was shelling on the beach when she spotted an unknown shadow rolling in the surf. "It was horrible," Mrs. Cashour said. "Once I realized the submerged object was a person, I ran home and notified the police." Sources indicate that the deceased freelance consultant, a Mr. Macklin Rudd of Maryland, sustained a fatal gunshot wound to the chest. Mr. Rudd served three months in the Maryland Correctional Institute for extortion. The police are actively pursuing leads in this ongoing investigation. Anyone with information about Macklin Rudd should contact Detective Shanelle Monroe, the detective in charge of the case.

At least the reporter hadn't dug up the connection between Bernie and Mac Rudd. I breathed a small sigh of relief.

Daisy Pearl plunked her bowl of butter

pecan ice cream down on the table and eased into a small chair. "Whatcha think about that?"

I pointed to the paper. "It says the dead guy was a freelance consultant, whatever the heck that is."

Daisy Pearl made a dismissive noise. "Sounds like he didn't have a regular paycheck. Let the Captain and Tennille worry about him."

"I have this sinking feeling they'll blame me for his murder. Because I found his body."

"Trouble is as trouble does."

I folded the newspaper inward and took a small bite of ice cream. "What the heck does that mean?"

"It means if you go looking for trouble, you'll find it. Leave it be, and stop looking over your shoulder."

The door opened and closed. "Is this a private party or can anyone join?" Russ Marchone pulled out a chair at our corner table and sat down. His khakis, light blue dress shirt, and blue striped tie showed off his muscled physique in an eye-catching way. Be still my beating heart.

In spite of his scowl, there was a softness about his eyes. My heart took me seriously about being still and actually stalled for a beat. Was he flirting with me?

I didn't know how to gauge his interest in me. Maybe I should take Daisy Pearl's advice and quit looking for trouble. I needed a friend. He seemed to be available. Was it possible to just be friends with a man?

"Afternoon, Mr. Pharmacist." Daisy Pearl beamed a three-hundred-watt smile at him. "What can I get for you? Ice cream? Cookies? Sweet tea?"

Russ sat tentatively, as if he was trying to keep most of his weight off of the airy chair. I could have told him that it would hold his weight. I sat at the same table each day, and Daisy Pearl always joined me. If the chairs held her massive girth, they would certainly hold him.

"What you got in here that's healthy?" he asked.

My eyebrows shot up. "You've never eaten here?"

Russ shot me a dark look. Ah, there was the Russ I knew. As long as he was dour and sarcastic, I was okay. It was when I looked too deeply in those warm brown eyes that I got in trouble, wishing for things that weren't possible.

Daisy Pearl lumbered to her feet. "People don't usually come in here for healthy. But I got it, just in case. One green tea and an organic apple muffin coming right up."

Russ turned his gaze on me. Heat washed through my body like my own private riptide, pulling and tugging until I didn't know which way was up. I went all shivery inside as I struggled to reorient myself.

"I read the article in the paper," he said.

I didn't need to ask which article. I sighed. "Yeah. Me too. Macklin Rudd wasn't a nice guy."

Russ went still. Reptilian still. I'd never seen a man be so still before. "There's a lot that's not said in the article."

It was my turn to freeze. "What do you mean?"

"I recognize the look in Rudd's eyes."

"What look?" Inhaling, I gestured toward the folded paper. "It's a standard mug shot."

The corner of his lips twitched. The softness fled from his eyes. In that instant I knew whatever he'd done in the military, it wasn't something one chatted casually about over ice cream. I also knew that he'd been darned good at it. Russ Marchone didn't strike me as a man who did anything halfway.

"You can tell a lot about a person from their eyes."

I made myself breathe again. "You're scaring me."

"Good. You need to be careful."

Thank God I had my eyeglasses on. They shielded me from his intense scrutiny. "I'm methodical, which is practically the same thing as careful. What else do you know about Macklin Rudd?"

He placed his palms down on the faux marble table. "He's a player."

"You lost me. A player? For what team? What do athletics have to do with this?"

"A player. Not for a sports team, for a much different organization. One on the wrong side of the law."

"Schorr and Monroe told me he'd done time in prison. That was in the article, too. I didn't need a decoder ring to understand that much."

The way Russ looked down his nose at me made me feel dumb as dirt. I tried not to take it personally, but darn it, this was personal. I shot him a stony glare.

"Here's my take on what happened," he said. "Mac Rudd tried to do an end run around his employers. They took him out. Made sure he went to prison to teach him a lesson. My guess is he stole something of theirs. Something very valuable. When he didn't give it back, they killed him."

Ice cream jitterbugged in my stomach. "God. That's awful. If that's true, why are the police interested in me? I didn't know Mac Rudd."

"You both lived in Maryland. There might be a geographical connection."

He was making good sense. I decided to tell him the rest of it. Heat steamed off my face. "There is, sort of. I saw Mac Rudd talking to my husband in Maryland."

His gaze narrowed. "Tell me more."

I relayed what I'd told the police. When I was done, I felt drained. Tired, like I was a hundred and fifty years old. I wanted to go home and crawl into bed. How could I work and smile at customers for another hour?

"Your husband knew Rudd. Now your husband is dead and so is Rudd. There could be another connection between the two men."

My stomach knotted and I voiced my fears. "Are you saying Bernie had underworld ties? I can't believe it. Bernie was an energy analyst for Jesseman and Associates, for God's sakes. He had a boss and a regular paycheck. He wasn't a crook. I'd have known."

That call to Mr. Valerio popped into my reeling thoughts. I'd called him. He hadn't known where I was. Oh, God. If Russ's outrageous claim was true, I'd just given the mob my phone number. Wait. I was overreacting. I knew those people. They'd eaten dinner at my house.

"You didn't know about your level of debt," he pointed out.

Bernie's mismanagement of our money wasn't the same thing as working for the mob. I leapt to my feet. "Listen up. I'm not rewriting my personal history. I had a good marriage. It was good, do you hear me?"

I ran outside before he saw the tears. Damn him. I didn't want to cry over Bernie again. I was finally at a point where I was surviving on my own, where I didn't wake up bereft or angry.

I needed privacy to sort through my thoughts. I couldn't face cheery holiday music or vibrant red and green decorations. The thought of standing here in the shop and breathing in scents of evergreen and baked apple pie disagreed with my queasy stomach.

I wanted to go home, so that's what I did.

I flipped my shop sign to Closed, locked up, and drove off in my Jeep. The startled spider clung to his web on my door as I drove fast. Too bad. If the spider couldn't take the wind, he shouldn't have built his web in such a precarious place.

Life was a bitch. I couldn't be worried about a spider when there was a slim chance

I might have been married to a mobster.

At home, I sat on my bed and rubbed my throbbing temples. God. What was I doing? I'd bought my craft shop on a whim, and the only thing I could glue together was my hair. Was I playing at life? Or was I hiding from it?

I could admit to myself that Bernie had been a jerk, but I wasn't stupid. Admitting to more than that meant I'd been operating in the dark for years. That I'd turned a blind eye to Bernie's flaws to save my marriage. Had I been that desperate for affection and companionship?

I drew Mama's fluffy down comforter around my shoulders. I didn't like seeing my past from this perspective. I preferred thinking the last ten years of my life had been worthwhile.

Bernie had stolen more than my heart and my money. He'd stolen my pride. It hurt to admit that, and it hurt even more that Russ had pointed it out to me. I was ashamed of being such an idiot.

My middle hollowed out like one of my sandy seashells. My dirty laundry was private; it wasn't for public consumption. Bottom line, I wanted my mom. My adopted mom. I wanted her arms around me and her hands stroking the hair on my head as she told me everything would be all right.

But it wasn't all right.

I was afraid it would never be all right again.

CHAPTER 12

Tuesday was a much needed oasis of calm. Not one sighting of Detectives Schorr and Monroe. Not one crank call. It seemed everyone knew I'd go crazy if anyone so much as whispered the word "murder" in my vicinity.

When I locked the shop for the day, Daytona and John Curtis Washington dashed up to me, vibrating with youthful energy and excitement. "Mary Christmas, come see our new baby," Daytona said.

"New baby?" Daisy Pearl hadn't said anything about being pregnant. I'd assumed her thickened waistline was a result of tending the ice cream and bakery shop for so many years. But still, I'd have to have been blind to miss something like that. I needed to find an ophthalmologist to have my vision checked.

"Yeah. She's from Gwinnett County, so we're calling her Gwen." John Curtis beamed his missing teeth smile, and my heart warmed. "Mama says Gwinnett is too much of a mouthful for an itty bitty thing like her."

An adopted baby. Someone's unwanted child. The tight-fisted, adopted part of my heart felt an instant kinship with the tiny baby girl. We were sisters of a sort. "I'd love to see your new baby. I'll be over soon as I finish locking up."

They dashed out toward the pharmacy, spreading the news of their new baby sister. Wonderful news. Babies caused grown people to *coo* and to *ah* and make silly faces. Me included. I'd have given anything to have had a child of my own.

Could I be an honorary aunt to little Gwen? Daisy Pearl and her family had been so welcoming to me. I really wanted to return the favor. Besides, Daisy Pearl listened to my troubles and gave me sound advice like I was family. She shouldn't have any problem with me giving extra attention to her new baby.

I looked around my shop for a gift. There were a few non-seashell ornaments. A tiny stuffed angel seemed appropriate. I wrapped it in a box and carried it next door.

"Come see my new baby," Daytona said as she dragged me to a beaming Daisy Pearl and Peachy. Other members of her adopted family circled the baby. I'd met John Henry and Tamiqua the day I had my meltdown in Sweet Things. The other slender teen watching the baby with great anticipation must be Tamiqua's sister, Ronelle. I knew John Curtis from my craft class.

The delicate baby in Daisy Pearl's arms was tiny, not more than a few weeks old. A smattering of black curls graced her adorable head. She peered out at the world with alert brown eyes and a tremulous mouth. A little fist flailed with feisty insistence.

My heart swelled as I looked down at her. Caught up in the wonder of how perfectly formed she was, I leaned close. The light scent of baby powder embraced me. Mesmerized, I teared up in earnest.

"She's beautiful," I whispered.

Pride beamed on John Curtis's face. "She's got ten fingers and ten toes."

I straightened. "Daytona said you were going to call her Gwen."

Peachy unwrapped my gift and held it up. "Look at this cute little angel. Thank you, Mary Christmas. It's the perfect gift for our newest angel."

"That's real nice." Daisy Pearl nodded her head in approval. "You wanna hold her?"

My palms went sweaty. I hadn't actually

ever held a baby before. "No. I mean, yes, I really want to, but I don't want to break her."

"It's okay. We'll talk you through it." Daisy Pearl patted the seat beside her. "Sit beside me."

I sat, trembling with the thought of holding something so small and precious. *Please don't let me screw this up.*

Daisy Pearl showed me how to support the baby. Once tiny Gwen was in my arms, I was a goner. In that second, something fierce and maternal clicked on, and I wanted to protect this infant from all the evil in the world. "She's so dear. How can you bear not to hold her even for a minute?"

Daisy Pearl laughed. "That baby will get plenty of holding in this large family."

"I didn't know y'all were even thinking about a new baby."

Daisy Pearl and Peachy exchanged a knowing look, and the tension ramped up in the room. Obviously I'd touched a sore nerve.

"Honey, we're never thinking about a new baby. They find us," Daisy Pearl said.

"Now Daisy Pearl," Peachy started. "You know this baby needed a home and ain't nobody gonna take care of her better than us."

Awareness dawned on me. Daisy Pearl took in the lonely and downtrodden. She celebrated life by opening her heart to those in need.

I glanced from one to the other. A whole lot of something wasn't being said, possibly because of the other adopted children in the room. Holding that tiny baby gave me a close connection to these people and this place. It was a welcome respite to celebrate life, to not worry about murders or lying husbands.

Daisy Pearl leaned over to glance at the baby. "Now look at that. She's done gone to sleep in your arms. You're a natural with babies, Mary Christmas."

Warmth filled me. I inhaled the baby's fragrance again, touched her soft skin. "My husband and I tried for ten years to have a child, but it wasn't meant to be. I'm so glad you have little Gwen. I plan to come over here and spoil her rotten."

Ronelle, the sixteen-year-old sister of Tamiqua, bounced over. "Can I have a turn now, Mama?"

I reluctantly handed over the baby. Gwen's eyes flicked open during the transfer, but Ronelle cooed her back to sleep. "Can she sleep in my room, Mama Pearl?"

Daisy Pearl laughed. "Girl, you won't be

thinking that when she starts crying at two in the morning. She'll stay in the room with me and Peachy for now. Once she starts sleeping through the night, we'll make other arrangements."

"I get first dibs," Ronelle said. "She can bunk in with me and Tamiqua."

"We'll see," Daisy Pearl said.

I congratulated them again and headed for home. Once I got in my Jeep, I thought about driving to the mainland and buying Gwen a cute little dress. I could afford it, if I was careful about my other expenditures this month.

Being careful with money wasn't new to me, but watching every dime I spent reminded me of being married to Bernie. Of the days I struggled to make ends meet. And of his betrayal of my trust by keeping secrets.

Thinking of Bernie soured my good mood. He'd brought poverty and despair into my life. And it looked like I was due for more heartache where Bernie was concerned.

I needed a drink, someplace I could unwind. I could do that at home, but happy hour at a beachfront bar on Hotel Row appealed to me. I drove to BareFootin', a low-key bar with a great view of the ocean. Happy hour meant I got two drinks for the price of one.

I nursed a couple of Coronas as the sun kissed the horizon. Silvery orange and molten gold rays of sunlight shimmered over the ocean.

You could have knocked me over with a sea oats plume when Russ appeared at my table. "Mind if I join you?" he asked, two beer bottles in hand.

Why would I mind? His was a familiar face, and we were friends. Friends hung out together. After thinking about Bernie, I needed a friend. "Pull up a chair. I didn't know you came here."

His face blanked for a moment. "This is the first time I've been in."

"Interesting." What was more interesting was that I'd been able to read his discomfort. I'd known he wasn't a regular here from the pinched expression on his face. Mr. Ultracool wasn't so cool after all.

"What's the occasion?" He settled into the nearest chair.

I still wasn't ready to admit Russ might be right about Bernie, so I steered clear of that subject. "Daisy Pearl and Peachy got a new baby."

"Ah. The new baby. Here's to the newest Washington." He raised his Budweiser and clinked it with my nearly empty Corona bottle.

I finished my beer and signaled the bartender for another round. This two-for-one deal at happy hour suited my lean budget. I downed another healthy gulp of my second beer. Two beers was normally my limit. Four would surely liquefy my brain. Three was dicey, but I felt the need to push my boundaries tonight.

"I researched Jesseman and Associates," Russ said. "The company has a Dun and Bradstreet number, but their phone number is out of service. Their physical address is an empty lot in the DC suburbs."

My heart stilled as arctic cold swept through my insides. The soft instrumental music flowed around me as before, only this time every passing note jabbed into my skin. The conversation in the bar shattered the rest of my illusions about the past.

Russ couldn't be right. I'd met Bernie's coworkers. I'd been to his Christmas party and met their wives. Russ couldn't rewrite my personal history this way. I flexed my cold fingers around my beer bottle. I wouldn't let him.

He'd crossed the line of friendship. "You had no right to do that."

With a casual shrug, he held my gaze.

"Facts are facts. I have a very analytical nature. I expect things to follow in orderly patterns. When they don't, I find out why. Tell me what you know about Bernie's work."

"I already told you. He was an energy analyst. He traveled the country checking energy consumption."

"Do you remember Valerie Plame? She was in the national news not too long ago."

This line of conversation was unsettling. Nausea churned in my gut. I abandoned my third beer and hugged my arms to my stomach. "I don't spend a lot of time following the news. Who the heck is Valerie Plame?"

"A middle-aged blond. She looked very much like a yuppie socialite, blond and personable, but she was a CIA operative. Her cover was that she was an energy analyst for a private company named Brewster Jennings and Associates. The CIA acknowledged her company was a front for investigations."

"CIA?" I heard my voice crackle. "Bernie? No way. He was always reading self-help books. Everything always had to be his idea. No way could he have worked for a large agency. His team was small, and they got along extremely well."

"MaryBeth, Bernie's situation is very similar to Valerie Plame's. Even the terminology for his work unit. Operatives work together in teams."

I ran my fingers through my short hair. "Bernie was no secret agent. He was a regular guy. Boxer shorts. Flannel shirts. Polyester suits from Penney's. We didn't have a life in the fast lane. We ate meatloaf and apple pie and scrambled eggs. He wasn't a top secret kind of a guy. He didn't have a passport."

"I know you believe that, but I'm not convinced. My gut instinct tells me that things in Bernie's life don't add up. From what you've said about his frequent travel schedule and his insistence on him phoning you while he was away, I'd say there's a really strong chance Bernie was CIA."

I shook my head. It was too much to take in. "Last time we talked, you said he was mob. Bernie's old work number is on speed dial on my cell phone. Let's call his boss right now and get this squared away." I dug my phone out of my purse and held the number two until it dialed the stored number.

Instead of the electronic voice mail proclaiming the extension numbers for various employees, a much different recording echoed in my ear. "The number you have reached is a nonworking number. Please check the number you are trying to reach and dial again."

I didn't think I could get any colder inside, but I did. Confusion fuzzed my thoughts. I didn't understand what was happening. Either way, CIA or mob, it was a nightmare. I flipped the phone closed.

Russ gazed at me expectantly. I shook my head. "The number is out of service. What you're saying seems too crazy to be true. People from his work came to his memorial service. No one ever mentioned CIA to me. If it's true, why didn't Bernie tell me about this before?"

Russ clasped his hands on the table. "I can't say exactly, but I can speculate based on recent events. One scenario might be Bernie was working undercover, and his cover was blown. In which case, the agency would no longer need him."

I gulped the rest of beer number three. Did Bernie's co-workers kill him? I gagged at the thought. "Are you implying that the CIA offed Bernie?"

"They don't make a habit of offing their agents. I believe they might have put him in the federal Witness Relocation Program."

My hands curled into fists under the table.

So much for unwinding at happy hour. "Who the heck are you to make such sweeping proclamations about my husband's past? Why should I believe you?"

"I can't make you believe me. However, I'm reasonably well informed about what goes on in the world, and I'm giving you the benefit of my opinion."

"Even if I am crazy enough to believe you, what about me? Why didn't they tell me? Why wouldn't they have moved me with him?"

"I can't say. Another scenario would be the mission blew up in Bernie's face, and he really is dead."

"You mean, like somebody else killed him? A bad guy?"

"Something like that."

I leaned close to him, made sure no one else was listening. "God. I don't know how you expect me to accept these wild ideas. The whole notion of Bernie being a secret operative is too fantastic." This conversation had ventured into the realm of mythology and legend — very entertaining but based on groundless speculation.

Russ swirled the remaining beer in his bottle then took a swig. "There is another scenario."

I gave a nervous laugh. "Let me guess.

I'm the secret agent in this one? I killed everyone?"

"This is no laughing matter." His eyes narrowed. "Given Bernie's acquaintance with Mac Rudd and your empty bank accounts, it's highly possible Bernie transferred his allegiance to the other team. His alleged death occurred after Mac Rudd got out of prison. If he were mixed up in one of Rudd's cons, some very nasty people would be after him. I can see where he'd want to go underground."

"I don't like it when you use words like 'alleged' and 'operative' when talking about Bernie. That's not how I remember him." I stood, but stumbled backward.

Russ must have anticipated my clumsy movement because his hands closed around my waist and tugged me upright before I fell on the floor. He held out his hand. "Give me your keys. I'll drive you home."

The room wasn't all that steady, but I didn't want his help. I was going to be self-sufficient for the rest of my life. "Don't be silly. Then your vehicle would be stuck here. I can drive home."

"Not happening. We can't have Mary Christmas going to jail for DUI."

The starch went out of my spine as I realized I'd downed four beers. I handed him my purse. "Go ahead, drive me home. But it's only fair to warn you, I'm a regular death magnet. People close to me end up dead, then I have to dispose of all their personal belongings. You've heard of angels of death? Well, I'm a custodian of death. The janitor who polices lifetime accumulations of belongings. And you know what?" I hiccupped. "It sucks."

He settled me in the Jeep passenger seat, adjusted the mirrors, and drove me home. For some reason, my thoughts refused to settle. The CIA and the mob didn't belong in my sheltered world. I couldn't integrate them into my thoughts. I needed to think of something concrete and immediate.

Russ was both concrete and immediate. His presence filled every nook and cranny of my Jeep. I crossed my legs at the ankles as his now familiar scent infiltrated my bloodstream. The desire to critique his appearance welled up inside me until it burst out of my lips.

I patted his leg. "Did I tell you that you have a cute butt? You do. But your nose is too sharp, and your eyes too all-seeing. That must get old, seeing everything."

In the dusky twilight, Russ shot me a considering glance. I considered him right back. I'd been wondering what it would be like to kiss him. Why not do something rash? Being good was boring. When we got to my house, I wasn't going to be responsible for my actions.

Rational thought resurfaced. Talking and acting crazy wasn't how I behaved. I had to think about something else besides kissing Russ. Anything to take my mind off of this abrupt sensual detour. "What about your truck? How will you get it?"

"No problem. I'll walk down the beach. It shouldn't take long to get back to Hotel Row."

He had a plan. Good. Because I had a plan of my own. As soon as we reached my house, I was gonna jump his bones. This day had taken an extreme toll on my mental health. Holding that baby had reminded me of how barren my life was. I wanted to celebrate life.

I should go for the gusto. Take a chance on Russ. If I didn't, my future would be as lackluster as my past.

Under my lashes, I glanced over at Russ. He would be an adventure I wouldn't soon forget. But, though he was attentive, he hadn't made any move toward cultivating a romance.

Pity.

Tonight, romance was very much on my

mind. As was kissing my male friend with the hot body.

What would it be like to make love to a man who was so tightly wound? Would he be insatiable? The need to know ate at me.

Life was short.

If I waited for Russ to make the first move, I might never find out what he was like. It was time to take action, time to take a life-affirming step.

When Russ opened my door, I slid out of my seat, wrapped my arms around his neck, and clung to him like a sandspur. "You know what? I've been wanting to do this for a long time." With that, I planted my lips on his and kissed him.

CHAPTER 13

I sighed, and the roar nearly deafened me. It was going to be a long day. Going for the gusto had netted me a killer hangover and a ton of embarrassment.

Russ hadn't kissed me back. He'd pried me off of his lips, made sure I was safely locked inside my house, and hightailed it out of there. I'd called him a few choice words behind my locked door. Then I'd passed out in bed fully clothed.

An expressway roared through my throbbing head. The enamel on my teeth ached. And my big floppy hat and dark glasses had failed miserably at dimming the morning sunlight and twinkling Christmas lights.

I knew better than to drink so much. Two beers was my normal limit, but I'd pushed the envelope last night. Now I was paying for my recklessness. I would've stayed home today for a personal mental health day, but that darned craft class was this afternoon.

I couldn't let the kids down.

Russ was next door in the pharmacy. His sleek black pickup had been in the parking lot when I arrived thirty minutes ago. I must have been out of my mind to kiss Russ. He didn't exactly protest, but he didn't warm to my embrace either. He'd been a perfect Southern gentleman about the whole thing.

Sickening man.

His lack of response confirmed what I already knew. No matter how fresh and new my haircut was, I was still boring and dull. Kissing me was not a thrill, not a moment to treasure, not even an event to write home about. He'd probably gone home and gargled with mouthwash after I'd assaulted him.

How would I face him again? I rubbed the growing ache in the back of my head. I needed a plan. I couldn't hide in here forever.

I should apologize to Russ.

Was an apology enough? I'd never been so forward with a man before. I had no way of knowing how offended Russ had been. Surely the situation called for something more than words. What would smooth out the awkwardness?

A gift might be nice. I brightened, then my hopes plummeted. He probably had everything he needed. I groaned and held my throbbing head. Great. What could I get for a man who had everything?

Something he didn't need.

I glanced around at the cluttered counters and overflowing cubbyholes in my craft room. Lots of raw crafting material in here. Not much that would be of interest to Russ.

All right. How about an ornament from the shop? I warmed to the idea. Only how would I know which one? He might already have a cupboard full of them. With reluctance, I opened the drawer of my imperfect seashell creations.

I hadn't been able to throw them out. The oyster shell Santas were too thin. The scallop shell angels were too blue. My cross-eyed Christmas mice looked comical. But I'd made them.

Why not give him one of each in a small basket? That way he'd be bound to like at least one item.

Humming along with "What Child is This," I tied a sassy red ribbon on the handle of a small woven basket, then lined the basket with green tissue paper. As I wrapped each homemade treasure in tissue paper and placed it in the basket, my spirits rose.

Hat and dark glasses in place, I strode

purposefully to Russ's pharmacy. He stood and met me at the counter.

The corners of his mouth kicked up briefly. "Going incognito today?"

He was speaking to me. That was a good sign. "The light is a little strong this morning." I lifted the basket up to his cluttered pharmacy counter. The red bow and green paper looked out of place against the orange pumpkins and Halloween witches. "I'm here to apologize for my forward behavior last night. It was inappropriate. I'm sorry for embarrassing us both."

He glanced at the basket. His expression tightened into a familiar scowl. "What's that for?"

I didn't understand the suspicion in his voice. "It's a gift for you. To go with my apology."

My hands gripped tightly together as last-minute doubts assailed me. What if he hated my second-rate craft efforts?

My heart would shatter if I saw the basket in the communal dumpster this evening. I exhaled slowly. His like or dislike of my gift didn't matter. The important thing was that I had tried to make amends. "Go on. Open it."

He glanced over at the gift basket. His fearful expression brought a smile to my face. At last, a reaction I understood. Not quite the forgiveness I'd hoped for, but fear was better than no reaction at all.

"It won't bite," I said. "I wasn't sure what you liked, but I'm certain you don't already have anything quite like this."

His dark brown eyes narrowed. "You didn't have to get me anything."

"I wanted to. Again, I'm sorry about last night. I hope we can still be friends."

"Friends," he repeated neutrally.

God.

Why was this so hard?

Yanking out my own teeth would be easier. I wanted to reach over the counter and shake a thank you out of him so that I could leave. If he didn't want to be friends, why didn't he just say so? I didn't have the time or patience to interpret his cryptic reactions.

My shoulders were practically touching my ears. I squared them and tried to calm myself. If he didn't want to be friends with me, fine. I'd done all I could do to make amends. "I hope you like the crafts I made. I've got to get back to my shop."

He looped two fingers under the basket handle and lifted it up. "Thanks, Mary Christmas."

I couldn't stand and watch while he

unwrapped each one of my mangled crafts. "See you around." I darted out.

During the day, the pounding in my head subsided, so I put my hat and sunglasses away. I replayed the Jim Brickman Christmas CD until I felt human. Late in the afternoon I picked up my mail from the post office. After viewing my bank statement, my headache returned full force. Four hundred dollars was missing from my checking account.

I drove over to the bank. Lawrence Ellerbe, the bank manager, took me in his office. "What can I do for you, Miz Cashour?"

"You can explain how check 1046 got cashed for four hundred dollars when I didn't write that check."

His genial expression vanished. "What's this?"

I waved my bank statement in his face. "Check 1046. Here it is on this month's statement."

He looked at me over the tops of his half glasses. "Did you lose your checkbook?"

I thought about leaning over the polished cherry desk and grabbing hold of his skinny navy blue tie. "I didn't lose anything. I don't know how that check got written. All I know is that I want my money back."

"Do you have your checkbook with you?"

I pulled it out of my purse and tossed it on his desk. "See? I have it right here. It isn't lost. And I'm on check 1027."

"Just a moment." He typed rapidly and the computer screen flickered. Soon, a printed image of the check was on his desk.

I scanned the page voraciously, shaking my head in disbelief. "This looks like my handwriting, but I swear on a stack of bibles I didn't write this check. Look at my account history. I never write checks to cash. I use my card at the machine outside when I want cash."

"You'll have to fill out some forms," Ellerbe said after he'd studied everything.

"Will that get me my money back?"

"The money will be credited to your account. What we do in cases like this is to freeze the account until we determine the extent of the damage. Are other checks missing?"

I flipped through my checkbook. The air drained out of me when I found another check missing. My voice caught in my throat. "Check 1049 is gone too."

"We'll stop payment on that one. You'll need to go through your supply of spare checks at home. And I recommend that you close out the account and open a new one.

Do you have any outstanding checks?"

"Yes." I opened my register. "Two. One to the phone company and one to the power company."

He made a note of it. "Would you like to open a new checking account today?"

"Yes." We transferred funds over to a new account, froze the old one, and thirty mind-numbing minutes later I stumbled out of there.

Ellerbe caught up with me at the door. "One last thing, Miz Cashour. You'll need to complete an incident report at the police station. Otherwise, there could be warrants issued against you for writing bad checks."

"But I didn't write any bad checks."

"That's why you need to complete the police report."

I called the cops as soon as I returned to the shop. Detective Monroe said they'd be right over.

As I set out wooden frames, seashells, and glue for the afternoon craft class, I couldn't stop thinking about that money. How did someone obtain my checks? I didn't leave my checkbook or my purse lying around. Who knew what my signature looked like? And why me? Surely other folks had deeper pockets than mine.

When Detectives Monroe and Schorr arrived, I filled them in. Detective Schorr wrote up the incident report as I spoke.

"No one else has signature authority on your account?" Detective Monroe asked. Her partner looked strong and buff beside her in his pressed jeans, black t-shirt, and linen blazer.

I shook my head. "Nope."

"Did you notice check 1046 was missing?"

"Not until the bank statement came."

"Are any other checks missing?" Detective Monroe continued.

"1049. We stopped payment on it. I don't know about the other checkbooks at home."

"Are your checkbooks ever out of your direct control?"

Her questioning of this most basic survival skill rubbed me the wrong way. I'd lived in an urban environment for most of my life. I knew to keep track of my purse. "I'm meticulous about keeping financial records and related materials in a safe place."

I pointed to the stretchy key chain on my wrist. "This goes to the locked file cabinet where my purse is stowed when I'm here. At home, I keep it in a kitchen cabinet near the pantry. My extra checks are stored in a kitchen drawer."

Detective Monroe examined the file cabinet lock and the locks on both doors. "Is your house locked up when you aren't there?"

"Sure." But a stray thought bubbled up from my subconscious. I didn't always lock up when I walked on the beach. "Most of the time."

The detectives exchanged a knowing look. "You reported a merchandise theft two days ago. Since there's no evidence of the locks being tampered with, there's a real possibility that someone else has a key. Did you change the locks when you took ownership?"

"No. I didn't know I needed to."

"It's a good idea. You don't know who the previous owner may have loaned keys to."

My mind reeled with the thought of a faceless stranger having a key to my private property. "Got it."

"I recommend changing the locks for your own safety and security. Whoever took those checks doesn't respect you or your property. Unless there's a deterrent, an opportunistic criminal will steal from you again."

My heart sank. I'd be spending money on security without hope of a financial return. This wasn't the first time someone had stolen from me. A shiver swept up my body. "Who would do this?"

"Someone who needs money." Detective

Schorr pushed the form across for me to sign.

Smart aleck. I already knew that much. My frustration boiled out as I scribbled my name. "That narrows the suspect pool down considerably. Who doesn't need money?"

"Don't shoot the messenger, hon," Detective Schorr said with a sly wink as he left.

Appalled, I stared at him. He'd never winked at me before. Was he flirting with me? I was way older than him. He'd never acted anything but professional with me before today. So why would Detective Hottie wink at me?

Memories of throwing myself at Russ came steaming into my head. Russ didn't strike me as a kiss-and-tell kind of guy, but I hadn't told anyone. My mouth went dry.

My reckless behavior was probably headline news all over the island by now. Reputations in a small town were fragile things. All it had taken was one extra beer, and I'd forever tarnished mine.

If Bernie were alive, he'd be furious about my attention-grabbing behavior. He'd always demanded I behave in a way that didn't cause comment. I'd allowed him to shape me into his perfect wife. And now, look at me. Without his guidance, I'd stumbled big time.

I'd drunk too much and assaulted a man with my lips. Appalling. Embarrassing. But not the end of the world.

Or was it in a small town? The locals might change their opinion of me. So far, I'd been associated with public drunkenness, fast behavior, financial trouble, theft, and murder.

Not the sort of person parents wanted their kids hanging around.

CHAPTER 14

Tinkling piano keys and softly blaring horns supported Diana Krall's jazzy version of "Sleigh Ride." I flipped my Open sign to Closed, locked the front door, and headed to my craft room. The kids should be here any minute now for the craft class — if they were allowed to come, that is.

John Curtis dashed into the back room, his long orange t-shirt half tucked into his droopy shorts. He glanced around the room expectantly. "Where's my shark?"

"What shark is that?" A flicker of hope lifted my spirits. Daisy Pearl had allowed her children to come. Maybe I wasn't black-listed.

John Curtis peered inside every bucket of shells on the back counter, disappointment etched on his face. "My shark. You said we'd paint Christmas sharks this week."

"I said, we'd see. This week's class is on seashell picture frames. You can paint your frame red or green before gluing on the shells if you want it to look Christmassy. Or you can make one that is more simplistic, more suited for year-round use, like the one Tyson started last week."

"Hear that, Ty?" John Curtis smiled his gap-toothed smile at Tyson who'd just entered the craft room. "She called you simple. Like Simple Simon."

Oh, dear. I'd better set the record straight, quick. "You misunderstood what I said. Simon's work is beautiful."

John Curtis laughed with enthusiasm. "Simon? Who's that?"

Heat steamed off my face. Class hadn't even started and I'd already put my foot in my mouth. "I'm sorry. I meant to say Tyson. His frame is beautiful. I'd like for each of you to work on a picture frame this week."

Jolene flounced in wearing a denim jumper and an oversized canvas hat with the brim flared up all around. She plopped down across from Tyson. Relief flooded my veins. The town hadn't placed me off limits to their children. "Welcome back, Jolene."

"Hey," Jolene said. She looked down at the craft supplies and heaved a dramatic sigh, as if it were the greatest inconvenience in the world for her to decorate a picture frame.

Part of me wanted to pull out the rest of my craft materials until I found something she wanted to make. But the other part of me said I'd be more successful in maintaining order if everyone worked on the same project.

I pasted a bright smile on my face. "We're making picture frames today."

Claudia and Steven Barber arrived next, greeted everyone, and found seats at the craft table. "Can I pass out the shells?" Claudia asked, her hip-length braid swaying as she perched on the edge of her chair.

Whew. Perfect attendance. Maybe my troubles weren't common knowledge. I beamed at Claudia. "Thanks, but shell selection is part of the creative process. Everyone is to fill their plates with the size, color, and texture of shells that they like the most."

"I get to go first." Jolene raced over to the back counter. She reached in the first bucket and grabbed a handful of shells.

Daytona and Claudia took longer making their selections. Both John Curtis and Steven Barber subscribed to the Jolene school of shell collection. Tyson already had a plateful selected from last time. He started meticulously fitting the next section of shells into his intricate pattern.

"Are you entering the kite contest?" Claudia asked Daytona.

Daytona sprinkled sand over the glue she'd applied to her frame. "Nope. I got me a brand new baby sister. I don't have time for kites."

Claudia precisely applied another brush full of red paint to her wooden frame. "My Dad helped me and Steven make kites. We've been to the beach a few times to try them out. Steven's tore up already."

Steven looked up from his frame. He'd arranged groupings of shells to look like Halloween faces, with double rows of coquina shells in the corners of the frame to look like screaming teeth. "It wasn't my fault. The wind was too strong."

John Curtis made a goofy face and wiggled his paint-laden fingers at Claudia.

"Yeah, and the scary man had nothing to do with it," Claudia said.

I froze. A scary man sounded like trouble we didn't need. "What scary man?"

"The scary man sleeping in the sand dunes by our house," Claudia said as she selected a white shell from her collection. "He had whiskers on his face so thick you couldn't even see his lips. And big glasses that made his eyes look beady. His brown hair was straggly-looking under his camouflage hat. He stank, too."

I trembled at her detailed description. This man sounded dangerous. He might be behind my recent thefts.

Steven groaned. "You didn't get close enough to smell him, Claudia."

Claudia tossed her long braid over her shoulder. "Doesn't matter. Boys stink. I'm sure he stinks worse."

My heart quickened. A raggedy stranger on the beach wasn't good news. "I hope you told your parents. Did the man threaten you in any way?"

"He didn't have to," Claudia said. "He looked scary when he stood up. Like a sand monster. I screamed and ran home."

I strolled around the table and kept my outward expression calm. My mind was spinning with what I should do. The last thing I wanted was to make the kids afraid. "Stay away from any people you don't know. The world is not a nice place."

"He better not come near my mom," Tyson muttered through clenched teeth.

Tyson's mom was confined to a wheelchair. It was adorable that Tyson felt so protective of her.

Jolene held up her glued-together fingers.

"I saw the scary man, too."

I stopped behind Tyson and looked over at Jolene. "Where did you see him?"

She pulled her fingers apart, completely engrossed in her project. "I took a shortcut home from school yesterday and saw him digging through the dumpster at Hotel Row."

"The bum was dumpster diving?" John Curtis hooted. "You were right, Claudia. I bet he stunk up a storm."

I calmed a degree. The stranger was a homeless man, not a master thief. "He must've been starving. Give him a wide berth, and tell your parents if he frightens you."

I remembered Claudia and Steven's address from their registration forms. They lived a quarter mile farther up the beach from me. We were both quite a distance from the hotel corridor. Was it possible this bum was my thief? I shivered at the thought.

Anything was possible. But how would he obtain my signature? How did he cash my check without showing identification? No, his being involved with the check fraud seemed unlikely.

After the kids left, it took me five minutes to straighten up the room. Much better than last week. Heck, I didn't even have a headache this time. Mercifully, there was nothing stuck in my hair either. I looked at the finished frames with pride. Though I hadn't made them, I could appreciate each one of them as a work of art.

Originals. That's what art was about. Tyson's frame would be a perfect composition. It was art too, but major league stuff. A boy who cared as deeply as he did about art and his handicapped mother would spend his life in touch with his creativity.

Inspired by the children's efforts, I sat down and decorated a frame. I dotted on fingerprints of red paint, then glued tiny little shells along the inner border. Art. I couldn't do it wrong.

Maybe I wasn't such a failure at crafts. Success was a matter of perspective. Not that anyone would pay money for my polka-dotted frame, but I wasn't planning on selling it. I could use some art on the walls at home.

Hmm. I pulled out two more unfinished frames and, using the same theme of small shells on the inner border, created different designs with the red paint. Now I had a grouping of folk art I could hang on the walls.

I carried a smile inside me all the way home because I hadn't had much to smile about recently. I needed to change my store locks, but that would have to wait one more day. My checks were still buried in a kitchen drawer. None were missing. My thief had been very deliberate.

Why target me?

It didn't make any sense.

Nothing was resolving. Events from my past didn't hold up to the light of day. It galled me to realize how little I knew about Bernie.

In my heart, I couldn't bring myself to accept the new information about Bernie. He'd been a good husband. Maybe a little too controlling, but at the time it had felt good to have someone to rely on. He'd been my rock.

What if Russ was right?

What if Bernie had been working for the CIA and was now in the Witness Relocation Program somewhere? Would I help if Bernie was in trouble?

Of course.

I frowned because I'd answered automatically, but my present-day feelings weren't so automatic. How could they be? I'd been through a lot these past six months. Russ's suppositions about Bernie kept running through my head.

I'd been married to Bernie for ten years.

If I didn't know him, no one did. There was no way Russ could be right about Bernie.

No way on God's green earth.

CHAPTER 15

"Christmas by the Sea," I said into the phone. "How may I help you?"

I waited. An ominous silence followed my standard shop greeting. Icy waves of dread washed over me.

"Hello? Anybody there?" I hoped like heck it was a little old lady needing directions from Hotel Row.

Emptiness echoed through the receiver. The hauntingly beautiful piano rendition of "What Child Is This" playing in my shop faded from my hearing as silence pulsed through the phone line. Though I remembered the police instructions for drawing out the duration of the call, now that the person was on the line, panic clawed at my gut.

"Who's calling?" Cinnamon and evergreen scents perfumed the air of my shop. I glanced around at the twinkling Christmas trees, half expecting a villain to lunge out

179

and grab me. My fingers tightened on the phone. "What do you want from me?"

No response. Oddly, the silence felt expectant, as if the person on the other end wanted to talk but couldn't. Impulse demanded I immediately hang up. I wanted to scrub my hands and my ears until the creepy feeling went away.

Except hanging up would defeat the purpose.

With my knuckles whitening beneath their harsh grip, I waited. The police needed time to trace the call.

With each passing second, my anger rose. Why didn't my phantom caller speak?

I didn't know anything about this person. If it was a male. Or a female. Black, white, Hispanic. He or she obviously knew me. How could I give them what they wanted so they would leave me alone?

I drew in a deep breath and released it. *Okay. Calm down. If you don't, you're going to blow this. There has to be something you can say to drag out the length of the call. Think.*

Thoughts raced through my head. Why did I automatically assume this person was evil? Couldn't the repeat caller have another problem? What if this wasn't a crank caller, but instead was someone who was painfully shy?

No, that wasn't believable. This caller wasn't misguided or shy. These calls were made for the express purpose of upsetting me. Harassment. I shouldn't try to pretty it up. It was ugly, and I wanted it to stop.

I listened for background sounds, anything that would give me a hint of who it was, child or adult. Nothing. Tension hung about me like a noose. Were the crank calls related to my thefts? Did the creep track my whereabouts with the calls? I should be able to figure this out, but all I could think about was slamming down the phone.

My heart fluttered. That creepy-crawly feeling of cold air scraping against my skin returned. Whoever was doing this to me deserved to be punished.

It felt like I had been on the phone forever. I glanced at the clock. Why hadn't I noted the time the call began? I didn't know if I'd been on long enough for the police to trace the caller.

I grabbed a handful of my hair, needing to hold onto something real. "Don't call me anymore. I can't help you."

Shaken by the continued silence, I put the phone on the counter and walked away. I rubbed the goose bumps from my arms. I had no pretension of having any psychic ability, but this experience was making me a believer in things unseen. Evil existed, as I'd just experienced, and it could be transmitted across phone lines. At least I wasn't alone this time.

I phoned Detective Monroe on my cell phone and explained the situation. "I just received another crank call here in the shop. I drew the call out like you said, but the person never spoke a word."

"You done good, Miz Cashour." Detective Monroe's crisp voice instilled confidence in me. "We'll get right on that trace."

"Thanks. I want this to be over."

I skittered around the shop for a few minutes, making sure all was well in my kingdom. I straightened up the plastic sharks in their bins, aligned the Christmas mugs just so.

If I didn't stay busy, I would be a nervous wreck. What else could I do while they traced the call? In the back room, I caught sight of the children's seashell frames. Thankful for the diversion, I started sealing them. The repetitive back and forth of the sealant brush provided an alternate focus for my racing thoughts.

The kid's frames were such cheerful reflections of their personalities. Bright and glittery for Daytona. Playful and boyish for John Curtis. Artsy for Claudia. Acute gender awareness for Steven. Jolene and her march to a different drummer.

And Tyson's work — well, deep currents of art there. His frame would be worth big bucks as one of his early works. If Tyson continued to come to my craft classes, I'd have to find new ways to challenge him.

The future.

I paused. Still a bit scary, but no longer terrifying.

Once this crank caller was arrested, and Mac Rudd's murder was solved, I wouldn't have any major baggage. Except Bernie. I might never know what happened to him. But I was at the point where I didn't care what he'd done. I wanted to move on.

The chimes on my front door sounded the first few bars of "The First Noel." Fear clutched my heart. Was it my stalker? I peered around the door of my craft room and was greatly relieved to see Russ. His alert gaze scanned the shop and settled on me. He prowled purposefully in my direction, his muscled strides eating up the floor.

Be still my beating heart.

Ignoring the rapid thumping of said organ, I managed a tight smile. "Hello, neighbor. What can I do for you today?"

"I tried to call just now, but your phone rang like it was busy. Is something wrong with your phone?"

I brushed past him and hung the phone up. "Nothing's wrong with my phone. I had a long call."

With Russ here, I didn't feel nearly so scared. I should've gone over to the pharmacy or the bakery to wait while the call was being traced. I wished I'd thought of that sooner.

Russ filled the doorway to my craft room. From his puzzled expression, he had more questions about my phone call, but I wasn't volunteering any information. Until I heard back from the cops, I wasn't sure I was capable of carrying on a conversation at all.

Wait. I didn't need to make conversation. He'd come over here. If I exercised a little patience, he'd tell me the purpose of his visit.

He shoved a box of cellophane at me. "I wanted you to have this."

"For me?" I chewed on my bottom lip as I studied the box in my hand. Chocolate truffles. My mouth watered at the thought of all that delicious decadence inside. "Yum. Thanks. Want one?"

Scowl in place, he shook his head. "No. They're for you."

"What's the occasion?"

He shrugged.

Okay. Clearly a meeting of the dating-challenged here. I'd given him a gift. Now he'd reciprocated. Did that mean we were even, or something else entirely?

Though it was midway between breakfast and lunch, I ripped the wrapping off and popped a truffle in my mouth. The treat melted on my tongue with heavenly bliss. I shoved the box at him. "Sure you won't have one?"

"I bought them for you."

His husky tone warmed me inside out. It hadn't slipped my mind that he was a man and he'd brought me chocolates. That date-like sensation skittered through my head. I needed to think about something else.

My gaze drifted back to the box. The enticing aroma of chocolate saturated the air above the remaining eight truffles. Would he think I was too indulgent if I ate another one? I surely wanted more. "I haven't seen these in the drugstore before. What aisle are they on?"

"We don't carry them."

"Oh."

My nerves scattered. He'd gone out of his way to buy a gift for me. He hadn't collected the things he couldn't sell and tried to pawn them off on me, which made his gift even more special. I quickly closed the lid on the chocolates so I didn't disgrace myself by eating the whole box in front of him.

Though I could.

Easily.

What now? I didn't have seating in my shop, but there were chairs around my craft table. Since I had no customers in my shop to require my attention, I gestured toward my back room. "Would you like to sit down?"

He ran his hand through his short brown hair. "I have to get back."

"Oh. Okay."

I fully expected him to leave, but he entered my craft room and paced the circumference of the room as if he were memorizing the lay of the land for a military maneuver.

Fortified by chocolate, I propped myself in the doorway and watched his long legs eat up ground. His barely contained energy reminded me of a caged lion. A predator. He'd be dangerous if cornered.

I kept my distance.

But the part of me that enjoyed my independence wondered what it would be like to cross his path. Would he move around me? Stop? Would his eyes darken as they looked into mine?

Warmth pooled in me at the thought.

He stopped by the exterior door. Light streamed in through the windowpanes in the top of the door, casting his stern face in shadow. "The thing is, I feel bad about what happened the other day."

Okay. The floor could open up and suck me down whole now and I wouldn't protest. I didn't want to talk about the Tuesday night kiss or his lack of reaction. It wasn't every day that MaryBeth Cashour made a pass at a man. My fumbling attempt at seduction wouldn't be repeated. I never wanted to feel that small again.

His words filtered through my humiliation. Wait. He felt bad about it? Nervous about where this was going, I nodded. "Go on."

"I shouldn't have been so blunt about your husband. I didn't mean to hurt your feelings, and I'm sorry for how I delivered the news."

He'd brought me chocolates because he was sorry? He hadn't mentioned me assaulting him with an unwanted kiss. I took a little breath. The world as I knew it wasn't ending.

In fact, it was just the opposite. The air

was rife with possibilities. A handsome man stood in my craft room, looking at me and really seeing me. Me, MaryBeth Cashour, not Bernie's wife or Naomi's daughter.

"That's okay. I knew you meant well," I managed to say.

"You believe me?"

I frowned, ignoring the little voices clamoring in my head that he might be right. If I believed him, my whole marriage was a lie. I clung to the safety of my interpretation of past events.

Ten years of marriage demanded I defend Bernie. "I didn't say that. Nothing could be further from the truth. My husband wouldn't have committed a crime and abandoned me. He wasn't like that."

"Take off your rose-colored glasses, Mary-Beth." His voice hardened. "Bernie Cashour wasn't the upstanding man of your memories. He kept secrets from you. He didn't put you first."

The chocolate truffle in my stomach soured. "I don't want to talk about the past. Thank you for the chocolates."

"I'm trying to do the right thing here." Russ rubbed the back of his neck. "I should've remembered the messenger always gets shot."

He stopped by the craft table and glanced

down at the shell-encrusted crafts. My mind whirred with frantic thoughts. Strangely, I wondered if he could tell who created each frame.

Russ studied them all, spending the longest time looking at my trio of red frames. "These are very good."

I didn't want to feel flattered. His interest in my crafts shouldn't make any difference in my opinion of him. Even though I was mad at him for disparaging Bernie's good name, I couldn't deny the spark of excitement his words brought me. "You like them?"

"Yeah." His brown eyes twinkled. "The bright colors remind me of some original folk art I recently acquired."

Warmth spread inside of me. He thought I was an artist. Flattering as that was, I couldn't allow him to keep that misconception. "They're nothing special. Not museum-quality art."

He looked up, his dark gaze locked with mine. "Don't sell yourself short, Mary Christmas. I know quality when I see it."

"But what about Tyson's frame?" I pointed it out for him. "It's much better."

He studied the intricate, precise mosaic of shells then shrugged. "Different. Not better."

The trickle of warmth inside me grew. I shouldn't be flattered. I wasn't a true artist. Heck, I'd never even had an art class.

A flowing instrumental version of "We Three Kings" came through the speakers. Not even gold, frankincense, or myrrh could compete with sincere praise. It was the finest gift of all. The corners of my lips turned up. "Thanks for the compliment."

For a long moment he watched me. Heat rose up my neck and swept across my face. It's a wonder steam didn't shoot out my ears under his intense perusal.

"Any time."

"So, we're friends again?"

His Adam's apple bobbed. "Yeah. We're friends."

With a quick smile, he left, but the sunshine of his words stayed in my heart. I had a friend. A male friend whom I'd kissed. A friend whose heated gaze implied something more intimate than friendship.

I traced the outline of my mouth and wondered where this was going. Friendship between a man and a woman. Intimacy. With Russ.

Lord, help me.

CHAPTER 16

The harsh rays of the setting sun had me navigating by the white line on the edge of the road as I drove west to the mainland that afternoon. Thankfully, most of the traffic was headed the other way. Not many islanders ventured to town this late in the day.

I wouldn't be on the road either if not for the summons from Detectives Monroe and Schorr. They'd traced my crank caller and requested my presence at the police station.

With each passing mile, my unease grew. I couldn't decide which was worse: finding out who made those harassing calls or being reminded of Bernie's death by the sea of police uniforms. I shivered.

Once I knew my crank caller's identity, then what? Would I learn why I'd been targeted? What caused this person to fixate on me?

My blood chilled at the possibilities darting through my head. *Please don't let the calls be related to Mac Rudd's murder.* I didn't want another connection to the dead thug. It was bad enough he and Bernie were connected.

My nerves refused to settle. Every driver seemed to be staring at me as if they saw something I didn't, like my head had a monster climbing out of it. I gripped the steering wheel tighter. Okay, so I wasn't as brave as I wanted to be. But I would finally have answers to my questions. That was worth a lot.

Images of the recently dead in my life scrolled through my head. Mac Rudd. Mom. Bernie. My shaky nerves shifted into overdrive. I needed to think of something else besides dead people. Anything else.

My tires clickety-clacked over the concrete sections of bridge. Five bridges broken by tidal flats connected Sandy Shores to the mainland. There was talk of widening the road, or even building another road at the north end of the island, but I hoped they didn't.

Higher volume roads would bring more people to the island. As a businessperson, having more customers appealed to me, but as a resident, I wanted to keep Sandy Shores as it was. Undiscovered. It was fine with me if the masses flocked to Hilton Head or Amelia Island.

I parked outside the McLinn County Police Department and made my way inside. A well-rounded officer manned the front desk. The fluorescent light gleamed on his bald head. His dark blue uniform was much different from the ones in Maryland. I allowed myself to breathe.

I could do this.

I tried to keep my pace normal, to pretend entering the station didn't turn my brain into a mass of quivering gelatin. "I'm MaryBeth Cashour. Detective Monroe asked me to come in."

He gestured to the battered chairs by the window. "Have a seat. I'll tell her you're here."

I nodded my thanks. Detective Monroe popped into the room before I had a chance to sit down. Her stern expression sobered me. She was all business today. Dark glasses weren't part of her office attire.

She waved me over. "Miz Cashour. This way."

Phones rang, detectives cursed, and piles of official-looking documents covered the institutional desks in the busy office area. The smell of overdone coffee saturated the air.

I clutched my purse to my side as I maneuvered around the labyrinth of furniture. The hair on the back of my neck tingled as I noticed the occupants of the room watching me. Was their interest the sort of noticing that came with being an observant police officer? Was my phantom caller a serial killer? Or had the police found some damning circumstantial fact that tied me to Rudd's murder?

The later thought took hold of my brain and wouldn't let go. A chorus of *oh-Gods* ripped through my head. I wasn't being paranoid. They were all staring at me. A shudder rippled down my spine. They knew something. Something bad.

Was it Bernie's body?

Had it finally surfaced? My misgivings increased with every step I took. Dread permeated my heart and weighed me down so that every step I took felt like walking through waist-deep sludge.

Whatever was coming, it wasn't good.

I hated bad news.

We joined Detective Schorr in a small room. "Please sit down," Detective Monroe said.

She didn't sit, but I wasn't sure my legs would hold me up if this really was about Bernie. I perched on the edge of a molded plastic chair, my feet soldier straight under my seat, my spine locked in a rigid ninety-degree angle to my legs. My elbows rested on the table.

"We located the person who made your harassing calls," Detective Monroe said.

"Who is it?" My voice sounded strained to my ears.

Detective Schorr opened a file folder. He slid a photocopy of a driver's license across the table to me. "Do you recognize this woman?"

She had long, frizzled blond hair, a crooked nose, and thin lips. Her eyes conveyed a bone-deep weariness, as if she carried the weight of the world on her shoulders.

I didn't know her.

My pulse thudded in my ears. I traced my fingers over the letters of her name on her Delaware driver's license. Why would she make the unsettling calls? "Arlene Nevin?" I met Detective Schorr's gaze. "Who is she?"

"You don't know her?" Detective Monroe leaned across the table, invading my personal space.

I inched back in my chair. "Never seen her before in my life. What does a resident of Delaware want with me? I've never even been to Delaware."

"You're absolutely certain you don't recognize her?"

"I'm certain. There's something in her eyes that I would remember," I stated with impressive calm. "She seems, I don't know, haunted almost."

Detective Monroe sat back in her seat. I had the sense there was more she wanted to say. "What is it?" I asked. "What do you know about her?"

"Her first husband is in the system," Detective Monroe continued. "He beat her to a pulp a couple of times."

The poor woman. I gulped. "That's awful, but what does she want with me?"

"Bear with me." Detective Monroe cleared her throat. "Her first husband shared a cell with Macklin Rudd."

"Oh." A shiver swept down my spine. I didn't like where this was headed.

I pushed the photocopied license back across the table. "Is he out now? Maybe you should warn —" I paused to glance at the sad photo for her name again. "— Arlene."

I felt an invisible wave of incipient bad news surge to a peak. I braced for disaster.

"Here's the thing. Arlene isn't in Delaware. We traced her through her cell phone and the tower system. She's here."

"Here?" My mouth went dry. "Then why

didn't she come see me instead of calling me?"

"She hopped a bus for the trip south and has been stranded at a mainland hotel with her two small boys."

Arlene must have mistaken me for someone else. I stood up. "As fascinating as this is, I don't see what this has to do with me. I want to press charges against her for the harassment. I'd like to do that and go home."

"Not so fast, Miz Cashour," Detective Schorr said. His broad shoulders filled the door frame.

It dawned on me that I couldn't exit without his permission. I hadn't done anything wrong. A frisson of alarm shot through me. They couldn't keep me here.

Detective Monroe tapped her little notebook against the palm of her slender hand. "Arlene is here at the police station. We want you to observe while we question her."

"Is that legal?" I shivered again.

"It's legal. We're holding her in interview room three."

I took another breath. I wasn't the one being questioned. "I'd like to know why she called me."

They led me to another area of the station. No hustle and bustle back here. Just overhead fluorescent lighting, ancient tile floors, and washed-out green paint on the walls. Muggy air weighed heavily in my lungs.

A large pane of glass sat directly in front of me. Through this interior window, I saw a short, whipcord-thin woman sitting with a brown-headed toddler in her lap. Another child of about kindergarten age climbed up on an adjacent plastic chair and jumped off onto the floor. All three were dressed in dirty, faded clothing. Both boys needed a haircut.

While Detective Schorr and I watched, Detective Monroe entered the room. Detective Schorr flipped a switch on the wall and sound blared from the room.

"Crisp, stop that," Arlene said. "Come over here and sit down, or I'll knock the snot out of you."

Detective Monroe set a manila file folder down on the table and introduced herself. There was an alertness about her that I hadn't seen before. "I'm here to question you about your recent cell phone usage."

The small boy in Arlene's arms hid his face in her ample chest. With her small bone structure, those thrusting boobs had to be implants. "What about it?" Arlene whined. "Did I go over my minutes? I'm supposed to have three hundred minutes a month."

"Is the phone in your possession?"

"Yeah."

"May I see it?"

Arlene dug in a voluminous bag, then handed a phone over. "I need that back. That's my only phone."

The active little boy tugged on Arlene's shirt sleeve. "I'm hungry, Mom."

"Not now, Crisp." Arlene shoved the child away.

The scene unfolding before me verged on unreal. It felt as if I'd been dropped into the middle of a reality television program. I envied Arlene her sons. The shy one on her boney lap tugged at my heart.

What kind of life would the kid have with her? Would she be able to care adequately for him, to provide the things he needed to grow up whole and healthy? Would she shower him with the love he seemed to be missing?

Detective Monroe took the phone, examined it, took some notes, and then set it down by her folder. "Has this phone been out of your possession in the last ten days?"

Arlene fanned her face with her hand. "Nope. It's my phone. I don't loan it out."

"Can you explain why you've made numerous harassing calls to Christmas by the Sea?"

Arlene stilled. "Am I in trouble?"

Detective Monroe leaned down in her face. "It's a misdemeanor to harass people with repetitive, threatening calls. What was the purpose of those calls?"

Arlene's lower lip jutted out.

"Or," Detective Monroe went on, "we could look at the big picture here. You have a record for assault and battery. You're miles from home, and these kids don't look like they've eaten or been bathed in days."

"They's boys. You have no idea how filthy they can get. You can't fill them up either. It's like feeding a giant tapeworm."

"So you say. But Child Welfare might take a different view."

The little boy on Arlene's lap started crying.

She set him down on the floor and he crawled back into her lap. "I can't take no more of this sniveling, Dooley. It's hotter than holy hell in here. Ain't you people ever heard of air conditioning?"

The child's name struck a chord with me. Dooley. Bernie used to constantly sing a song with the name Dooley in the lyrics. Something about hanging down your head, Tom Dooley. My stomach knotted.

Was Bernie our connection? Needing to know, I pressed my forehead to the glass, as if that would help me hear better.

"Look, you can't take my kids from me," Arlene said, her voice shrill and loud. "My man done run out on us, and my kids are all I got left. You can't have my kids."

Detective Monroe fiddled with her folder. "Your husband is missing?"

"Yep. Said he had unfinished business on a God-forsaken island named Sandy Shores in Georgia. That was three weeks ago. Ain't heard hide nor hair from him since."

"And how does repeatedly calling Christmas by the Sea help you to find him?"

Arlene chewed on her bottom lip. I silently willed her to answer. I had to know how we were connected.

When Arlene remained silent, Detective Monroe pushed a photo across the table at Arlene. "Do you know this man?"

From behind the window, I recognized Macklin Rudd's mug shot. Arlene shook her head. "Nope. Never seen him before."

No hint of recognition had registered in her facial features. I believed her.

Detective Monroe filed the photo and drew another one out. "What about this man?"

Bernie's photo. My breath hitched in my

throat at the sight of his smiling eyes. God. I missed him. He'd been a puke, but he was my puke.

"That's my husband!" Arlene shrieked. "Oh, God. Where'd you get that picture? Did something happen to my precious Bernie?"

CHAPTER 17

Her husband? Her Bernie? Pain ripped through my heart. I couldn't catch my breath. No, it couldn't be. She was lying. She had to be. But from the shattered expression on her face, I believed her response was truthful.

Emotions rioted within me. Bernie was my husband. How dare another woman claim to be married to him?

"Your husband?" Monroe asked.

"Yep. Bernie Nevin. Is he in jail?"

"No, ma'am. When was the last time you saw him?"

"I already told you. Three weeks ago. He came in from his truck driving job and said he had to come down here. When he didn't come home or call me, I came looking for him."

I held onto the wall for support. Bernie was alive? He was supposed to be dead. Not living with another woman in Delaware.

He had another wife and two sons. My stomach twisted and turned as I gasped for breath. He'd made love to another woman. He'd had a secret life. He had secret children.

He'd betrayed me on every level.

The room spun around me. My stomach lurched. I had to get out of there, fast. "I'm going to be sick," I said to the empty room.

Dazed, I stumbled through the station and out into the murky twilight in the parking lot. Chills wracked my bones. Cold sweat dotted my forehead, moistened my palms, pooled in the small of my back. Bile burned my throat.

I wanted out. Out of this dull and boring body. Out of this lackluster life.

Bernie. Married to another woman. I'd been cuckolded. He'd lied to me. Broken his wedding vows. Stolen everything I had.

Heat flushed my face. My fingers curled into tight fists, and I barred my arms across my chest to hold the hurt in. Only, it wouldn't stay put. The ugliness was coming out whether I wanted it to or not.

A tidal wave of heat and dizziness hit me. I tried to get my bearings, but the world wouldn't stop spinning. I stumbled, falling on my knees on a little grassy strip near my Jeep.

My stomach emptied. I wanted to die. No. I wanted Bernie to die. Like he supposedly had. The bastard.

"We need to talk," Detective Schorr said.

Through the tangle of my hair, he appeared larger than life and twice as invincible. I felt so small and used up. My mouth tasted sour. I shivered with cold. I wasn't going down for another one of Bernie's messes. "Not without a lawyer present."

Waving away his extended hand, I scrambled to my feet. My sweaty shirt clung to my back. "Look, I'll fill out your forms, whatever it takes, but it has to be tomorrow. I can't think straight right now."

"You don't look too steady on your feet. Come back inside and let me get you a glass of water."

I shot a worried glance at the stucco building and dug blindly for my keys. Through some miracle, my fingers ran across them on the first pass through my purse. "I won't go back in there unless I'm under arrest. Am I?"

Schorr stared at me. "We'd like to finish this up. It won't take much more of your time."

If he got me on his turf again, no telling how long he'd keep me. I had to get away. I had to get some perspective. "Forget it. I'm spent." I jumped in my Jeep and sped away.

As I drove over the island causeway, the headlights of the oncoming cars blinded me. I put on my dark glasses, distancing myself from the cold, cruel world.

I didn't want to be alone right now. I wanted to talk to someone. I wanted my mom. My mom who wasn't my real mom.

Crap. How did my life get so messed up? I ran my fingers through my hair, my chopped-up hair that was supposed to be the new me. How could I be the new me when I didn't know who the old me had been?

Apparently I wasn't a Weaver, though I'd been raised by Naomi and Vern Weaver. It appeared I might not be a Cashour either. I didn't know if Bernie married me before or after he married Arlene. How did Bernie have two last names? Which one was real?

If I wasn't his widow, was I still his wife?

Or was I his mistress?

Did he have wives tucked away in every state?

Anger coursed through my veins. Where the hell was Bernie? Why had he done this to me? I deserved to be treated better than this.

These questions pounded through my

head as I cruised past the bars on Hotel Row. Drowning my sorrows in alcohol wouldn't help matters. I needed a clear head to figure this out. I needed to talk to someone. A friend. A female friend.

The closest thing I had to a female friend was Daisy Pearl. But she had a new baby and a pile of children. What would she want with my troubles?

I'd stayed away from her before to keep her free from the taint of my problems, but I had nowhere else to turn. I parked in her front yard amidst a fleet of old cars.

In the waning twilight, Tamiqua rocked the baby on the porch. I couldn't summon the energy to move. Three of Daisy Pearl's cats greeted me. A big tabby jumped on the hood of my Jeep, circled, and lay down. A petite Siamese stalked across the yard, tail twitching, and stopped ten feet away, her blue eyes drilling into me. The third, a meowing tom, came over and put his paws up on my door. His ears were tall enough for me to see his face as he batted at the spider web.

I wanted to respond to them, but a flood of tears drowned me. When I'd calmed a degree, Daisy Pearl and her whole family stood beside my Jeep.

"Mary Christmas, what ails you, child?"

Daisy Pearl asked.

So many kind faces looked in at me. How could I articulate my loneliness to someone who had so much family? I tried to talk, really I did, but between the lump in my throat and my quivering chin, I couldn't get a word out.

"I cain't stand to watch her heart break," Daisy Pearl said. "This poor child needs some loving. Tamiqua, hand Ronelle the baby, and you and John Henry help her out of the car and up on the porch with me."

Everyone started moving, and in moments I found myself sitting on the porch glider with Daisy Pearl, her comforting arm around my shoulder. I must have cried for another million minutes before I could hold it together again.

"I'm so sorry," I managed to squeak out. "I didn't know where else to go."

Daisy Pearl patted my shoulder. "That's okay, baby. You came to the right place. Tell me what happened to upset you."

I swiped my palm over my damp cheeks. "I shouldn't burden you with my troubles."

"You shouldn't hold them in either. What's so terrible on this Thursday evening?"

After a shaky exhale, I found the nerve to explain. "The cops found my crank caller. She's my dead husband's wife. My husband who isn't dead after all, but missing."

The glider stopped moving. "Say what?"

I sniffed in a broken breath, reached for my gold locket, then stopped. That locket no longer represented Bernie's undying love for me. Another stab of hurt speared my broken heart. "I saw his other wife today at the police station. She has two little boys. God, I don't know what hurts worse. Bernie's betrayal, or the mountain of lies he told me. I don't even know if my marriage is legit."

I stared up at this woman who had so much compassion, hoping she had answers for me. "Who am I, Daisy Pearl?"

The glider moved in a slow, soothing rhythm. "You're a fine young woman who's standing on her own two feet. That's who you are."

"But my name. What if my name is a lie? What if all these years Bernie was married to her, too? How could I have been unaware that I shared him with another woman? How could I have been so clueless?"

"That Bernie is a dirty rotten scoundrel, and you're well shed of him. You don't need to have his kind of baggage weighing you down."

"It gets worse. Arlene — that's her name — she was married before, and her first husband served time with our dead guy."

Daisy Pearl stopped the gentle rocking motion of the glider for a moment. "Huh."

I nodded in agreement. "No kidding. Somehow, this whole big mess is related, and I'm caught right in the middle of it."

"You gotta be strong. That's what you gotta do."

"I'm not a tower of strength. It took everything I had to move south and start over."

She gave me a reassuring smile. "Looks like you're doing fine to me. You got a good job, a roof over your head, and food to eat. And people who care about you."

True, but her words didn't make me feel warm and fuzzy. They reminded me I was shouldering my burdens alone. "I have no family. I don't even know who my real parents were."

"Now let me tell you something about that." Daisy Pearl waggled her index finger at me. "The couple who raised you, they're your real parents. Being there, doing the day-to-day stuff, that's what makes a parent. The person who spits out a baby and moves on, that's not a parent."

I swallowed my immediate knee-jerk retort. Daisy Pearl had adopted a ton of kids. She was right. I did have parents. I'd become so lost in my anger at discovering their deception, I'd denied the love my parents had blessed me with. "I needed my mother tonight so I sought you out. Thank you for reminding me of just what a parent is."

"That just proves what I was saying earlier. You're a fine young woman with good sense. That man of you'rn, he was blind if he didn't see what a jewel he had. I say you're due for a little ice cream therapy."

Bernie was blind.

I liked that mindset. I would've done anything for him, but he'd thrown me away. He'd been blind, deaf, and dumb to miss my many charms.

I didn't want him to be a part of my life ever again.

"Daytona!" Daisy Pearl bellowed.

Daytona's pig-tailed head peeked around the screen door. "I'm here, Mama."

"Mary Christmas needs a bowl of chocolate ice cream."

"I don't want to put you to any trouble," I said, loving the sense of belonging Daisy Pearl instilled.

Daisy Pearl squeezed my shoulder. "No trouble at all. That's what family is for."

Family. It wasn't entirely about blood relatives. It was about caring and listening and supporting. The day-to-day things my mom had done for me, that Daisy Pearl continued to do for her adoptive children.

Here at Daisy Pearl's house, I was sheltered from the storms of my life. The others joined us on the porch, Daytona climbing into my lap and singing to me as I polished off the best chocolate ice cream ever.

The mess with the dead guy and Bernie and my past was out there, swirling like a distant hurricane on the horizon. But here in this safe harbor, the howling winds of death and betrayal couldn't touch me. I looked around at the now familiar faces and felt encouraged.

I still had to sort out the past, but I wasn't alone anymore. My life mattered to the Washington family.

And they mattered to me.

CHAPTER 18

Friday morning dawned clear and mild. The parking lots in Hotel Row had already begun to fill for the weekend, which meant I'd have a steady stream of sunburned customers late this afternoon and through Sunday. Busy was good. It meant I didn't have time to think about my bigamist husband.

He'd screwed me over royally. I hoped he stayed missing. Hell, maybe he'd moved on to his third wife by now. That seemed to be the way he operated. Find a woman. Marry her. Desert her.

I didn't care what he did or where he was as long as he stayed away from me. I'd have to kill him if he showed his face around here. He'd taken a large part of me to his supposed grave. I wanted my sense of self-respect back.

Refusing to ponder the two-timing bastard further, I checked to make sure I had plenty of change and merchandise bags. The money looked good, but with Christmas approaching I needed to order more bags. More sales meant I needed more stock in inventory.

Damn. Unless a miracle happened, my stock would soon look like the stuff I gave Russ. He said he liked it, but he could have been saying that to be nice.

Maybe I should put some of it out to see if it would sell. Naw. I wasn't ready for that level of rejection.

The resonant tones of Anne Murray filled the shop. I hummed along with "Joy to the World" as I wrote out an order form for more bags.

A dark car pulled up immediately in front of the shop. Detectives Monroe and Schorr stepped out of the car. My stomach sank, and I groaned aloud. "What now?"

Couldn't I have one cop-free day? It seemed like every time I stood up, I got knocked down by another wave of bad news from theirs truly. Gritting my teeth, I stared at the flashing lights on my angel tree and waited.

The detectives approached my door. Panic skewed the music in my head to a demented verse. *Joy to the World the cops are here, let them, their guns employ. Let every crook, fade into the woodwork, far as the eye can see, far as, far as, the eye can see.*

"Miz Cashour?" Detective Monroe stood not three feet from me. She didn't bother to remove her sunglasses.

I started at her close proximity. I'd been so lost in MaryBeth-land I'd completely spaced out and missed their entry. A senior moment. That's what it had to be. They happened to everyone. I was not losing my mind.

"Yes? What can I do for you today?" Mentally I put on my own Terminator sunglasses. I had a tough guy side too. Somewhere in this thick head of mine.

While trim Detective Monroe flipped open her notepad, Detective Schorr barred his brawny arms across his chest, the fabric of his linen blazer stretching taut. "We need to ask you some more questions about Bernie Cashour," Monroe said.

Bernie was in this up to his neck. He wasn't taking me down, too. "It sounds like I might need a lawyer."

"Your call. But we can stop any time you feel uncomfortable if you agree to proceed."

My stomach knotted, and I grimaced in pain. "I already feel uncomfortable, but go ahead and ask your questions."

So much for my tough-guy mask. "Do you

have any idea what it's like to find out that your husband of ten years was a fraud? I don't even know if my marriage is legitimate. I could have been his mistress all those years. Maybe one of his many mistresses."

Detective Monroe slid her dark glasses up on her sleeked back hair. Her voice softened. "For what it's worth, it appears his Bernie Nevin identity was established after the Bernie Cashour identity."

"Is that supposed to comfort me?" Did that mean he found me boring? Or incompetent? I hated these doubts. The questions they provoked. I hated that Bernie had lived out a fantasy life with another family.

My hand fluttered over my mouth. God. He had another family.

I couldn't just stand here and do nothing while they ripped my life to shreds. I needed action. Under the detectives' watchful gaze, I paced around my shop, fiddling with this, straightening that.

If I moved fast enough, Bernie's exploits couldn't touch me. "This isn't about identities to me. This is about betrayal and abandonment. If you find Bernie, you tell him I'm filing for divorce. I want nothing to do with him ever again."

Detective Monroe tapped her notebook

against her palm. "That's just it, Miz Cash-our. He's disappeared. We need to question him. That's why we're here."

They followed me around my shop, two cats stalking a frightened mouse. My heart ached. This entire disaster was Bernie's fault. He'd left me with problems I couldn't fix.

He'd vanished with our savings, leaving me to deal with our creditors. Me, who he'd deemed incapable of balancing a checkbook because I didn't do it his way.

Why couldn't he just stay dead and get the hell out of my life? If it wasn't for him, I wouldn't be having daily visits from cops. God.

My life sucked.

I stopped next to the oyster shell Santas. "Look, I'm no expert on Bernie. He conned me for ten years. I don't know what was truth and what was a lie. If you want to find out about Bernie, you better ask Arlene." The woman in his other family. "She wants him back. I want nothing to do with him."

Detective Monroe frowned. "Tell us about his last business trip. What can you remember about it?"

A puff of air snorted out of my nose. My hands went to my hips. "You want gritty details from my sham of a marriage? Here's a factoid for you. Write this down. We were supposed to go to my mother's for her birthday. Right when we were leaving he got this emergency call. He told me there had been a nuclear accident. That I wasn't to leave the house for any reason. That I should watch the news. I didn't want to stay home. We quarreled. Then he left."

Heat rose to my face as I recounted my greatest humiliation. I moved back behind the safety of my sales counter.

I'd missed my mother's birthday because I'd believed Bernie's lie. No. Another one of Bernie's lies. Mom had sounded so hurt when I called to tell her I wasn't coming. In hindsight, I realized she'd been waiting to tell me about her cancer in person. Once Bernie disappeared, she must have decided she couldn't burden me with additional bad news.

God.

I'd missed so much in life because I'd heeded that liar.

I believed everything he told me. He must have laughed long and hard about my gullibility. Never again would I believe another word that came out of his lying, two-timing mouth. To me, he was as good as dead.

"Tell us more about the call he received," Detective Monroe said. "Did he take it in front of you?"

It hurt to open that particular page of my memory book. But I did it because I wanted this to be over. "No. He stepped out on the patio."

"Didn't that tip you off that something was up?"

My chest tightened. I held on to the counter to stop from trembling. "Not really. He did that with his business calls. In the beginning, he made excuses about why he took his calls in private. Like, he didn't want to interrupt the TV program we were watching, or he didn't want me to be bored with the dry technical details of his job. Stupid me. I never suspected he had this whole other life. I believed his lies."

"We need to get to the bottom of this. From our conversation with Mrs. Nevin, it appears Bernie was a business acquaintance with her first husband. That's how she met him."

I mentally reeled from the implication. It didn't seem possible. And yet, Russ had tried to tell me this very thing. When was I going to pull my head out of the sand? If I didn't start paying attention to the big picture, I was going to be in big trouble.

No time like the present to make a change. I inhaled slowly. "Are you saying Bernie consorted with criminals? That he had underworld ties?" Bile rose in my throat. I'd slept with him. Cooked for him. Cleaned for him. Hemmed his pants to thirty-one-inch inseams. Miscarried three of his babies.

And it was all a big, fat lie.

The room started to spin. My head seemed an impenetrable glop of melting cotton candy. I stumbled over to the stool I kept behind the sales counter and sank down before I keeled over. A crushing weight squeezed against my chest. After a few deep shuddering breaths, I pulled myself together enough to speak. "You must think I'm the biggest fool in the world."

Detective Monroe cleared her throat. "We think Bernie's disappearance has a direct bearing on the murder of Macklin Rudd. Anything you can tell us will be of interest."

I raised my hands in surrender. "Don't you get it? I know nothing. All the events in my past are lies. The man I loved conned me. He was an adulterer. And now you tell me he had underworld connections."

Detective Monroe flipped through her notebook before she spoke. "We've researched the time frame after Rudd's prison term. It appears Rudd and Jimmy Lee Bryan — that's Mrs. Nevin's first husband — worked together in collections for the

Bertelli family, a known crime syndicate."

The pressure on my chest eased. I still wanted to lash out in anger over Bernie's many lies, but the cops didn't deserve my emotional outburst. They were only doing their jobs.

Now that the conversational focus was off me and my failures, my brain started to work. "If Rudd and this Jimmy Lee Bryan character were mob, wouldn't their continued association after prison violate Jimmy Lee's parole?"

Monroe shook her head in denial. "According to the Parole Board, both of them drew regular paychecks from different employers. The fact that the companies were owned by the same consortium wasn't known at the time."

"You make this sound like some big, well-thought-out strategy. Is the mob that sophisticated?"

Detective Monroe scowled at me. "You bet. During that time frame, several large thefts occurred in the Northeast. It may be that Rudd and Bryan double-crossed the Bertellis. The mistake cost Rudd his life and Bryan his freedom. Bryan won't talk. That leaves Cashour. We need your help."

My head reeled from the new information. How could I have missed that I lived in the eye of a dangerous storm? "I'm sorry. I can't help you."

Monroe put away her notebook and nodded toward the door. "There's a reason these people followed you down here. Once we learn why, we can solve this murder."

I'd indulged them long enough. Time to get my questions answered. "Arlene's two boys. Are they Bernie's kids?"

At first I didn't think either detective would answer. Then Detective Schorr cleared his throat and spoke. "Bernie Nevin adopted the two boys last year. A year after he married Arlene."

"Oh." That news sank in slowly. He'd married me before he married Arlene. So he'd cheated on me with Arlene. But I still didn't know if my marriage was legal. Or if he'd fathered the boys out of wedlock. "Did he have other wives too?"

Detective Schorr's Adam's apple bobbed. "At this time, we haven't uncovered any additional identities."

I didn't need an interpreter to read between those lines. Other wives might be out there. I ached with flu-like intensity. My husband was a liar.

Possibly a thief.

Definitely a bigamist.

After the cops left, I tried to pull my

thoughts together. The relief of being higher on the wife pecking order than Arlene was short-lived. A good chance existed that I was still legally bound to him, which meant his messes were my messes. I needed help before the next wave of Bernie's lies blindsided me.

Lucky me. Help walked in my door in the virile form of Russ Marchone. The words to "O Holy Night" filled the shop. Was Russ my star shining brightly in the night?

Get a grip, MaryBeth. You're a married woman. You have no business thinking about Russ as your personal hero until Bernie's mess is cleaned up.

"You okay in here?" he asked.

His glittering eyes were too intense for me. They seemed to poke through my brain and uncover my secrets. I averted my gaze to the tiled floor. "I'm fine."

"You don't look fine."

I shot him a nasty glare. "You wouldn't look fine if you had cops for breakfast either."

Russ leaned against the sales counter, the muscles in his biceps straining against his forest green polo shirt. "What did they want?"

I reluctantly met his insistent gaze. "They wanted to know about my husband's underworld connections."

His eyes widened for a moment. "Whoa. Rewind. Your husband?"

"Yeah. He's not dead. Just missing." I shrugged. "Go figure." I sounded casual, but saying those words opened emotional wounds.

Damn Bernie.

How could he do this to me?

Russ stared at me so long I broke into a cold sweat. Did I have "sucker" tattooed on my forehead? With trembling fingers, I lined up my countertop accessories in perfect parallel rows. The stapler next to the tape next to the pen jar. Just like Jolene and her regimented seashell art. I couldn't help myself. When I got nervous, I straightened, organized, and sorted, anything to busy my hands so I didn't have to think.

"What are you going to do?" he asked.

"I need a good lawyer. You know any who can get me a quickie divorce from a resurrected, rotten, two-timing husband?"

A muscle in his face twitched. "I might know someone. I'll check into it." He headed toward the door.

I stared after him as he left. He wanted to help. I tried to feel relief that he hadn't condemned me when he learned the truth. But as he sauntered out the door, hormones smothered all coherent thought but one. Russ Marchone had an excellent butt.

CHAPTER 19

A fire engine red convertible parked at my shop's front door on Saturday right as I opened for the day. A perky redhead wearing cobalt blue bounced out of the car and stretched up tall. She looked vaguely familiar, but I couldn't place her.

My first thought was, oh no, someone else from my old life in Maryland followed me south. Only I couldn't remember who she was.

Please God, not another one of Bernie's wives.

She wore high-fashion wraparound sunglasses, trendy above-the-ankle slacks, and spiky pink heels. Definitely not someone I knew from Maryland. No one from my old life dressed like a sex kitten for work or play.

Her eyebrows were nearly the same color as her hair, so it was possible that her bright autumn hair was natural. She seemed so familiar. But her name hovered just out of reach.

She breathed in huge gulps of salt air. Her gaze lingered on each beachside palm tree and the nearby ocean. Then she drew herself up straight and marched right toward me.

Uh-oh. I hightailed it away from the window so that I was safely behind the counter when she entered.

I pasted on a benign customer smile. "Good morning. Welcome to Christmas by the Sea."

The redhead spun slowly on her heels. "I like what you've done with the place, Mary-Beth."

Holy shit. She knew my name. Which meant I should know hers. I wasn't good at bluffing. Best to come clean right off. "I feel like I know you, but I can't place you. Have you been in the shop before?"

"You might say that." She smiled slow and graciously. "I'm the poor schmuck you bought this goldmine from."

I shook my head vigorously, "Justine? You look so different than before." Oops, that didn't come out right. I hastened to soften my unfortunate remark. "But different in a good way. Great, in fact. Twenty years younger. How have you been?"

"Oh, I've had quite an adventure, but I'm

227

ready to come home now."

"Come home?" My heart stuttered as a full orchestra swelled through the airwaves. Horns and strings carried the melody and the unspoken lyrics to this Christmas hymn came to my mind: let nothing you dismay.

Too late.

A bomb of dismay exploded in my gut, followed closely by a sense of outrage.

This forest of fake Christmas trees replete with twinkling lights and painted seashells belonged to me. It wasn't hers anymore.

Her bright pink nails fluttered through the air and landed theatrically on the side of her jaw. "Oh, dear. I've said the wrong thing. The shop is yours, dearie, free and clear. I took the money and I'm not sorry one bit. I got what I wanted, which was to travel and to have men swoon at my feet. Only, it wasn't nearly as satisfying as I thought it would be. I miss making my crafts, miss seeing the children's faces when they come through the shop. You know what I mean. I could see it in your face the first day you walked in here. I knew you understood."

Whatever she knew, I certainly wasn't getting it now. But at her assurance, my anger dissipated. She wasn't trying to take my shop from me. So what was her business here? My brow furrowed. "I don't understand."

She smiled at me, a smile that reached all the way up to her heavily mascaraed eyes. "You get this place. I could tell right away. I'm good at sizing up people, and I knew you were perfect for this shop."

I nodded, not so much agreeing with her as stalling for time. Until I knew what she wanted, I'd be noncommittal. My immediate feeling of protectiveness toward the shop had surprised me. Christmas by the Sea wasn't just a job anymore.

It was my life.

Living in the moment was my entire reality. My past was a mess, my future a big unknown, but today, I knew what today was all about. I owned a Christmas shop, and I went to work there each day.

"And because you get this place, I knew we could work together. I guess I always knew I'd be coming back. What do you say, MaryBeth?"

I stared at her in shock. "You want to work for me?" Working together sounded like a very bad idea. Two cooks couldn't function in the same kitchen, and I suspected the same was true of craft shops.

"I love this place." Justine walked around touching the things she'd made: a wreath of seashells, a scallop shell angel, a Christmas shark. "I bet you could use a hand here. I know it got to me after a while, always having to be here. I could fill in when you need a breather."

Yep. It was a bad idea all right. Though she stated her intent was to help, she wanted to run my shop and boss me around.

I had spread my wings when I bought this place. They weren't ready to be clipped. I enjoyed choosing what I was going to do and how I would do it. I didn't need anyone coming in here and telling me what to do.

I'd changed since I moved here. Grown. Become tougher mentally. This wasn't just a shop. It was my salvation.

A ready-made answer came to me. "I can't afford to pay another staff person."

Her hundred-watt smile dimmed a bit. "You wouldn't have to pay me much. I'm not in this for the money. I want to paint my shells, to bring Christmas cheer to everyone again."

Hmm. I studied my sneakers. Maybe a collaboration wouldn't be the end of the world. My inventory was dwindling at an alarming rate. I needed painted shells. But still, she was used to running this place. Better to tell her what my real reservation was.

"I'm sure you could run this place with

one hand tied behind your back, but the thing is, I'm doing it my way. I like being my own boss."

She nodded. "I want you to be the boss. That's the part I hated, that business side of things. You and I would be a good team, MaryBeth, because I'd focus entirely on the creative side of the business. We can work something out when it comes to wages. It wasn't fair of me to walk in here and spring this on you so suddenly. Why don't you sleep on it over the weekend? I'll swing by on Monday morning, and we can have another chat."

I shook my head in denial. "A few more days won't change how I feel."

She reached across the counter and clasped my hand. "There must be something I could say to make you consider taking me on. I could replenish inventory if you don't want help in the shop. In fact, that's what I'd rather do. Come in here and paint in the back room when you need to get caught up. I wouldn't interfere with the daily operations. I'd be on the reserve list for when you needed a day off, or if you had a doctor's appointment or something. Please, think about it."

She looked so earnest I couldn't flat out tell her no. After Bernie's deceit, I was probably too wary of her motive for showing up again. I threw my hands up in resignation. "Okay. You wore me down. I'll think about it. But I'm not making any promises as far as pay. Money is really tight right now."

Justine breezed into the craft room and started opening drawers. "You're a little low on supplies. And a glue gun is missing. Did it finally kick the bucket?"

This was why I didn't want to hire her. She was already trying to wrest control from me. "Yeah. I know I'm low on craft supplies, but I can order more."

She paused at the back door. "I can't tell you how many days I stood here at this window, praying for five o'clock. It felt like life was passing me by. Do you ever feel like that? Like life is a swift river current, and you're marooned on an island in the midst of all that flowing water. That's how I felt about Sandy Shores. I loved living here, but I had to get out and see the world."

An unwanted surge of sympathy hit me. I completely understood her need to spread her wings. "Is that what you did?"

"Yep. I saw the world. Well, Vegas, but they've got everything out there. I'll tell you my stories when I come to work on Monday."

I drew in a large breath between my teeth,

not wanting her to be too hopeful. "Justine —"

She shushed me with her hand. "Not another word about my working here. Tell me the news before I go air out my house. Did anything exciting happen while I was gone?"

I closed all the drawers she'd opened. "You mean like having a dead guy wash up on the beach at my feet?"

She gave me a little shove. "Get real. That didn't happen. Stuff like that never happens around here."

"It does now. Detectives Monroe and Schorr come here almost every day with a question about the murder case."

"Dang. I'll have to call my nephew Schorr and grill him. Why'd things get interesting once I left? I couldn't wait to leave this oversized sand dune, but once I was away, I couldn't stop thinking about Sandy Shores."

God. Why did she have to say that? Now I felt sorry for both of us. We were two peas in a pod. I reached for my gold locket and then remembered I hadn't put it on today. The new MaryBeth didn't need an emotional crutch. The new MaryBeth looked out for herself.

I drew myself up tall. "It's good to see you, Justine. Even if I don't hire you, I hope you'll still come by and visit me."

Justine patted my arm. "Don't fret, sugar. It will all work out. I have a good feeling about you and me."

Gentle harp strings were plucking out the melody of "Away in a Manger" as she swept out of the room. The shop seemed chilly and empty at her departure. I had the urge to run after her and hire her on the spot, but that was an emotional reaction. It wasn't rational and well thought out.

Daisy Pearl would want me to find a way to keep Justine here. But money was a problem. So was the authority issue. Hell. How was I gonna make everyone happy, when the most unhappy person would be me?

CHAPTER 20

I worked late on Saturday because I couldn't figure out what to do about Justine. And because I'd been dealing with cops and connections, it occurred to me that her reappearance might have a sinister motivation.

I didn't want her to be connected to the murders, but her timely arrival struck me as coincidental. She might have been recalled from Vegas by her nephew, Detective Schorr, to be an undercover agent in my shop. Once she ratted me out, she'd get the shop back.

This wasn't helping. Worrying about things never made them go away. Justine's arrival would sort itself out. I'd have to have a little faith in humanity.

Faith.

It seemed a stretch after all I'd been through. People weren't inherently good. They were opportunistic and mean. Twilight thickened as I locked my shop and drove home the long way, along the sea wall so that I could hear the ocean waves.

It might be a nice evening to walk on the beach. The tide was out, so there'd be lots of beach. Lots of flies, too. Maybe I'd save the beach walk for another night.

To get back over to Breezeway Drive, I cut through a housing development where children were out riding their bikes on the lighted sidewalks. I noticed a set of headlights in my rearview mirror remained constant.

My unease returned.

Someone was following me?

What if Bernie's other wife had upped the ante? She could be royally pissed about getting caught making those calls to me. I sucked in my bottom lip and glanced once more at the reflection in my mirror.

If it was Arlene and her boys, I didn't want to come face to face with them now. When we met, if that unfortunate day ever came, I wanted bright lights and lots of people around. Not the darkness of my isolated house.

Instinct made me circle the populated development again. The headlights stayed with me through every turn I made. I could pull into someone's drive and call the cops.

My heart pounded in my ears. My stomach twisted and turned like a roller coaster ride. Was there a stalker on my tail? Some mobster following me who'd kill for the sport of it?

No way was I going to my house alone.

I needed protection. A big bodyguard type. Someone lethal, intense, and close at hand. Only one person fit that description. And had a nice butt, to boot. I punched in Russ's number on my cell phone. He answered immediately.

"It's MaryBeth. Someone's following me. I'm afraid to go home." I heard a hitch in his breath before he answered.

"Where are you?"

His no-nonsense voice reassured me. My headlights flashed on the elementary school parking lot. "I just turned off Airport Road onto Jolly Roger Road. What should I do?"

"Call the cops." Russ swore aloud. "No, wait —"

"What?"

"Schorr and Monroe were in the pharmacy this afternoon. There's a big dress-up event on the mainland they're working this evening. It'll be half an hour before a cop could get over to the island. I can be there in five minutes."

My blood ran cold. I couldn't face my pursuer alone. It was getting darker by the second. The lighthouse beacon flashed across the sky, illuminating the deserted parking lot to my left. "I'm scared, Russ."

"Fear is good. Embrace it. Fear will keep you sharp until help arrives. Keep moving. Stay in populated areas. I'll meet you at your house in five minutes."

"I want this car to stop following me."

"I'm leaving the pharmacy now. I'll meet you at your house. If you get there first, don't stop. Circle around until I arrive."

Help was on the way. I didn't have to face this crisis alone. I exhaled shakily. "Thanks, Russ."

After another lap around the development, I headed home. Russ, my hero, stood in my driveway as I pulled in and parked on the crushed shell drive. The car following me gathered speed and passed us in a blur.

I hopped out of my Jeep and ran to Russ. I thought about throwing myself into his arms, then I remembered he wasn't my husband, or even my lover. He was my friend. I stopped short of colliding with him. "Did you see the car?"

His sharp teeth flashed in the darkness. "I couldn't make out the tag number, but it was a dark-colored Saturn. Navy blue or black. The driver wore a baseball cap and glasses and a beard."

"A beard? You think it was a man?"

He took a moment to reply. "How many bearded ladies do you know?"

"You got me there." His down-home sensibility grounded me, made me feel like I wasn't going crazy. "Okay. A man followed me home. Why?"

"You must have something he wants."

I pressed my hand against my racing heart. "That's crazy. I don't own any valuables." I rubbed the goose bumps on my arms. "I hate being scared like this."

"You need to report this incident. Call the cops. I'll check the locks on your doors and windows."

From the safety of my well-lit kitchen, I called and reported my problem. After ascertaining the situation had been diffused, the dispatch person told me to come in right now and fill out an incident report. I hung up.

Shivers ran up and down my spine at an alarming rate. He could be out there, right now. I stepped away from the darkened window.

What I wouldn't give for a football field's worth of floodlights and a six-foot-tall chain link fence with concertina wire on top. A dozen pit bulls would be nice, too.

Russ frowned his way into the kitchen,

stopping to lean against the counter. I frowned right back. "I've got to drive over to Brunswick and file a police report."

"You need deadbolts for the front and back doors," Russ said. "You could also use wooden dowels in the windows to reinforce the aging locks."

New locks weren't cheap. I had a tiny bit of savings in reserve, some just-in-case money, that I really wanted to keep. I didn't want to get in the same financial hole as before where I owed money to everyone and his brother. My meager assets were oozing through my fingers like globs of wet sand-castle sand. But with God knows who stalking me, I didn't have much choice.

My chin quivered. Damn it. I was not going to cry. Russ already thought I was mentally unbalanced. Crying about lock replacement would cement that idea in his head. I summoned up a brave face and nodded my agreement.

Russ jammed his hands in his pockets. "It's not the end of the world. I'll go to town with you, file the report, then we'll stop at the home repair store and get the items you need. I can install them for you tonight."

So much for my brave face.

He knew I was a gutless wonder. I didn't want to be an open book to any man. And my friendship with Russ was moving into an uncomfortable dependency.

I didn't understand the rules of this "friendship" game. I didn't have an offensive strategy, and my defense wasn't so hot either. It worried me that I'd called Russ first instead of the cops. That was how the old MaryBeth had operated — she didn't make a move without masculine approval.

The new MaryBeth stood on her own two feet.

It was about time I remembered that. "I called you tonight because I was scared, but now that the car's gone, I can handle the rest of this by myself."

His eyes darkened dangerously. "MaryBeth, don't refuse my help. We're friends, remember? Friends help each other."

I chewed on my bottom lip. I wasn't keen on being alone, but I didn't want to become so dependent on him that I couldn't think for myself. I could figure out how to install dowels and deadbolts. "It seems like too much to ask. I don't want to abuse our friendship."

"Let me be the judge of that."

My spine stiffened. "Don't get all chauvinistic on me. I'm learning to do things on my own. I know firsthand how easy it is to rely on someone else. I wouldn't have called you tonight except I was scared out of my gourd."

The air thickened with tension. "What makes you think the danger is past?"

I gestured out toward the road. "The car is long gone."

He shook his head. "You're smarter than that. Whoever was following you wanted you to see them. They wanted you to be scared. You asked me to help. That's why I'm here. You need to file that report at the police station, so let's go."

He had a good point. I collected my purse and locked the house. "How come I never noticed how bossy you were before?"

Russ cranked up his truck. "How come I never noticed how stubborn you were before?"

He had me there.

I glanced around his pickup in wonder. I'd never been in his vehicle before. Coins littered the floor along with empty soda cans. An old pair of gym shoes rested behind the front seat. A stack of old newspapers filled the console space between us. "What's all this?"

He took a long moment surveying the empty road before he pulled out onto Breezeway Drive. "My mother collects newspapers. I bring her the leftovers from the pharmacy."

"Oh." What did one say to that? My curiosity wouldn't let the subject drop. "What does she do with them?"

He eased the truck onto Breezeway Drive and headed for the causeway. "She uses them for her papier-mâché art classes."

My stomach dropped down to my unpainted toenails. "She's an artist?" God. I'd given an artist's son my crummy painted seashells.

"That's one label for her. Mostly she's bossy and stubborn and manipulative. But she means well."

From his description, his mother didn't sound very likeable, but his voice had softened when he talked about her. He cared for her. My heart panged again, only this time with a shaft of jealousy. Russ had a real family.

On the causeway, he sped up considerably. Wind blew my hair into my face. It tangled under my glasses, so I rolled my window partway up.

"Too much wind?" he asked.

I flicked the hair away from my face and shook my head. "Too much hair. I can't see a thing."

His laughter warmed my shivery heart.

"You should laugh more," I told him.

"You're much too serious all the time."

He flicked me a sideways glance. "Life is serious. No getting around that."

True. I'd been through a lot of life recently. When was life going to let up on me and focus on someone else?

After filing the police report, we swung by the hardware store, where I purchased the locks. We had a comfortable dinner at a buffet-style restaurant, then headed home. Russ's headlights illuminated the crushed oyster shell drive and flashed on my house.

The door to my house stood ajar.

Russ immediately killed the headlights and backed the truck out on the road. "Stay here." Russ's voice was low and dangerous. "Lock the doors. Call the cops."

Shivers tripping down my spine, I grabbed for his arm and missed. "Wait!" I whispered back. "You shouldn't go in there. We should wait for the cops to come."

Russ withdrew a handgun from under his seat. His lips twisted up in a mirthless smile. "I'll be right back."

He kept a gun in his truck? "Russ!"

"Stay in the truck." He vanished into the night.

Shivers tripped down my spine. I fumbled my phone out of my purse and dialed 911.

"This is MaryBeth Cashour. I filed a police report on a stalking an hour ago. I just returned home, and someone has broken into my house at five-three-seven Breezeway Drive on Sandy Shores. Please send the police immediately."

"I have your information. It's important that you stay on the line until help arrives at your location."

"I'm afraid someone might hear me talking. My friend went in my house. I'm worried about his safety."

"Ma'am, don't hang up. We need to keep the lines of communication open."

The urge to help Russ mounted. A gunshot reverberated through the damp night air, followed by a splintering of glass. Russ. Russ was in trouble. I had to help him. "I heard a gunshot. I have to help my friend." I hung up.

I needed a weapon. The new deadbolt on the truck seat was heavy. That was better than nothing. I grabbed it out of the box and crept in the darkness toward my house.

Between the new moon and the cloud-covered sky, I couldn't even see my own feet. No street lights back here either. I had this little peninsula of salt marsh to myself. The majority of the houses were two blocks over on the beach side of the long, narrow island. Nothing but me and a ton of mosquitoes back here.

Russ's warning for me to stay put echoed in my head, but a gun had fired. That changed things. I had to know if he was all right.

Insects feasted on my neck as I navigated around a thick clump of pampas grass guarding the entrance to my driveway. I smacked them. Too late, I realized the smack of flesh on flesh could give my location away.

I froze and listened to the night.

The only sound I heard was the frenzied beating of my heart.

I started forward again, stumbled over something, and fell. A muffled yelp tore from my throat as my shin banged on a hard, foul-smelling, irregularly shaped object. A conch shell. I'd forgotten I'd thrown this monster out here last week to cure.

I'd have an ugly bruise tomorrow, but at least I'd be alive. I didn't know if I could say the same for Russ. I scrambled to my feet, inching forward until I encountered my Jeep in the driveway.

The slap of rapid footfalls sounded. My breath hitched in my throat. I crouched behind the far side of the Jeep, deadbolt in my right hand. Adrenaline roared through my veins.

A person crashed into the other side of the Jeep. I wanted to bean the intruder with the deadbolt, really I did. But he had a gun. Thoughts of rescuing Russ were overwhelmed by an urgent self-preservation message. Hide!

I covered my head and cowered beside my tire.

Cursing in a deep voice, the intruder spun off the other side of the Jeep and ran toward Breezeway Drive. He tripped over the upended conch shell, cursed again, and kept running.

My heart pounding in my throat, I exhaled slowly. Someone had run out of the house. Where was Russ?

My glasses steamed up. I huffed little breaths of air up my face to help the lenses clear. I inched my head above the hood of the Jeep and listened in the foggy silence. Fresh air gradually cleared my field of vision.

No Russ. I could make out the side of the house. The white paint gleamed a dull gray in the darkness. I saw nothing more.

What now?

Find Russ and make sure he wasn't bleeding. Or dead. My legs trembled. God. Russ couldn't be dead.

An intruder had run past me, but was he working alone?

Without warning, an arm wrapped around my neck, and a metal cylinder pressed into my rib cage. I didn't think. I smashed the deadbolt into my attacker's head.

A grunt. The arm around my neck slackened.

Frantic, I kicked backward with all my might, catching his knee. Silently, we fell together, my attacker taking the brunt of the fall and then rolling over and covering me with his body.

The deadbolt fell from my hand. "No!" I cried, groping for it in the sandy grass, but coming up empty.

His palm covered my mouth, and I bucked hard to get out from under him. Only he didn't budge.

Oh God.

I was gonna die.

I was so gonna die.

"Be still, MaryBeth."

I cringed at Russ's whispered command. I'd beaned him with the deadbolt and kicked the crap out of his knee. Friends didn't attack each other like that.

Could this night get any worse?

CHAPTER 21

"Are you okay?" I whispered, my heart in my throat.

"My head hurts." With a groan, he rolled off me, sat up, and rubbed his temple. "What the hell did you hit me with?"

The cool night air brushed against my skin, further inflaming my overwrought nerves. I didn't like being wrestled to the ground, but I liked being alone even less. Shivering, I sat up beside him. Oyster shell fragments fell from my hair. "The new deadbolt. Sorry about that. What happened in there?"

"While I was checking out the house, I located your intruder in a bedroom. I tried to subdue him, but he got away from me."

Sirens wailed in the distance. Help was on its way. I took another breath. "I heard a gunshot. Did you shoot him?"

"Nope. He fired at me —"

"Fired at you!" My heart slammed against

my chest. Oh, God. Oh, God. "Are you okay?"

His mouth kicked up a bit. "I'm fine. But you're going to need a new window."

"I don't care about the window. That can be replaced. You could have been killed."

I could have been killed, too, I silently added. A gunman had been in my house.

As the police car approached, the siren's wail increased. Russ moaned. "I can't take that racket. I wish they'd turn that thing off."

The poor man. Guilt poked at me. It was my fault his head hurt. "Let me get you an ice pack and some ibuprofen."

I stumbled to my feet and wobbled into my Jeep. "Whoa. I need a moment for my head to clear."

Russ stood and leaned against the Jeep. "Good thing you parked here."

Thunder rumbled, then the heavens opened. Fat raindrops pelted my head. We needed shelter fast. I nodded toward the house. "Is it safe to go inside or should we wait outside?"

"Your intruder is long gone."

That was good enough for me. I grabbed Russ by the arm. We ran for the open door. When I turned the house lights on, the house remained pitch black. I strained to see through my water-speckled glasses. "Now what?"

"He must have flipped the circuit breaker." Russ's voice was clipped with pain. "Where's your panel box?"

I fumbled my way toward a chair at the kitchen table and pulled it out. "Here." I pushed Russ toward the chair. "Sit down. I can deal with the panel box."

Russ ignored my command. "Do you have a flashlight?"

"Yes." With a shuffling gait learned from years of finding my way to the bathroom without my glasses, I crunched over debris on my floor until I stubbed my toe on the refrigerator, then went one drawer to the right. My fingers closed around the flashlight.

I flicked it on. A narrow shaft of light swept through my kitchen. Cabinet doors hung askew. The cereal box lay toppled on the counter, with oat circles scattered everywhere. A bag of rice had been slit. Grains of rice littered the floor. The cap had come off my all-purpose cleaner under the sink, and the pungent smell of fresh pine filled the air. "Oh. My. God."

Russ took the light from me. "Where's the panel box?"

I directed him to the metal box on the

laundry room wall. In seconds, the air conditioning hissed to life. The refrigerator hummed. I grabbed us each a dry towel and used mine to wipe the moisture from my glasses. I flipped on light switches as we headed back to the kitchen.

After I got Russ a bag of ice for his head, I took a moment to survey the kitchen. Over by the sink, smashed dishes littered the floor, along with broken Pyrex bowls, pots, and frying pans. The small marble fish my mother had sculpted lay near the stove in two pieces.

A sob escaped my lips. I bent and picked up the broken fish. Sadness stilled my lungs. My fish. My beautiful green fish. A silent tear rolled down my damp cheek.

Shells crunched as the cops pulled into my driveway with lights flashing and sirens blaring. I put the fish down and went to the door. Detectives Monroe and Schorr trotted up the steps in formal evening attire. They approached the house with weapons drawn, Schorr in a tuxedo and Monroe in a spangly gold lamé number. I felt like I'd stepped onto the set of a James Bond movie.

I motioned them in. "Russ chased the intruder out."

"We were off duty when your call came in," Monroe said, her cop eyes flicking around the ransacked room as she spoke. "What happened here?"

I updated them on the evening's events. "After filing the police report, we shopped for locks and grabbed dinner on the mainland. When we returned, someone was inside my house."

Detective Monroe turned to Russ. "Is that when you got hurt?"

Russ adjusted his ice bag so that he could see Detective Monroe. "That's when I left MaryBeth safe in my truck to call the cops while I took a look around. I treed the intruder in the house, we scuffled a bit, he broke free and fled, firing back at me as he ran out the door."

"I couldn't wait in the truck once I heard the gunshot," I admitted. "So I got out and edged closer to the house. Someone ran out of the house right when I got to my Jeep."

"You wouldn't have been in danger if you'd waited in the truck," Russ said.

Detective Monroe turned to Russ. "The intruder hit you in the head with his gun?"

Russ winced. "MaryBeth hit me in the head with a deadbolt when I surprised her in the yard."

I felt heat rising in my cheeks. "He grabbed me from behind. I didn't know if he was friend or foe, so I defended myself."

A smile tugged at Detective Schorr's clean-shaven face. "You did the right thing, Miz Cashour. Looks like you've got a decent right jab."

"Tell me about it." Russ shifted the ice pack to cover the egg-sized lump on his temple.

"Is anything missing?" Detective Monroe asked.

"Everything I own is torn up. Until I sort through the rubble, I don't know." My gaze caught on two small chunks of green marble, and my chin started quivering. "He broke my mother's marble fish."

Detective Monroe cleared her throat. "If we knew what your intruder was after, then we'd have a better chance of identifying and catching this guy."

I got the message. She didn't have time for me to fall apart. I summoned extra resolve from somewhere. "I know I'm starting to sound like a broken record, but why me?"

Detective Schorr shot a dark look at his partner. "We'd like to answer that question as well, Miz Cashour. We've called in a crime scene unit, and they should arrive shortly. From the looks of this place, it will take all night to process the scene. Do you have a friend you can stay with tonight?"

"Me," Russ answered.

He'd made another decision for me, but truthfully, I'd rather stay with him tonight than be alone in a hotel room. "Thanks, Russ."

"Can I seal that broken window before we leave?" Russ asked. "We're supposed to get more rain tonight."

"Sure. I'll give you a hand with that."

While Russ and Schorr taped a black garbage bag over my broken living room window, Monroe and I went from room to room. "Let me know if you see anything missing," Monroe said.

My belongings were in a shambles. My home had been violated. I couldn't stop my teeth from chattering. I found my windbreaker on the floor and I donned it. "Without sorting through the mess, I can't tell anything."

We walked into my bedroom. Drawers were open, my no-frills lingerie was tossed around the room. My jewelry box had been upended. Necklaces and rings spilled across the dresser and onto the floor. My bed had been stripped.

Two naked pillows lay on the bed. On one pillow was a head-shaped indention. On the second pillow was a gleaming gold object. "My wedding ring!" I moved to pick it up.

"Don't touch it!" Monroe cautioned. She took photos of everything. With a practiced gesture, she swept the ring into a small plastic bag. After she'd photographed the bed, I sat down on it.

Like an incoming wave, anguish flooded my heart. I put my fist to my mouth to keep from crying out. If I could just wake up from this bad dream, everything would be okay. Only this wasn't a dream, this was real and dangerous. I shivered as cold sweat moistened my brow, my palms, and the channel of my spine.

I had to pull myself together. The connections were here if I knew where to look. The most obvious connection to me and my wedding ring was Bernie.

Had he been here, lying on my bed? I leaned over and sniffed my pillow. I couldn't tell a darned thing. All I wanted to do was to crush the pillow to my hollow middle.

"What? Do you see something on the pillow?" Monroe asked.

"There's nothing to see. Why would someone strip my bed and then put the pillows back?"

"People do funny things, but the arrangement of the items seems personal. And going by the list of suspects in this ongoing murder investigation, the most likely intruder is Bernie Cashour. Do you see anything else that might point to him?"

Other than the ring on "my" side of the bed and the head imprint on "his" side? There was no doubt in my mind who my intruder had been. "Why would Bernie sneak around my place?"

"He may be trying to retrieve one of his possessions."

"I don't have anything of his. Look around. There's no guy stuff anywhere. I'm so frustrated I could scream."

"I'd appreciate it if you didn't," Monroe said. "Let's get you out of here."

"What about clothes for tomorrow? Can I take my things with me?"

"Make a list of what you want. I'll bring it over to Marchone's place once the crime scene unit finishes processing them."

Under her watchful eye, I pointed out an outfit for tomorrow. "I'd also like my travel bag of toiletries. It's in my vanity's top drawer."

"No problem." She ushered me out to the porch where Russ and Schorr stood.

"We're being ejected," I said to Russ.

Russ nodded soberly. "About damned time."

My nerves kicked in again as we got in his truck. I was going to spend the night with

Russ. Not the same as sleeping with him, but I'd never had a sleepover at a man's house. I moved my purse over so I could hitch my seat belt. "Maybe you should drop me at a hotel."

"Don't go waffling on me, MaryBeth. We're going to my place."

"I don't mean to be indecisive. I just realized how big of an imposition this is. I'm sure you weren't expecting to have an overnight guest."

"Take a deep breath, MaryBeth. It's going to be all right."

Easy for him to say.

I kept my mouth shut except for compliments about his tidy two-story, three-bedroom beachfront cottage. The clean lines of the modern furniture suited him, as did the burnished leather wraparound sofa in his den. "Very nice."

"Oh. Uh. Thanks." He gestured up the stairs. "You can have your choice of the master bedroom or the guest bedroom."

It was clear he wasn't hitting on me, but there was a part of me that wanted to sleep with Russ, a part that needed the closeness of human contact tonight. For a moment, I allowed myself the fantasy of sleeping in his strong arms — and much more. I had the feeling Russ brought a bone-deep thoroughness to everything he did, and sleeping with him would broaden my horizons.

My fantasy reel screeched to an embarrassing halt as I realized Russ was waiting for an answer. "The guest bedroom will be fine."

"Would you like something to eat or drink? Is there a TV program you'd like to watch?"

I managed a smile. "No. I'm beat. The sooner I get to sleep, the sooner I can put this day behind me."

"We're in agreement on that. There are some extra toothbrushes and the like in the guest bathroom. Make yourself at home."

I put my hand on the banister. "Thanks again, Russ. For everything."

"No problem."

I scooted up the stairs, took a turn in the spotless bathroom, then dragged my sorry butt into the guest room. The muted roar of ocean waves drew me to the window. I looked out at the white-headed cresting waves. I opened my window a smidgen, and the soothing sound of the waves became more distinct.

The queen-sized bed seemed huge. Not as cozy as my double bed, but I could adjust to the larger space for one night. My thoughts returned to my bed and my pillows.

Bernie had been in my house. I was sure of that. For him to trash my stuff like that, especially my mother's fish, which he knew meant the world to me, he must have been in a fine rage. My chin went up. I didn't have to worry about his temper anymore. I didn't care what the law said. He'd abandoned me. In my eyes, he was no longer my husband.

But what did he want?

Why had he been in my bed?

Was he planning to shoot me with his gun?

This wasn't helping me settle down for the night. I needed routine thoughts. My cell phone. I should recharge it. I kept a charger cord in my purse so that I could charge my phone wherever I went.

While I was looking for the charger cord, I noticed a narrow slip of paper poking out of my change purse. What was that?

By the thin light of the bedside lamp, I recognized the slip as a fortune from a Chinese cookie. How'd that get there? I couldn't remember the last time I'd had Chinese food. I withdrew the slip and looked at it.

Written above the faded, inked fortune was a scrawling mismatch of printing and script that I recognized as Bernie's hand-writing: *Trust no one. The cops are in on this.*

CHAPTER 22

Why had Bernie left me a message? How could he expect me to blindly follow his orders after he abandoned me for a new life and another woman? I owed him nothing. I crumpled the note in my fist. It would serve him right if I took this note to the cops.

If Bernie's warning was correct, I couldn't trust the cops. But if I didn't tell the cops about the note, I was withholding evidence. I hated lying. I hated that he'd put me in this situation.

Raindrops slapped against my window, muting the roar of the surf. I stared at the crumpled paper in my hand, wanting to swear out loud, but fear of Russ overhearing kept me silent.

Damn you, Bernie.

What was I supposed to do now?

Why should I believe a word he said?

He couldn't just waltz back in here and expect to pick up where he left off. The new

MaryBeth wasn't that gullible.

Why had he put my wedding ring on the pillow? Was he sending me another message?

I shoved the note back in my wallet. If he saw me now, he'd have plenty to say about how I was living my life. I balanced my checkbook with pink ink. I filed my bills in a shoebox. I had colorful dinner plates instead of his prescribed white ones. And I didn't have dessert after every meal.

It hadn't escaped my notice he'd broken every single geranium red dinner plate during his rampage though my house. Bernie's violation of my privacy welled up within me. Suddenly, I couldn't stand being alone in this room. Maybe I could quietly make a cup of hot tea in Russ's kitchen and try to regain a semblance of peace.

When I opened my door, I noticed the hall lights were still on. I padded downstairs. Russ sat sprawled on the sofa, the ice pack discarded on the end table. He didn't speak, but his eyes tracked my progress as I entered the room and halted a few paces away.

"I couldn't sleep," I offered in explanation. "Is it all right if I make some hot tea?"

He unfolded from the sofa and headed to the kitchen. "I'll make it for you. I was just thinking about getting something to eat.

Would you rather have ice cream?"

Now that he'd mentioned ice cream, I craved it. I followed him. "Ice cream it is. How's your head feeling?"

"My head's fine."

His curt tone implied otherwise. He sounded unhappy. I wasn't so happy either. My resurrected, gun-wielding husband was either trying to kill me or save me. Was Russ worried about the same thing?

My eyes lit up when I saw the carton of chocolate ice cream. This was much better than worrying alone in my room.

"You want to talk about this evening?" I asked.

He pulled out clear bowls, spoons, and a heavy duty ice cream scoop. "This is big-time stuff going on here, MaryBeth."

Ah, his pissy mood was out of concern for me. "I didn't mean to bring trouble to your island."

"Trouble has a mind of its own. Thing is, we don't know who the players are. Without good information, we're sitting ducks. The guy in your house tonight, he knew some moves, or I would've had him."

"Did he hurt you?"

A muscle twitched in Russ's cheek as he dished out the ice cream. "Only my pride."

Damn Bernie. I didn't want him hurting

my friends. He'd fired a gun at Russ. That was deadly serious.

His eyes narrowed. He put down the scoop, tension radiating from his body. "You know something. What is it?"

I chewed my bottom lip. Russ had put his life on the line for me. He wasn't a cop. And I trusted him. "The intruder put my wedding ring on my pillow. I think my resurrected husband was in my house, lying on my bed, waiting for me to come home."

Russ watched me a long moment, then nodded tersely. "What was he looking for, MaryBeth?"

I shrugged. "I don't know. I sold all of his belongings. If he's looking for his favorite chair or his church suit, I don't have it."

"My guess is he got that message as he searched, and that enraged him further. By his actions, I'd say he's a desperate man. You have something he needs. As long as he believes that, you're not safe."

I shuddered. "But I don't have any of his stuff. Heck, I barely have any of my things. I squeezed everything I owned into my Jeep for my trip south."

"Until we figure out what he wants, you shouldn't stay alone at your place."

"I don't have any choice. My list of friends down here includes the Washingtons, Gabby

265

my hairdresser, and you. That's it. I'm not bringing trouble to the Washingtons' door, Gabby's too old to protect much of anything, and I've already bothered you tonight."

"You need a dog. A big dog that could take a bite out of anyone stupid enough to bother you."

"Dogs cost money. I can't afford a dog." That's what I said, but I'd always wanted a dog. Bernie had been allergic to animals, so we'd never owned a pet.

What was I doing here? Bernie was my problem. I'd deal with him. "Thanks for putting me up tonight, but I'll manage on my own tomorrow. I'm not your responsibility."

Russ shoved a heaping bowl of ice cream at me. I wasn't sure I could eat a bite, not with Russ looking at me like I was his next course.

"What if I wanted you to be my responsibility?" he asked.

"What do you mean?"

Once the question slipped out, I wished I'd kept my mouth shut.

His gaze connected with mine, hot with intent. A look that had my pulse soaring sky high. "When I asked you about sleeping in the master bedroom, I wasn't planning on vacating it."

"Oh." My pulse thundered in my ears. I could go jump in his bed and have wild sex. I was attracted to Russ. I'd certainly thought about being intimate with him. The surprise was that he'd thought about it too.

Had I changed so much that I could spend the night in his bed?

Was the new MaryBeth so adventurous?

Heat flooded my face. I couldn't quite catch my breath. I clutched the sleek counter for support. I answered as truthfully as I could. "I don't know what to say. This is happening so fast. With the stalker and the shootout in my house tonight, I don't know that my decision-making faculties are working."

Disappointment flared briefly in his eyes as he carried both bowls of ice cream to the table. "If you have to think about it, you're not ready. Eat your ice cream."

"How can you eat after that?"

He shrugged. "Ice cream is a poor substitute for sex, but I'll settle for it tonight."

I wished he'd quit talking about sex. I sat across from him and stirred my ice cream. "My life is a mess right now. I don't understand my past, and I can't envision my future. Friends matter to me, and I don't

267

want to do anything to mess up our friendship."

His eyebrows shot up as he spooned the ice cream in his mouth. "Is this the no-sex talk?"

I groaned at his word choice. The image of him lying protectively on top of me in my yard flashed in my head. Was he thinking about how snugly his body fit on top of mine? I knew I was. "When I kissed you, I was a widow. Now it appears I'm not. I may be married. Or maybe my marriage isn't legal. Whatever the case, my life is a mess, and I shouldn't lead you on."

He put down his ice cream spoon and placed his palms flat on the table. "Too late. You led me on when you kissed me. We've been striking sparks off each other since we met. You can deny it if you like, but we both know it's true."

My spoon clattered into my bowl. All this plain speaking had pushed me past my safety zone. "I have not led you on. What kind of chauvinist bull crap is that?"

He leaned in close, and I got a full whiff of the unique musky scent that was Russ. "The kind that gets you to kiss me again."

"I was under the influence of alcohol when I gave you that kiss."

His brown eyes twinkled. "Yeah, but you

weren't drunk. Just uninhibited."

He had a point there, not that I would admit it out loud. "Well, all my inhibitions are back, bigger than ever. I feel bad enough about you getting shot at tonight. Don't make me feel guilty over leading you on. Because you know that's a lie."

"Lies." He gazed steadily at me. "You really don't like them very much, do you?"

"You do?" The note from Bernie burned in my mind. I couldn't tell Russ about it, but was withholding information the same as lying? It was an omission. That wasn't lying.

"For the most part I'm a black and white kind of guy. I believe in following rules. Pharmacists tend to be very linear thinkers."

"Not me. I tend to think in circles, but I'm trying to fix that. I'm through with being a victim. I've decided to attack my Bernie problem head-on."

He studied me across the table. "How so?"

"I'm going to call folks in Maryland and see what I can find out about Bernie."

"I don't like you sticking your nose under all these rocks. Consider me your after-hours shadow until this is resolved."

Darn it.

He was crowding me again.

"I'm not your responsibility, Russ. I'll never find out what went on during my marriage if I don't start asking questions. Bernie cheated on me. He lied to me. He stole our savings. I need to know why."

He reached across the table and cupped his hand over mine. "Answers aren't all they're cracked up to be. What if the why really hurts?"

"Then it will keep me from making the same mistake twice. I have to understand the past before I can move forward."

He gave my hand a gentle squeeze and let me go. "For what it's worth, I think you're a brave woman. You could have stayed in Maryland, kept your job, and never ventured out of your comfort zone. Instead, you chose to mix things up. You chose to live large. You describe yourself as dull and boring. I don't see you that way. I see an exciting woman on the verge of coming into herself."

My heart raced at his words. He liked who I was. What a novelty not to have to pretend to be someone else. I pressed my hand against my chest to slow my racing heart. "You'll turn my head with such talk."

"One day you'll believe it's true. You've changed, MaryBeth. You're not the timid person who landed in Sandy Shores. You're a capable woman. You single-handedly took on a craft business. You started that Wednesday class for kids. And you're going to hire Justine back."

I shook my head in wonder. "How'd you know about Justine?"

"I saw her in the parking lot today. But more than that, I knew she'd be back. She's a homebody. She wants the comfort of her familiar routine now that she's got the wanderlust purged from her soul."

I raised a hand. "You're scaring me. Do they teach analysis and psychology in pharmacy school?"

"I got a bit of everything in P-school. Had to know what the problems were to know what the meds should be."

His job had always intrigued me. "Don't you ever wonder if you'll put the wrong pill in a pharmacy bottle? Or type in the wrong dose and kill someone?"

"Let me tell you a little secret. Prescription filling is mostly computerized. That plus all the checks and balances make it very hard to screw up that big."

"But you do screw up?"

He scowled. "I don't like how this conversation veered off-track. We were talking about your life."

"Thanks for reminding me." I grimaced.

"You know about my previously dead husband. About my adoptive status. And about Justine turning up. My life is practically an open book."

"Except for whatever sent you sneaking downstairs tonight."

My heart went nuts again. Was he talking about sex or did he know about the hidden note? Either way, I didn't want to talk about it.

I hurriedly put my bowl in the sink, avoiding his eyes. "Thanks for the ice cream."

"Any time. And MaryBeth?"

I turned to face him.

"My door is open if you change your mind."

Yikes!

Temptation flashed like a blinking carnival arcade, larger than life, as thrilling as any whirling ride. My resolve to spend the night alone faltered. There was no doubt in my mind that going to bed with Russ would be life-changing.

I grew warm all under. Lordy. I had to get out of here fast. I'd had all the life-changing I could take in one day.

Besides, I couldn't be intimate with Russ. Bernie's note said to trust no one. Not that I trusted Bernie, but I couldn't start an affair with Russ tonight, not with so many loose ends staring me in the face.

"Good night." Heart pounding in my throat, I rushed upstairs to the guest bedroom.

CHAPTER 23

Sunday, Sunday. Not as low key as a Monday, but not a high traffic sales day like a Friday or Saturday. I'd started lifting the rocks of my life, and creatures were skittering out of the darkness. Being proactive scared me silly, but I had no choice if I wanted to overcome the wrong turn I'd taken in life.

I'd awakened in Russ's guest bedroom this morning determined to dig until I found the truth. Living here at Sandy Shores had opened my eyes. No longer was I the broken woman who'd bought a gift shop on a whim. I was on a journey of self-discovery, and damned if I'd let the past ruin my new start.

Russ had escorted me to work this morning in his usual scowling silence. I flicked on the shop lights and thought about my next step in the truth-seeking process, calling Bernie's friends and co-workers. Even if

I opened a hornet's nest, that was better than not knowing.

This late in the morning, most people were headed to church or, like me, feeling guilty about not going to church. If I got anyone's answering machine, I could call again later in the day.

For today's music, I selected an instrumental piano CD with an array of traditional hymns to lead off the set. Other choices I loaded into the multiplex CD player were also of soft, background-type music. I didn't want any distraction while I was on the phone.

The first person I dialed was Shawn Ellis, Bernie's slimy college roommate. His answering machine picked up. I listened to his glib message with a sinking heart. Here was my first test. I could hang up and not sound like a desperate woman, or I could stick to my plan.

I swallowed around the lump in my throat at the sound of the tone prompt. "Shawn. Hello. This is MaryBeth Cashour again. I'd like to talk to you. Call me."

He picked up the phone before I finished saying my number. "MaryBeth?"

My head bobbed in surprise. "Shawn? I thought you weren't home."

"I screen my calls." He yawned. "How you

doing, babe? How's tricks on your island?"

I winced at the undisguised interest in his voice. Shawn's biggest claim to fame had once been how much he could drink without passing out. And there was that whole God's gift to women mindset he had. Ugh.

If there was a God in this world, I prayed he'd apply Shawn-repellant on the borders of Maryland to keep him there. "I don't own Sandy Shores. I just live here."

Time to get down to business. I gripped the phone tightly and spoke whisper soft. "This is going to sound strange, but I believe Bernie was in my house last night."

Shawn chuckled lightly. "He's haunting you? Want me to come down there and exorcise his ghost?"

His patronizing irritated the crap out of me. "You'd have to exorcise his body, too. Bernie's alive, Shawn."

"He's alive?" In the silence that followed, I could almost feel the wheels turning in Shawn's head. "That shit! He owes me a thousand dollars."

My mouth went dry. "You loaned him money?"

"Yeah. Two months before his funeral, he said you'd gone crazy and maxed out your credit cards. I didn't mention the debt at the service because I figured that would be a shitty thing to do. Then I heard you were broke, and I realized I'd never see my money again."

His words knifed into my heart. "Bernie lied to both of us. He didn't deposit your loan in our joint checking account, and I didn't know about the overdue bills until he was long gone. Did you keep the check? Maybe we can tell where he cashed it and trace him that way."

"God-damn it." Shawn shouted into the phone. I held the receiver away from my ear. "I shouldn't have loaned him a dime. I should've known he'd rip me off. That welsher tried to pull a similar scam back in college but I found out about it and busted his chops."

Bernie had been scamming folks since college? That certainly explained our lack of friends from that period. How could I have been so blind?

Focus, MaryBeth. You can't change the past, but you can sure as heck write your own future. "Do you still have the check, Shawn?"

"No. I tossed that worthless piece of crap in the trash. I remember Bernie cashed that check on the day I wrote it."

"Has he contacted you since the funeral?"

"Hell, no. He'd know I expect him to pay me back that grand he borrowed."

"If you do hear from him, would you call me?"

"Wait a minute. What makes you think Bernie was in your house in the first place?"

"Because of the mess he made. And Shawn, he took my wedding ring out of my dresser and put it on his pillow. That's how I know."

Shawn swore aloud, an inventive mix that had me wincing.

I had to know if Shawn knew about the rest of it. I forged on. "There's an ongoing homicide investigation down here. Lots of stuff I never knew about Bernie is coming to light." I paused to gather my courage to say this out loud. "He had a whole other family, can you believe that?"

"Another family?" Shawn sounded taken aback.

His surprise gave me hope that I hadn't been Bernie's only dupe. Misery truly loves company. "Wife, kids, car. No wonder we were broke. It can't be easy to support two families on our meager incomes. And he had another job, a secret posting that was his real job, not his job at Jesseman Associates."

"Bernie wasn't an energy analyst?"

"The police believe his analyst job was a cover for his clandestine activities."

Shawn whistled. "Cover? Are we talking about slinking around? Spy stuff? Bernie?"

"Yeah. I know. Strange, isn't it?"

"God, I wouldn't suspect Bernie of a double life in a million years. He was a welsher, sure, but a spy? That's like, science fiction or fantasy."

"That was my first reaction too. Bernie liked everything done a certain way. His way. He sure had me fooled."

"What did he do? Sell national secrets to the Chinese?"

"That's the crazy part. I don't know. Bad people are down here looking for him, and, because they believe I know something about his double life, they're also looking for me. Shawn, did you ever hear Bernie mention Macklin Rudd?"

"Who's he?"

"A dead man. That's who he is. But he knew Bernie." I took a deep breath. "How about Arlene Nevin? Do you know her?"

"Let me think. I knew an Arlene once. A leggy brunette with big tits. A real party girl. Dropped out of school to have babies with a townie."

The description fit. Bile rose in my throat. "Did Bernie know her?"

"If it's the same Arlene, we all knew her. In the Biblical sense. She'd screw anyone

279

for twenty bucks."

I gagged. Bernie had married Arlene? How the mighty had fallen. Anger churned in my gut. "Never mind. If you remember anything else about Bernie, anything that would help me find him, please call, okay?"

"Sure thing. Say, would you be interested in a long weekend in the Caribbean?"

Yuck. I wasn't that desperate for a vacation, but I couldn't afford to alienate Shawn at this point. "I can't get away right now, and I wouldn't want to involve you in this murder investigation."

"Some other time then."

I hung up the phone fast and scuttled away from it, shuddering with revulsion. Aack. Gross. I was not sleeping with Shawn Ellis. Not in this lifetime. I had standards.

I tried Bernie's work number again. Disconnected. Funny. Three of his colleagues had come to the funeral. None of the numbers I had for them worked either.

Frustrated, I tossed my address book back in my purse. So much for taking the initiative. The only new thing I'd learned was that Bernie's current wife had slept with men for money. And Shawn Ellis had hit on me. Neither fact would help me find Bernie.

The obvious source of information slowly

dawned on me. To find Bernie, I needed to talk to Arlene. The cops said she was staying at a budget hotel over in Brunswick. Was she still there? The question was, did I have the courage to face her and those two little boys?

Boys that might very well be Bernie's biological sons, even though he'd only adopted them two years ago.

Pain lanced through my heart, taking my breath away. I'd gotten pregnant three times with Bernie, but I had nothing to show for it. If Bernie had kids with the promiscuous Arlene, then that further proved I was barren. Worse, he'd never been faithful to me. He'd never cared about me. All he'd cared about was what I could do for him.

Tears welled up in my eyes. God, when would the hurt and betrayal end? Why couldn't Bernie have stayed dead?

When the door chime sounded seven notes of "The First Noel," I wiped my tears away and greeted my customer. I blinked at the heartwarming sight of ten-year-old Tyson Price.

His straight blond hair fitted his head like a cereal bowl, and he smelled ocean-breeze fresh. He was the son I could never have. "Tyson. This is a pleasant surprise. What can I do for you?"

"I was wondering if I could work some more on my frame. I know it isn't a class day, but Mom's sister is here so I have some free time. Is it okay?"

Poor kid, always taking care of his sick mom. "Sure. Let me get the supplies out for you. Come on back in the craft room."

"Thanks."

"It's no problem at all. What have you been doing today?" As I spoke, I put Tyson's frame, his plate of pre-selected shells, and a bottle of craft glue on the table.

Tyson slid into his chair. "Me and my dog Andy went down on the beach this morning."

I sat across from him and managed a smile. "Did Andy chase the birds?"

"Yeah." Tyson grinned. "His mission in life is to free the beach from seagulls."

"Does he ever catch them?"

"No, but that doesn't stop him from trying."

"It's nice you have Andy to keep you company."

Tyson nodded soberly. He glued on a shell. Then his face clouded. "I saw the scary man again today. Andy chased him off the beach."

The scary man. The one the kids said was sleeping on the beach. What had Claudia said about him? He had a beard, glasses, and straggly brown hair.

My brain made an unwelcome connection. The man following my Jeep had a beard. Bernie's hair was brown. He wore glasses. Was he the scary man on the beach?

"Where did you see him?"

Tyson dragged his fingers through his shells. "Eden Beach."

My heart missed a beat. Eden Beach wasn't far from me. "Did you notice anything else about him? What was he wearing?"

"Jeans. A dark blue shirt. Camouflage hat. Sneakers. He sure ran fast when Andy started barking."

He sounded like a beach bum. Not like the Bernie I knew, the Bernie who insisted his jeans were pressed and starched. Did I ever really know him?

I knew he was afraid of dogs. Had been ever since a pit bull bit his leg as a boy. The Bernie I knew would've run from a large dog like Andy.

Hmm. Another connection.

"Stay away from that guy. Keep Andy away from him, too."

Fire burned in Tyson's eyes. "You think he might hurt Andy?"

"He's a stranger. We have to assume he's

dangerous. I don't want you to be scared, but be careful around strangers. Call the cops next time you see him. He's probably a harmless drifter. As winter sets in, he should move further south."

That's what I said, but my thoughts spun out of control. If it was Bernie, what was he doing scaring children? Should I tell the cops? Or would I be signing our death warrants if the cops found him? God, I hated not knowing what to do.

He'd dragged me into his mess, and I accepted that my fate was cruelly linked to his. But he wasn't going to put the island children at risk. They were innocents.

"He was down by the fishing docks when I rode my bike in a few minutes ago."

I glanced toward the front door. The fishing docks were visible from outside the shop. I rose. "I'm going to see if I can spot him. I'll be right back."

Tyson followed me out. Both of us scanned the docks. There was no one in sight. "He was there a few minutes ago."

Disappointed, I went back in my craft room and washed my hands, wishing I could rid myself of Bernie so easily. "I don't doubt you, Tyson. I was hoping I could see him though. I'd like to see this man who's scaring you kids. Let me know if you see him again. We should ask the cops to check him out."

"Whatever." Tyler slouched in his seat and picked up a shell. He positioned it exactly where he wanted it then glued it in place.

Through the speakers, fluid harp notes plucked out the tune of "Away in a Manger," and I unconsciously hummed along as I sat with Tyson. My door chime rang. I trotted back to the sales floor. "Welcome to Christmas by the Sea."

Two familiar cops stared at me. My tightly wound nerves made me giddy. "We have to stop meeting like this," I deadpanned. Neither detective cracked a smile at my feeble humor. "What can I do for you this morning?"

"Our interview with Mrs. Nevin led us to an associate of your husband's, a Mr. Ed Sawyer."

That got my attention. I'd been trying to reach him. Bernie's warning about cop involvement popped in my head, but I ignored it because I wanted to know what they knew. "You talked to Eddie?"

"We talked to the Henrico County Police in Richmond, Virginia, where he's currently detained."

I tried to understand the ramifications of this, but the dots wouldn't connect. Eddie and Bernie had worked closely together for years. I'd had Eddie over to dinner countless times and he'd entertained us with wild stories. Were they all lies?

"What did he do?" I asked. "Shoot off his mouth at someone who didn't have a sense of humor?"

Detective Monroe reached in her back pocket for her small notepad. "He was picked up for outstanding felony warrants after a routine traffic stop."

"Oh." Butterflies flitted around my stomach. From the cops' grim expression, I surmised they'd learned something else unsavory about Bernie. "What? What did he tell you?"

"Mr. Sawyer led us to believe Bernie had gotten mixed up with some big-time crooks. He swears Mac Rudd stole something from an organized crime syndicate and gave it to Bernie for safe-keeping. Sawyer's statement jives with the evidence we have on Rudd's bullet. It matches other unsolved murders in New Jersey."

"The mob killed Mac Rudd?"

"Looks that way. We have no witnesses who can place Rudd in the area, only the plastic Christmas shark, which ties him to this shop. Our only viable lead to solving his murder is the missing item that allegedly came into your husband's possession."

The butterflies in my stomach took flight. Were the cops telling me the truth? What they said felt true. And rotten. Like Bernie. He was a cancer that tainted everything he touched. "Bernie had something that didn't belong to him?"

"Yes. According to Mr. Sawyer, Rudd was ordered to get the item back from Bernie, only Bernie was dead. Do you remember Bernie bringing home an unusual item?"

"What do you consider unusual? A gargoyle statue? An old Army trunk? A new car? Japanese beer?"

Detective Monroe looked up. "Do you have any of those items?"

I shrugged. "Nope. Sorry."

"Do you have boxes of his belongings that we could look through?"

"After his death, I couldn't afford to be sentimental. I sold everything at a yard sale."

Detective Schorr recoiled. "You kept none of his stuff?"

"Nothing."

He shuddered. "Man. That's cold."

Detective Monroe frowned, then tapped her pad against her leg. "What can you tell me about Mr. Sawyer?"

"What do you want to know?"

"Where he hung out. Places he and Bernie went together. That sort of thing."

I'd always liked Eddie. It was hard to believe he'd conned me, too. "He had a one-bedroom apartment on the wrong side of the tracks. Eddie pinched his pennies because he was saving up for early retirement. I had no idea he had outstanding warrants."

"What about hangouts?"

"Bernie and Eddie were in a Tuesday night bowling league at Turtle Lanes in Frederick. Sometimes they stopped off after work for a drink at the Raw Bar."

Detective Monroe scribbled down the information, her gaze on my face as she wrote. "What about other known associates?"

The nasty way she said "associates" made me think she meant "felons." Because I didn't have anything to lose, I gave her the phone numbers for Bernie's coworkers. "The thing is, these phone numbers aren't any good."

"You called these people recently?" Monroe asked.

I nodded. "This morning."

Detective Schorr muscled his way closer. "Why'd you do that?"

Instinctively, I edged back a step. "I want answers. I'm tired of being in the dark."

"These aren't nice people we're dealing

with," Monroe said. "They'll shoot first and ask questions later. Leave the investigating to us professionals."

"The things you tell me, they're hard for me to accept. Eddie, for one. He was such a sweet guy. He brought over pizza and ice cream. I can't tell you how many nights we spent just talking about nothing on our patio."

"You and your husband didn't go out to restaurants or visit attractions?"

"Almost never. If we had a special occasion, we drove over to Annapolis to eat."

"What about the Bethesda area? Did you and Bernie ever go there?"

"No. My gynecologist referred us to a fertility specialist near Georgetown, but Bernie refused to consider it. He said he didn't want a two-headed kid."

"You went along with that?"

"I allowed Bernie to guide me in a lot of things." I stared down at my stubby hands on the sales counter. "I realize now that I made a big mistake, but Bernie always sounded so sure of himself, and he got upset if events didn't go according to his plans."

It hurt admitting these shortcomings out loud. Bernie had been a bully, but I'd let him bully me. No one had held a gun to my head. I'd willingly gone along with whatever he said. Because it was the easy way. But no longer.

I looked into Detective Monroe's sunglasses, the twinkle lights reflecting off them like crazy. "I'm a coward. Bernie's temper scared me. I let him tell me what to do. I wasn't unhappy living that way. Bernie took care of me, I took care of our home. I thought that's what marriage meant."

"Has he contacted you since his alleged death?"

"I haven't spoken to him."

That was the truth, though it was a lie of omission. The warning in Bernie's note kept me from saying more. He didn't deserve my loyalty, but I wanted to talk to him, to get answers for myself. If the police were involved, they might shoot first and ask questions later. Then where would I be?

I wanted to know why he'd faked his death, why he'd lied to me for ten straight years, why he'd left me that cryptic note. Bernie owed me that much.

For the first time ever, I wasn't worrying about igniting Bernie's temper. He'd better worry about soothing mine.

CHAPTER 24

Chocolate cupcakes were the perfect mid-morning pick-me-up. The first one went down easily. So did the next one. I hummed in satisfaction as the rich flavor flowed down my throat and settled my nervous stomach.

"Good thing swimsuit season is done, the way you're snarfing down those cupcakes," Daisy Pearl said. She held baby Gwen nestled in the crook of her arm as she sat with me at Sweet Things.

I chased the cupcakes with a swig of coffee. My waistline was the least of my worries. "Hey, I'm entitled. My house was broken into. I have a bullet hole in my window. Justine's back in town. It seems my dead, philandering husband is alive, and the cops expect him to contact me any moment now."

Daisy Pearl shook her head. "Jumping up to a size sixteen won't fix your problems. First of all, your dead husband is alive?"

"Yeah." I filled her in on yesterday's events. Except for the note. I wasn't telling anyone about the hidden evidence in my purse. "After my house was trashed, I found my wedding band sitting right in the middle of my pillow. I haven't worn that ring since I moved here."

"The cops know about the ring on the pillow?"

"They know about it. It's been processed as evidence."

"Man, there is some bad mojo following you around."

My shoulders slumped. "God, you're right. I brought Bernie's mess down here with me. I've put you nice people at risk."

"Don't you worry. What comes around, goes around. Give them enough time, and the Captain and Tennille will stumble onto the right answer."

"They don't seem to be stumbling around to me. When they stare at me through those reflector sunglasses, I want to crawl under a rock and hide until they're gone."

"Hmph. They wouldn't get away with that with me. I'd snatch those glasses off their scrawny noses in a heartbeat. Is Shanelle giving you a hard time about your not-so-dead husband?"

I thought back on Detective Shanelle

Monroe's penetrating questions about Bernie and me. "Maybe."

Daisy Pearl nodded. "She's a man-hater all right. Don't pay her no never mind. She like to tore up my son John Allen. Broke his heart, ripped it out, and stomped it to pieces. She won't come in my shop unless it's business cuz she knows I'll give her what for."

"Are we talking about the same woman? She seems cold and dispassionate to me."

"She's cold all right. Like a snake in the grass." Daisy Pearl shuddered. The baby's eyes flared wide and she fretted. "Now look what that mean old Shanelle made me do," Daisy Pearl said. "Poor little Gwen was nearly asleep."

As Daisy Pearl crooned to the baby, I finished my cupcake. I tried to picture Detective Monroe as a steamy temptress who went around breaking men's hearts. I didn't succeed. She was a robot of a person. And an endless font of questions.

Once the baby was settled, Daisy Pearl fixed me with another all-seeing look. "What about Detective Hottie?"

Detective Kent Schorr was hot all right, but I wasn't a sucker for the muscle-bound, rolling-gait kind of man. I preferred men with more natural musculature. For years,

Bernie's slight build had been the embodiment of my perfect man. Not anymore. The thought of him brought a sour taste to my mouth. I quickly put him out of my mind. "What about him?"

"He hitting on you?"

I swallowed wrong and had to drink the rest of my coffee before I could speak again. "God, Daisy Pearl, is sex all you think about?"

"Honey, it's all they think about. Don't you doubt it for a red hot minute."

"He's too young for me, but he does seem quite friendly when he finally says something."

"Uh-uh-uh. I just loves me a man that don't have much to say."

"You're interested in Detective Schorr?"

"Heck, no. I got me a good man. But I ain't dead. I like to look. Nuttin' wrong with looking."

I glanced down at my empty coffee cup. I'd already had a cup with Russ and now this super-sized cup. If I drank more coffee, I'd have the jitters all day. Dang. Why did I want things that were bad for me? Why didn't I ever long for more carrots or broccoli?

Daisy Pearl must have caught my wistful expression. "You want some more coffee?"

I pushed my chair back from the table, intending to stand up. "No, I'm already at my limit. I should get back to the shop."

Daisy Pearl clamped a hand on my wrist, her strong fingers manacling me like hand-cuffs. "Not so fast. I didn't get the Russ report. I wanna know about the sleepover at his house last night."

Did she have eyes in the back of her head? How'd she know that I spent the night at his house? "I called Russ when I realized someone was following me home from work. He stuck with me all evening, then he appointed himself as my after-hours body-guard."

Daisy Pearl let me go and rocked the baby in her arms. "You have a thing for him?"

My heart stilled. My feelings were private, and I intended to keep them that way. I needed to distract Daisy Pearl from her inquisition. Why wasn't there a busload of tourists pulling into the parking lot right now? "I called him because I was worried."

"You could have called the police."

"The cops already think I'm nuts. Heck, they think I'm part of the crime wave."

"I see."

Her terse answer made my full stomach knot. What did she see exactly? Did she think Russ and I were having hot sex?

Daisy Pearl fixed me with a meaningful stare. "Russ now, he's not a man to be trifled with."

What the heck did that mean? "I don't understand your concern. I was in trouble. I phoned a friend."

"Men don't think that way. You called him. He came. He likes you."

Heat rushed to my face. Did Daisy Pearl know about the kiss? She seemed to know everything else. "We're friends. He helped me."

"He followed you into work this morning. Did you sleep with him?"

Did she have people spying on me? I hastened to explain. "It isn't what you think. I needed a place to stay because the crime scene unit was at my house. Russ wouldn't hear of me going to a hotel. I slept alone in his guest room." I hated that my voice sounded so shrill. No telling what Daisy Pearl made of that.

"Why didn't Russ shoot your burglar?"

Thank God he hadn't. I'd had enough talk about guns and sleepovers. I sneaked a longing glance at the door. "I really need to open my shop."

"Not so fast. What about Justine?"

"What about her?"

"You gonna let her work in the shop?"

My hands spasmed together in my lap. "I don't know. I honestly don't know."

"Justine belongs in that shop. Why don't you want her?"

Heat blasted off my face, moistening my nose, causing my glasses to slip. I shoved them back up. "My reason sounds small and petty, but I can't help it. I'm finally my own boss. I don't want anyone telling me what to do again."

"Justine's not like that. She needs to be around people, and she's really good at making crafts."

"And I'm not," I said with a sigh. "You don't have to remind me of my failures. I know I'm not crafty."

"I never thought that for a minute. What would it hurt to allow Justine to help out?"

"My mother used to say, too many cooks spoiled the pot. Justine and I have different ideas about how things should be. I respect that she used to own the shop, but it's mine now."

"Are you listening to yourself? The woman who came south on her own and started a new business won't befriend a lonely older woman?"

"I'm a coward. I'm not the brave woman you think I am. I'm small inside. Small and hurt and wishing I could have my invisible life back."

"Your old life sucked."

I winced at the truth. "But I didn't have to make hard decisions. Bernie took care of all that for me."

"Don't get stuck looking over your shoulder at what used to be. You're Mary Christmas now. You've opened your heart to the local children. You're responsible for that shop and for yourself."

I couldn't sit still any longer. I jumped up, discarded my trash, and paced the room. "I'm not the person you want me to be."

"You're who you think you are. Nothing more. Nothing less."

The door was within reach. I could leave right now. Only I didn't want to leave. I wanted Daisy Pearl to understand why I couldn't live up to her expectations.

"I'm scared," I admitted.

Daisy Pearl's face softened. "It's all right to be scared."

Easy for her to say. She didn't have the police breathing down her neck. Or drowned husbands coming back to life. Or dead bodies washing up at her feet. "What if I make the wrong decision?"

"Life isn't so black and white, baby." Daisy Pearl's voice softened. "You make a choice, you change direction. If you don't make a choice, you freeze and life passes you by."

The sounds of the bakery receded. "You think I'm frozen?"

"I see the strength in you, waiting to be tapped."

"That's not what I feel. I feel the cops' suspicion. I feel Russ's interest. I feel your expectations. I don't know what to do. All I know is that I don't want to be passive anymore. I don't want life dragging me down. Only I don't know how to be brave like you."

"Bravery isn't complicated. It's simple. One step at a time, one decision at a time."

"But how will I know if I'm making the right decisions?"

Daisy Pearl rose, the sleeping baby in her arms. "Because every decision you make will be the best one you can make at the time. That's all you can do, sunshine. That's all you can do."

As she disappeared in the back of her bakery, I stood there absorbing her earthy wisdom. I could continue to drown my sorrows in molten chocolate cupcakes, but that wouldn't change my plight. I'd still be the fraidy-cat little girl who got pushed around by the bullies of the world.

I didn't want that for my future. I wanted

to live, and the way to live was to take risks, to make choices. I chose to go next door and open the shop. I chose a CD of a children's choir singing songs about a snowman and chestnuts. I chose to call Justine and invite her down to the shop.

CHAPTER 25

Russ escorted me to and from work each day, making a big show of checking each destination for intruders. He installed my new locks, and now my home was as secure as a fortress.

I hadn't seen the cops since Sunday.

I hadn't heard from Bernie.

Life was good.

Late Tuesday afternoon I knew I'd made the right decision by hiring Justine. She'd been churning out crafts nonstop for two days.

At four o'clock, Justine stood and stretched like a sleek cat. As she rolled her neck in a slow circle, her silver hoop earrings banged on her thin shoulders. "I can't thank you enough for this job. I wasn't sure you'd hire me."

I opened another drawer to continue my supply inventory. We were low on acrylic paint, tulle, squiggly eyes, red ribbon, and wooden frames. "My hesitation had nothing to do with you. It was about me. I've lived a sheltered life, and it's taking me a while to figure some stuff out about myself."

"Whatever the reason, I'm thrilled to be here. And I'm equally thrilled that I get to do crafts, and you handle the administrative headaches." She pushed her chair under the table. "Would you like to come to dinner tonight?"

I shoved the drawer shut. "Thanks, but can I have a rain check? I'm going to be at the shop for a bit longer tonight setting up for tomorrow's craft class."

Justine's well-drawn eyebrows arched high under her bright red bangs. "And you have young Russ next door waiting to escort you home. Say no more."

Heat steamed from under my collar. "Young Russ is a grown man. And we're just friends."

A sly smile crossed her glossy lips. "Um-hmm. I may be old, but I'm not dead. He's a fine young man, a good provider, and he's got a good head on those hunky, broad shoulders."

"Really, Justine, I'm not looking to marry Russ. He's a decent guy, and yes, very nice on the eyes, but that's all there is to it."

"Hell. What's the matter with you young

people today? If I had a red-blooded man like Russ sniffing after me, I'd tie him in my bed and leave him there for the next fifty years."

Okay. Too much information. I didn't need the image of sixty-year-old Justine making love with Russ in my head. Best to change the subject. "Are you coming in tomorrow?"

"Can't make it. I have two home improvement contractors stopping by to give me estimates. Now that I'm done catting around, I'm going to spruce up my little cottage." Justine did a suggestive little wiggle. "I've always been a sucker for a man in a tool belt."

I opened another drawer so Justine wouldn't see me blushing. Her frankness about sex and sensuality embarrassed the heck out of me. "I'll see you Thursday morning then."

"Toodles." Justine waggled her fingers at me and slipped out the back door.

At her departure, the shop seemed blessedly peaceful. I'd gotten used to this being my space. Granted, I needed Justine's help to replenish my craft stock, but she talked nonstop. Would I have to start wearing ear plugs to work?

Ah well, I had another hour to kill until

Russ was off work. The front door of the shop was locked. The Closed sign hung in the window, the Christmas music was turned off. It was just me and the wondrous silence in the craft room.

The rolls of red and white plush material piled near the sink called to me. I ran my fingers across the bolts of soft fabric. I was pretty sure Justine had intended this material for new tree skirts, but another idea tickled my thoughts.

Though John Curtis wanted to paint plastic sharks, I couldn't look at them without thinking of Mac Rudd rolling in the ocean. But the plush fabric, I could easily see that as Christmas stockings. The kids could decorate them with sequins and beads. If I cut out the fabric now, I could hand-stitch the stockings together tonight.

I stood at the back counter and drew up a pattern on tissue paper. If I drilled small holes in some seashells, the kids could sew them to the stockings, too.

A blast of air blew across the nape of my neck as the back door opened. "I'm sorry, we're closed," I said as I turned.

At the sight of the unshaven man, my breath caught in my throat. With one glance, I knew this was the scary man the kids had been talking about.

I took in the flannel shirt, the camouflage hat, the oversized glasses, the sandy hair. And the gun.

Why hadn't I checked the back door lock after Justine left? I reached behind me for a weapon. All I found was a handful of red plush fabric. That wouldn't stop a bullet. Why hadn't I installed a phone back here? I needed to call the cops. I edged toward my sales floor and the telephone.

As if he read my thoughts, the man cut between me and the open doorway. "Dammit, MaryBeth. Why the hell did you move to this God-forsaken place?"

I gulped. That voice sounded familiar. I pushed my glasses up the bridge of my nose and squinted at the ragged mustache and beard. A dirty strip of gauze was wound around his left hand. "Bernie, is that you?"

He stepped closer, brandishing the gun in my face. "Were you expecting someone else? Like the snarky pharmacist next door?"

His rumpled clothes reeked like a dead skunk. Unkempt whiskers covered his lips. I saw a lot of gray in his ragged beard. The old Bernie always insisted on every hair being in place. He'd plucked out the gray hairs on his head. How had he gone from Mister Perfection to Mr. Who Gives a Shit?

There was so much I wanted to say to

Bernie. So many questions I wanted answered. But the questions would have to wait. Anger churned in my gut.

Screw the gun. If he thought I was the weak-willed woman he'd once known, he had another thought coming. "I was expecting that my husband of ten years would be faithful to me." My voice vibrated with outrage. "That he wouldn't fake his death and wipe out our bank account."

He touched my hair with the barrel of the pistol. "What in the hell did you do to your hair?"

I swatted the gun away like it was a mosquito. "My hairstyle is none of your business. Where have you been?"

He shoved the gun in my face. "Shut up. You've ruined my life. Ruined it, you hear? I can't show my face anywhere, and it's all your fault."

My spine stiffened. "I don't have to take your crap anymore. Leave my shop immediately."

Fury blazed in his eyes, and he jabbed the gun into my left breast so hard that I might as well be having a mammogram. His bandaged hand grabbed my shoulder. "Shut up, bitch. Where's my stuff?"

My anger morphed into a numbing fear. I'd never really known this man at all.

"What stuff?"

"My stuff. My clothes, my personal items, my laptop. Where is it?"

I cringed inside. But I wouldn't back down. My chin jutted out. "I don't have it. Why'd you leave me that note?"

"Dammit MaryBeth, don't make me shoot you. Where's my stuff?"

He couldn't shoot me because he needed something from me. I was safe as long as I held that power over him. My courage returned. "First of all my name doesn't begin with dammit. Second of all, I don't have your stuff. I sold it."

His eyes flared beneath his oversized glasses. "Sold it? Why in the hell would you do that?"

Even the gun jabbing into me couldn't completely quell my anger. "Do you know how many bills you left me with? I sold everything and barely had enough money to pay our creditors."

"My belongings weren't worth much. I know you. You're a pack rat. You wouldn't get rid of anything that might be useful some day. Where's my stuff?"

I shrugged. "It's gone. I had yard sales. People from all over came to buy our used furniture. I couldn't afford the mortgage payment and the home equity loan you'd taken out. The bank repossessed our house. When all was said and done, I had just enough money to rent a car to get me to my mother's."

His eyes narrowed. "My stuff is at your mother's house?"

"Mama is dead, her house is sold. I told you. I don't have your stuff. Why did you let me believe you were dead? Didn't you love me?"

A muscle in his bearded cheek flinched. "What do you know of love?"

That hurt. Coming from the man I'd loved unquestionably. "Not much, apparently. I was in love with the man I thought you were, but the police told me about your underworld connections. We were married for ten years, Bernie. Was all of it a lie?"

A wild look came into his eyes. "You married me for better or worse."

My heart tightened with pain. I gave a rough laugh. "How much worse can it be to have you come back from the dead and threaten to shoot me because I didn't keep your bowling shoes and your polyester suits?" I fought for composure. "What's with the ring on the pillow and the note in my purse?"

"I didn't want you telling the cops it was me."

"Too late. They already know it was you."

"You're supposed to be wearing your ring."

"Get a grip, Bernie. You don't own me. You're dead, and I'm a widow, remember?"

"I took on a new identity, but I'm not dead. Where the hell is my stuff?"

His repetitive questioning was tiresome. I threw my hands up in the air. "Are you deaf as well as dumb? I don't have your stuff. Tell me what you're looking for, and I'll try to remember who bought it."

His jaw went slack. "Shit. Shit. Shit."

"I don't want you or your gun in here. Get out."

"Goddamn cops. They're everywhere. When they're not watching you, Wonder Dog next door is on guard duty. What are you afraid of?"

"Just about everything. I'm afraid of whoever killed your criminal associate Mac Rudd. I've had crank callers. I've been stalked. I've had break-ins in my store, my Jeep, my house."

Bernie's eyes got large behind his glasses. "They're here? Shit. They said they wouldn't mess with you, not yet anyway. We don't have much time."

"We? No way." I pointed to the door. "I'm not part of your fraudulent lifestyle. Go away. Crawl back into whatever snake hole you crawled out of and leave me alone."

"No can do. I've got to have that picture."

He had me there. "What picture?"

"The picture from my office."

"I sold your office pictures at the yard sale. I don't have anything from your office. Look around if you don't believe me. I've got the house and the shop. That's it."

I prayed that getting shot in the heart wouldn't hurt. I wasn't afraid of dying, but I was a real weenie about pain.

His voice roughened. "You're still my wife."

"Think again. Arlene is your wife." At his look of surprise I went on. "Didn't think I'd find out about her, did ya? Unlike me, she's afraid for your safety. She wants you back. Go home to her and leave me alone."

Some of the starch went out of Bernie. "Arlene needs me. Those boys need me."

I didn't want to ask, but I had to know. "Are you their real father?"

"I take care of them."

My fist banged on the counter. "That's not what I asked. Are those boys your biological children? Were you sleeping with her the whole time you were married to me?"

He sneered. "I did a lot of things you

never knew about. You were outside the need-to-know circle."

"Need-to-know circle? So it's true? You're a spy? I'm not buying it. Here's what I believe. You screwed up. You ran off and left me. Now you want me to put your life back together for you. You know what? It ain't happening."

His eyes blazed. "I didn't screw up. My cover was blown. I faked my death so the Bertellis wouldn't come after you."

"Not believing that either." My voice wavered as emotion overcame me. "If you're really a government agent, they would've relocated us on their nickel. Why did you leave me penniless? Why did you abandon me?"

"There was a mole in the agency. We couldn't risk the Witness Relocation Program. I had to finance my own future."

"You dumped me to save your own skin. Admit it. Your future meant more than the trust we'd shared for ten years."

"Don't twist my words. I did what I thought was necessary."

"I was your cover in Maryland, wasn't I? I was the housekeeper you came home to after running all over creation doing God knows what with mobsters."

"It wasn't like that."

"Yeah? Tell me what it was like."

"I can't. The less you know, the better off you'll be."

I snorted with disbelief. "God, you're such a liar. Why shouldn't I call the cops right now and turn you in?"

"The Bertellis play for keeps. I tried to keep you out of this, but they found me." He held up his bandaged left hand. "They cut off part of my finger. They said if I don't get them the frame by noon tomorrow, you're their next target."

I recoiled. My insides iced as I glanced at the dirty bandage again. I counted the fingers on his hand. Twice. Oh God. It was true. He was missing a finger. I tucked my fingers behind my back. "We've got to call the cops."

"It was a Jersey cop who hacked off my finger."

I tried to swallow but my mouth was too dry. "A cop?"

"A cop. We're not telling the cops anything."

"Surely that was just one bad apple. The cops here are nice. They wouldn't do that."

"They're all connected. If the cops catch me, I'm a dead man."

I balled my hidden fingers into fists. Fear ate at my belly, fueled my anger. "You lying bastard. I don't trust you."

He dragged the gun barrel across my lips, reminding me who held the upper hand. "Don't get hung up on the truth. It isn't an absolute."

I was sick of the sight of him, sick of his rants. I wanted to push him away, to hurt him as much as he'd hurt me. He didn't deserve my loyalty or my honesty. "You're a liar and a fraud."

"What the hell has gotten into you, Mary-Beth?"

"Independence. You threw me to the wolves. I learned to fight my own battles."

For a moment I thought I'd pushed him too far. The cold gun barrel jabbed into my breast like an auger, then he dragged the gun along the neckline of my stretchy T-shirt. Using the fingertips poking out of the dirty bandage, he tugged the gold locket out from underneath my collar. "You still wear my necklace. You care for me."

Denial sprang to my lips. "I love this necklace. I do not love you. You broke my heart and abandoned me. You aren't my husband."

He dropped the necklace. His fingers closed around my throat and squeezed lightly. My fear returned full force. Was this the end?

Would I see a bright light or a tunnel?

Would memories flash before my eyes?

None of that happened. Instead, Bernie kissed me hard on the lips. "If you tell anyone I was here, I'll kill you, necklace or not."

He hit me in the head with his gun, and the room went dark.

CHAPTER 26

I opened my eyes. A dark forest of metallic chair legs dominated my field of vision. Cold seeped up from the yellowed tile floor through my cheek. My shaky inhalation was the only sound that reached my ears. The scents of evergreen and cinnamon perfumed the air.

I blinked myself fully awake. I was in my shop. That was good. When I looked around to see if I was alone, the movement brought intense pain. Reaching up, I fingered the lump on the back of my head and yelped.

What happened to me?

I'd been working on tomorrow's craft, and someone had come in the back door. Someone scary looking. The scary man. The kids' scary man was Bernie.

It was coming back to me now. Bernie had threatened to kill me. He'd kissed me, and he'd knocked me out cold.

Damn him.

Holding my aching head, I slowly sat up. My throat was sore. I remembered his fingers tightening around my neck. Would there be bruises?

Gaining my feet, I peered anxiously in the reflective surface of my paper towel dispenser. The darkening imprint of his hand was visible. Horror welled up like a surging tide as I stood there, staring at myself.

Unless I came up with a picture of his I didn't have, the mob would kill me tomorrow, or at the very least, cut off one of my fingers. I shuddered. I wasn't ready to part with a single digit. It seemed to me there was only one option.

Call the cops.

But what about Bernie's warning?

Screw Bernie. I dug out my cell phone and dialed Detective Shanelle Monroe. "My husband was just here," I whispered into the phone. "He had a gun, and he threatened to kill me if I called the cops."

"Where are you?" Monroe's voice fired right back through the line.

"I'm still at work. Waiting for Russ to escort me home. I can't be seen with a cop. Bernie said he's watching me."

"No problem. Do I have permission to enter your home?"

My home seemed to have a revolving door

these days. What was one more visitor? "Sure."

"Good. I'll have Schorr drop me off at your place on the way to your shop. He'll discreetly follow you and Marchone home this evening, then stake out the perimeter while I'm in there with you."

"I'm scared. Bernie has this nasty bandage on his hand. He said a Jersey cop chopped off his finger and that I'm next."

"Did you find out what they want from you?"

"Yes. It's a picture from Bernie's office. I don't have it." My chin quivered. "Bernie said the mob will grab me tomorrow and cut off my fingers. I don't want to die. You have to help me."

"We'll help you. Stay calm. You did the right thing by calling us. We're on our way."

I ended the call. How the heck could I stay calm with a lunatic husband and who-knows-how-many mobsters wanting a piece of me?

Calm. I took a ragged breath. What would a calm person do?

She'd think of a way to keep Russ from seeing the bruises on my throat. I knotted the arms of my sweater around my neck. There. I'd accomplished something.

I checked that the door was locked and

watched the clock. Russ would be here any minute. Do I tell him what was going on? Or do I keep him in the dark?

If I told him, he'd insist on staying with me tonight and tomorrow, and he might get hurt. Bernie had shot at him the last time Russ had helped me. No. I'd better keep Russ safely uninformed.

He came right on time. "You look a little pale, MaryBeth. Are you all right?"

I hitched my purse over my shoulder, keys in hand. Dark storm clouds weighted down the late afternoon sky. Thunder rumbled off in the distance. "It's been a long day. I could use a hot bath and a bowl of soup."

"Do you need to pick up anything on the way home?"

We stepped outside, and I locked the shop. "No, thanks. I want to be home before the rainstorm hits tonight."

"I'll be right behind you."

I nodded and drove home. Questions mounted as Russ checked out my house. Was Detective Monroe inside already? Would Russ sense something was up?

I chewed on my fingernails as I waited in my Jeep. Moments later Russ gave me the all clear. Wherever Detective Monroe was hiding, Russ hadn't seen her.

"You sure you don't want me to stay over?"

"No, thanks. I'll be fine."

"You remember I'm taking my mother to the podiatrist tomorrow morning after I drop you off at work?"

"I remember. Go home and relax. You're looking a little peaked yourself." Wonder of wonders, he left.

The first thing I did was close all the blinds and curtains. "Detective Monroe? He's gone." I whispered as I went through the house.

I heard a slight rustle, and she swung down out of the small attic opening like a trapeze artist. Her eyes quickly scanned the room. "Don't turn on any lights. Let's go in the bathroom and talk. I want to hear everything that happened."

I sat on the john, and she perched on the side of the tub, notebook in hand. I told her what happened and showed her my bruises.

"You want to press charges?"

"Yes."

She inclined her head. "We'll put out an all points bulletin and pick him up. There can't be too many flannel-shirted, bearded men running around the island."

My fingernails dug into my damp palm. "If we pick him up, what about the mob?"

319

"We haven't had reports of any members of the Bertelli family on the island."

"Bernie said they're coming after me tomorrow. He said I couldn't call you because the cops are in on this."

"He's wrong about that. Schorr and I aren't in on anything. We'll keep our reports local for now. The Captain has to know, but I trust him with my life."

"What about protective custody? What about Witness Relocation?"

"There are problems with those options. What we'd prefer to do is to have you stay in place where you'll be under surveillance. If we believe Bernie Cashour, then you aren't in danger tonight. Tomorrow is when everything goes down. That gives us time to set up undercover agents at the front and back of your shop, and to do a license checkpoint on the island causeway. No one will get on the island without us knowing."

I understood her plan all too well. She was fishing for mobsters and little ole me was the bait. It made sense. Why should she settle for Bernie when she could catch the mob in action?

"Will I be safe here tonight? What if the mob has my house bugged?"

"I did a cursory check when I got here, but I'll check again now." She walked around the house, careful to stay away from the windows, flipping things over, looking everywhere thoroughly, and finding nothing. "You're good to go. This place is clean."

I must have looked unconvinced.

"We can change the plan. You can go with me now. We don't have to do it this way."

The thought of spending the night here alone seemed unbearable. I was sorely tempted to go with her. But I wanted to catch Bernie. And I wanted to make sure I didn't have to worry about the mob for the rest of my life. "No. We stick with the plan."

The sky opened and rain pelted down. Detective Monroe checked her watch. "I've got to run. Call me on your cell if you get worried."

She left via the side porch exit before I could answer. I was plenty worried. What would she think if I called her before she even cleared my flower beds?

Bernie's threat kept reverberating through my head. He was going to kill me. I burrowed deeper under the covers. I rolled over on my stomach. But no matter what position I tried, sleep refused to come.

Damn him for doing this to me. Double damn him for using me all those years. If he'd told me what picture everyone was looking for, I'd have half a chance to get myself out of this mess. Instead, I was a sitting duck.

When would the mob come for me tomorrow?

God. I hated being helpless.

According to the garish red display on my bedside clock, it was half-past midnight. I padded into the bathroom and closed the door before flipping on the lights. In the mirror, I observed the purplish bruises on my neck.

Bernie was tangled up in something that could get both of us killed for real. Was he out there right now? Hiding in the sand dunes, watching my house? And if he was outside, would he protect me or lead the bad guys on a victory raid? Since I didn't have the picture, I wasn't sure whose side Bernie was on. He may be alive, but the Bernie I'd loved was dead.

If he was out there, I hoped he was drenched from the constant rain.

I wasn't his property, and I certainly wasn't his wife anymore. I'd sold my car to pay for his empty coffin, and he didn't even have the grace to be dead.

It was my own fault I'd been so naive. One of my girlfriends at work had tried to tell me how controlling Bernie was. When I'd mentioned Patty's comments to Bernie, he'd made me promise not to speak to her again. I'd gone along with his wishes, instead of really seeing the true man I'd married.

Back then I didn't want to acknowledge how much he controlled me. Back then, I liked being taken care of. But that was the old MaryBeth. The new MaryBeth made her own decisions.

How could I get myself out of this mess? Bernie wanted a picture from his office. I couldn't fathom why a picture would be that important.

I squeezed my eyes tight. What could I remember about his office junk? There were several framed pictures in the boxes his co-workers had handed me at the memorial service.

One of them was a shot of us dressed up for a New Year's Eve party three years ago. That photo had been in an ugly black plastic frame. I'd saved the picture and sold the frame for a quarter.

Another framed picture was an aerial photo of the Chesapeake Bay. That poster-size print had sold for three dollars at the yard sale.

There had been a copy of the Declaration of Independence. I'd marked that one three dollars, but the history teacher who bought it had bargained me down to a buck-fifty.

The other picture had been of his dream car, a cherry red vintage Mustang. But the frame looked arty, like the ones my mother made. It was heavy too. I remembered taking the car picture out of the stained glass frame and using the frame for something else.

What were the odds that this was the picture Bernie was looking for? A one in four chance. But it was the only lead I had. There must be some people in the background of the photo, people that didn't want to be seen in any photo together. A tingle of excitement shot through me.

If I found the photo and gave it to Bernie, I'd have my life back. So where was the vintage Mustang picture? If I didn't sell it, I still had it.

Somewhere.

It was coming back to me now. I'd put our New Year's Eve photo in a pretty stained glass frame and packed it away. Where was it?

I walked back into the dark bedroom and made sure the curtains were tightly drawn. If someone was out there, I didn't want them to know I was prowling around my house in the middle of the night.

Why couldn't I remember where I put the picture?

With a flashlight, I started going through my dresser drawers and my closet. But Bernie had already searched this house and he hadn't found the picture. Nothing was under my bed either. Nothing but dust bunnies.

I sneezed.

Dang. I hadn't moved in all that long ago. Was this early onset of dementia? I certainly had grounds for losing my mind with all the recent upheaval in my life. I flopped down on my bed and tried to retrace my thoughts.

When I moved in, I had unpacked my meager belongings myself. At the time I'd set up housekeeping, I'd been too upset about Bernie's death and his theft of our savings to want to see his face on a daily basis.

So where was the picture?

It wasn't in plain sight, nor in a cupboard, or Bernie would have already found it. Where was it then? What wasn't in plain sight?

There had been an odd storage space in this room. On the wall across from the bedroom window. I'd placed the dresser in front of it to cover up the ugly entryway. I shoved at my dresser, but it wouldn't budge.

I lugged the drawers out and stacked them on the floor. Then I pushed with all my might until the dresser slid out of the way.

My heart rose in my bruised throat. If this was the picture that Bernie wanted, I had to be careful. One man had already been murdered for the missing item. I didn't want to meet a similar fate.

I flicked open the latch and peered inside the cobwebbed storage area. It was actually the access port to the shower water pipes, but I'd squeezed some personal items in here. My high school yearbooks. An un-framed eight-by-ten portrait of me with my adopted parents done just before my dad died. My perfect attendance certificate from Sunday School. The stack of sympathy cards from my mother's funeral. My old thirty-five mm camera. My wedding album.

As I lifted each item out of the small space, my heart leapt with remembrance. These precious things connected me to my past. I was glad I'd kept them. One day I would want to look through them. But not today.

The picture frame was on the bottom of the stack. I'd wrapped it in a well-worn beach towel. I had to lift it with two hands because it was so heavy. Unfolding the soft terry cloth covering was like opening a present on Christmas morn. Anticipation rushed through my veins.

The pretty stained glass panes were just as lovely as ever. I held the frame so that the flashlight illuminated the brilliant cobalt blues, the stunning reds, the glorious yellows. From the center of the frame, Bernie and I looked out at the photographer. Bernie looking arrogantly sure of himself. I looked besotted with Bernie.

Ugh.

Couldn't think about that now.

Was it the frame Bernie wanted or the picture of his dream car? I studied the frame. The stained glass rectangular border was transparent. No room to hide anything there. The tubular inner support seemed unbroken.

Must be the car photo. I removed the back of the frame and withdrew the car photograph, which I'd stored underneath our New Year's Eve photo. There were no people in the picture. No hidden numbers, no secret message, no license plate either.

Damn Sam.

I'd so hoped I had the right picture here, but I didn't see anything unusual about this photo or frame. Disappointment swamped my senses. Tears welled in my eyes.

I rested the frame on my legs. I'd had a

one in four chance this was the item Bernie wanted. One in four meant that three of the chances were that this wasn't the right frame. I'd guessed wrong.

What would happen if the underworld didn't get their property back? Would they kill Bernie? Would they kill me?

A pins-and-needles sensation radiated from my legs. Stained glass was heavy, but this frame was heavier than all four of my yearbooks combined. I took another look at the frame. With the photo removed from the middle and the glass out, there wasn't any particular place that caught my eye.

Numbness invaded my legs. No tiny key to a storage locker. No hints to where the lost mob property was. The only remarkable structural feature was the tubular support frame rimming the inner edge of the stained glass.

I traced my fingers along the edge of the smooth metal. They glided over the polished surface. That was when I noticed that the bottom corners of the tube seem to be bisected, like a ninety degree angle of a sleeve to a garment. I tugged on the bottom section.

It wiggled.

My heart skipped a beat. I was onto something here. Or I might be destroying this beautiful frame. I hesitated for only a moment. My life was worth more than this frame or its hidden contents.

I tugged with all my might. It wouldn't come off. A hammer would help me open it. I padded into the dark kitchen and retrieved a hammer from my kitchen toolbox. I tap-tap-tapped on the frame until it gradually came apart in my hands.

A deluge of sparkly gems showered down on my legs. Whoa Nellie.

What was this?

Was this what everyone was searching for? My hands played through the gems, and rainbows of light dazzled my eye. Diamonds and lots of them. They were all shapes and sizes. Tiny ones that glittered. Larger diamonds that resembled teardrops.

The diamonds must be what everyone was looking for.

They had to be worth a fortune.

What now? I could give them to Bernie. No way. He'd lied to me repeatedly. I could give them to the police, but then the mob guy would show up and cut off my fingers. I could give them to the mob if I knew how to contact them, but they'd probably kill me for knowing about the diamonds. I could run to the far corners of the earth with my windfall.

Choices.

What was the right one?

God, if I kept the whole lot, I'd never have to work again. I couldn't spend them either because I'd be very dead.

Bad choice.

I needed to get these diamonds to the cops. No matter how scared Bernie was of the rogue New Jersey cop, the ones here weren't part of an organized crime syndicate.

Was it as simple as calling Detective Monroe up and having her come over and get them?

She'd said I was safe here tonight. With the steady rain, I was inclined to believe her. I was safe, and the jewels were safe for tonight.

I didn't want the mob to show up here. No more gunfights in my house. I needed to get the diamonds out of here. I'd take them into work with me and call the cops from there.

I needed to be clever. Creative even, or I'd find myself fingerless.

The best place to hide the diamonds was in plain sight. I could wrap up the picture frame in a box to use as a gift under one of my Christmas trees in the shop. But the gems, how could I get them out of here?

I believed folks were watching the house tonight. Bernie. The cops. Maybe even the mob.

It was imperative that I acted like nothing was wrong. My regular routine consisted of picking up shells in a colorful pail, then taking those shells into the shop.

So, if I dumped the gems in my pail and covered them with seashells, that should look normal. And if I wrapped up several boxes for fake presents, that shouldn't appear out of the ordinary for a Christmas shop owner.

I got an extra pail out of the laundry room. I'd collected these shells a few days ago and left them home because I had so many itty-bitty shells at work. I dumped the shells in a coffee cup, layered the sparkly diamonds on the bottom, then covered them up with the sandy shells.

I checked the time. One in the morning. Now that I had a plan for getting this stuff out of here, I wanted it to be daylight already.

I stacked my personal belongings back in the storage area and sealed it shut. After shoving the dresser back in place, I loaded in all the drawers.

Now I needed to find wrapping paper and boxes so that I could disguise the frame.

Problem. I didn't have any wrapping paper. What did I have?

Toilet paper. Computer paper. Plastic bags from the grocery store. Paper towels. Freezer wrap. Aluminum foil.

Foil would work for Christmas paper.

Okay. I had foil. Now I needed boxes. I didn't keep empty cardboard boxes at home, but my kitchen contained boxes of food. I had a cereal box, a box of instant mashed potatoes, a box of leftover pizza.

I emptied them all. The frame I put in the sturdy pizza box, then I wrapped all the boxes up in foil. For bows, I used the spindle of red yarn in my junk drawer. Satisfaction hummed in my veins as I tied off the loops of yarn. My packages were ready for public viewing. Now what?

It was still four hours until daylight.

If I had a computer at home, I could surf the Internet and find out more about the diamond theft. But my ancient laptop was at work.

Russ would know what to do. I could call him right now and have him look up diamond heists on his home computer.

No. I wouldn't rely on a man to get me out of this mess. I was doing okay on my own. The new MaryBeth Cashour didn't need a man to solve her problems. The new

MaryBeth was empowered and proactive.

My thoughts swirled in the near darkness of my bedroom. For ten years, I'd done everything in my power to make Bernie happy. I'd kept conflict out of our home. I'd had supper on the table when he arrived, prepared the meals he preferred, cooked, cleaned, and shopped.

My slavish devotion hadn't been enough to keep him in my bed. Or to engender his loyalty. What it had been was a colossal waste of my time.

I gritted my teeth. I would get through this.

Then I was going to divorce my dead husband. When they asked me what grounds, I'd tell them to take their pick. Adultery, desertion, cruelty. And any other grounds I could think of.

I flopped back down in bed and watched the torturously slow parade of numbers on my alarm clock. Daylight couldn't come fast enough for me.

CHAPTER 27

The following morning, I pretended all was well when Russ arrived to follow me to work. He eyed the shiny packages. "What are those?"

"Fake presents. Thought I'd spruce up the displays. It won't be long 'til Christmas."

"Sure you're all right?"

I thrust my dark glasses onto my nose. My performance so far deserved an Oscar. "I'm fine." Or I would be as soon as this day was over. He nodded and tailed me to the shop.

After I placed the shiny foil-wrapped packages in the front window of Christmas by the Sea, I went through the motions of opening up for the day. For music, I chose soothing instrumental guitar renditions of non-secular songs.

But the softly plucking strings scraped on my nerves. How could they settle when I had a fortune in diamonds in my back room?

I'd dressed in a kelly green twinset and tan pants and sneakers. A coordinating scarf covered the bruises on my throat. I'd washed my hair, put on mascara. I looked like I did every day of the week.

Unless you looked really closely at the dark circles under my eyes or noticed my trembling hands, you wouldn't know I'd been up all night. Part one of my plan had been successful. I'd gotten myself and the diamonds out of my house. Part two depended on Detective Monroe.

I called her on my cell.

"Monroe."

I heard loud voices in the background. "What's going on?"

"I'm lining up extra help in the squad room. Schorr just phoned in and said you got to work safely. He's watching your shop as we speak."

It felt good knowing he was out there. "Any luck finding Bernie?"

"We haven't sighted him today. But he can't hide for long on an island. We'll catch him."

"Late last night, I remembered a place in the wall where I'd stored some personal items. The shower access panel behind my dresser. I found what they're looking for. The frame was filled with diamonds."

"Hey, knock it off in here. I can't hear myself think," Monroe yelled. The voices quieted. "Say that again."

I repeated my story.

"Where are the diamonds now?"

"In my shop. I don't want to let them out of my sight until you come and get them."

"Good girl. I'll be there in twenty minutes. Sit tight."

"No kidding."

Twinkle lights blinked on and off. I picked up a duster and darted around the room. Twenty minutes and this would be over.

The shop phone rang. I checked the time. Nine-thirty. Too early for business calls. The hair on the back of my neck snapped to attention. With increasing dread, I picked up the receiver. "Christmas by the Sea. How may I help you?"

"I've got the kid." The man's raspy whisper was worthy of a *Godfather* movie. "Bring the picture frame to the dumpster behind the Blue Heron hotel in ten minutes or the kid is dead."

My blood chilled at the clipped words. "What kid?"

"The blond kid with the big dog. The boy that fishes from the marina dock."

I couldn't swallow around the lump in my throat. My hand spasmed on the phone.

Dear God. They'd snatched Tyson Price. His poor mother couldn't take a shock like this on top of her chronic illness.

Hell, I couldn't take the shock either. I had to do better. I didn't recognize my caller's voice. I went over to the front window and looked out. There were no people sitting in parked cars watching the shop. "The boy has nothing to do with this. Let him go."

"He's our insurance policy. Come alone. If you bring those two cops or your pharmacy friend, the kid is dead."

Tyson could be maimed or killed if I made the wrong decision.

Damn Bernie's sorry hide.

Why hadn't I turned in the diamonds and myself to the police last night? Tyson would be safe now. God, I never should've tried to save the world. I should have turned everything over to the cops as soon as possible.

Another innocent had been dragged into his mess. Bernie had a lot to answer for when this was over. If we survived. "How do you know I have the frame?"

The man paused long enough for my heart to stop beating. "We know. Bring it, or the kid and his dog are dead. Don't do anything foolish. We're watching you."

The line went dead.

I staggered over to the counter and sank onto the wooden stool. This wasn't making any sense. If this man knew I had the frame, why didn't he storm my house and take it last night? Why wait until the light of day?

Unless he'd somehow overheard my cell phone conversation with Detective Monroe. My heart sunk.

I scooted behind a Christmas tree and glanced out the front window. About a block away, Bernie leaned against a clunky car. He stared in my direction.

Detective Schorr was nowhere in sight. I should've told the cops about Bernie's note right from the start. Now it was too late, and I had to try and sneak out of here without Schorr or Bernie seeing me leave.

God, help me. Tyson's life hung in the balance. He was only ten years old. Much too young to die. I needed coffee, but I didn't dare waste the time to go next door for a caffeine infusion.

Besides, Daisy Pearl would know something was wrong in a heartbeat. Anyone who had raised two dozen children had a highly developed sense of Mom-radar.

My mom had always known when I was in trouble. So what if she'd hidden the evidence of my adoption? As far as she was concerned, she was my real mom. She'd been there for me in every sense of the word.

Funny how that was so crystal clear right now.

I'd been furious with my mom for not being forthright with me, but now I saw that her omission had nothing to do with lying to me. It had everything to do with how much she loved me as her own daughter. My adoptive status meant nothing to her.

Okay. Enough already. I had to lock up the shop and drive over to the defunct Blue Heron. Nausea and terror rippled through my empty stomach. I felt so inconsequential the stiff wind of today's northeaster could easily have blown me over. My hands shook as I pulled the pizza box back out of the window. A beam of sunshine caught the foil and mirrored a shaft of blinding light into the street.

When Bernie startled at the bright light, I knew he'd seen my hurried movements. He headed for the shop. Crap. Not now. I didn't have time to deal with Bernie. A kid's life was on the line. The diamonds were the only bargaining chip I had to save his life.

I ran to the craft room and collected the pail of shells and diamonds. For good measure, I dumped more shells into the diamond pail. I noticed several of Jolene's congealed glue globs were in the mix. Gotta love that kid.

Then I raced out and jumped in my Jeep. No sign of Schorr. So far, so good. Bernie rounded the building just as I was pulling out. He dove onto my hood. I had no choice but to slam on the brakes, though I can't say the idea of running him over didn't cross my fevered mind.

I rolled down the window and yelled at him. "Get off!"

"Did they call you?"

"I don't have time for this. Get off my car."

His bearded face was inches from my windshield, his brown eyes full of desperation. "They've got Arlene and the boys. Tell me you have the frame."

Not another complication. More lives were on the line. Would the bad guys go on a rampage and massacre everyone on the island? "Shit."

"The frame, MaryBeth. You have it?"

I was so scared for Tyson, so scared for myself. I didn't want to feel anything for trashy Arlene and her sons. But the thought that curled through my mind was the fevered look in Bernie's eyes. I'd never seen him this worried before, not even when I'd been hospitalized for my first miscarriage.

Part of me wanted to soothe him and the

other part of me screamed he was the reason for this disaster. I had to stay focused. "They've got one of my art students. I've got to go."

"I'm coming with you."

I glanced at my watch. Four minutes had passed since I had received the phone call. "Get off my car."

Bernie slid off the hood and opened my door. "Move over. I'm driving."

I didn't budge. If they saw Bernie, they'd probably kill Tyson. "Like hell you are. This is my vehicle. You lost your rights to boss me around when you died."

"You don't know who you're dealing with, MaryBeth. I do. Now move."

"He said to come alone."

"They'll get over it."

Damn him. I didn't want him to come along, but he wasn't listening to me. I moved, carefully straddling the pail of seashells and diamonds that I'd placed on the floor of the passenger side of the Jeep.

He slid into my vacated seat. "Where are we going?"

My stomach did another flip flop at the word "we." How many times had Bernie said that word to me before and not meant it? "The Blue Heron. The hotel that went bankrupt. The dumpster's in back."

He grimaced. "I know it well."

I thought he was waiting for me to get my seat belt buckled. I hurriedly fumbled for the strap and clicked the hitch. "Let's go."

"Not so fast. What's the plan?"

I adjusted my glasses. "The plan? I'm giving them a picture frame, and they're letting Tyson go. That's the plan."

"You said you didn't have the frame yesterday."

"After you left, I remembered that I'd squirreled some personal items away in the wall. I found them late last night. I kept this particular frame because it reminded me of the colorful frames Mama used to make."

"It's trimmed with stained glass?"

I nodded.

"That's the one I need. Where is it?"

"Wrapped up in the back seat."

"Good girl. You might have just saved our lives."

I glanced at my watch again. "We've got to go. He said he'd kill Tyson if I didn't get there in ten minutes."

"They won't kill the kid."

"How do you know?"

Bernie finally shifted into drive and pulled out of the parking lot at a snail's pace. "Because murder is messy. Valerio doesn't want the cops breathing down his neck."

My mouth dropped open. "Valerio? Your old boss at Jesseman and Associates? He's behind all of this? He's connected to the mob?"

"Yeah."

Oh my God. No wonder Valerio had asked for my address. He didn't know where I was until I'd called him looking for Bernie. A wave of dizziness washed over me. I wanted to hit something. So I did.

I punched Bernie in the arm. He deserved that and more. "I cooked dinner for him in our home. You brought the mob home for dinner?"

He flinched. "Get a grip, MaryBeth. Valerio holds our lives in the palm of his hand."

Suddenly my skin seemed too tight. "Not just our lives. Other people are involved. Did he kill Macklin Rudd?"

"Rudd was an idiot. He double-crossed Valerio."

We passed the first hotel on Hotel Row. The scales of the sexy mermaid on the Welcome sign danced hypnotically in the sunlight. My stomach lurched something awful. Nausea and cold chills wracked my frame. I fumbled for the door handle. "Stop the car!"

Bernie stopped. Even through the swirl of nausea, I realized I couldn't leave the diamonds in the Jeep with him. I bolted from the Jeep, plastic pail in hand, and had dry heaves on the sand dune behind the sexy mermaid. Wind whipped my pants against my legs like a sail straining against a headwind. Sweat oozed from my pores.

God. If I messed this up, these men would kill us all, just like they'd killed Mac Rudd. They'd asked me for the frame. I was willing to give them the frame, but if they didn't have the diamonds, that might give me enough time to get Tyson to safety. Okay. I'd leave the diamonds here, under the mermaid sign.

I dumped out the seashells and the diamonds, then made sure the diamonds were well buried. I wiped the drool from my mouth, picked up the empty pail, and stumbled back to the Jeep.

"What's with the pail?" Bernie asked.

I had to keep my cool. Bernie wouldn't think much of my plan to thwart the diamond thieves. I reached for my seat belt twice before I got it. "After I was sick to my stomach, I covered everything up with seashells."

Bernie shook his head. "God. You'll never change. The world isn't a neat and tidy place. A little vomit won't hurt a sand dune. Especially in this wind. It'll be buried before we leave the parking lot."

I gazed out the window at the storm clouds hovering over the well-endowed mermaid. One could only hope.

CHAPTER 28

Dark storm clouds hung low in the sky. Beyond the low-lying sand dunes, whitecaps foamed against the windswept shore. With this storm system blowing in, the beach was deserted. My chances of being rescued by a casual passerby were nil.

I didn't know what happened to Detective Schorr. Looked like I had to rescue myself.

And Tyson.

A dark sedan with tinted windows waited in the Blue Heron rear parking lot. The car should have seemed small in the wide open space, but it looked like a giant, evil toad. My stomach lurched again. My head whirled with doubt. Maybe I shouldn't have hidden the diamonds.

But then I wouldn't have anything to bargain with, and I needed leverage. I clutched my hands together in my lap and prayed.

Bernie parked two car lengths away from

the sedan. He shot me a patronizing look. "Stay here." He reached back for the gift-wrapped frame.

God. I hated it when he talked down to me. I didn't care how dangerous this situation was, I wasn't letting Bernie call the shots. I snatched the foil-wrapped box out of his hand. "I'll carry the box."

His jaw dropped open. He fisted his empty hands. "Don't be a hero. Heroes get shot."

I wish I had a camera to capture his thunderstruck expression. If I died right now, at least I would know that I'd shocked him so much, he'd finally let me have my way.

He wasn't getting the package back. A man who faked his death rather than stand up to these guys six months ago had no credibility with me. Nausea assailed me again. I fought it back, clutching the package to my chest. My chin jutted forward. "They are not getting this picture frame until I see Tyson Price."

I sounded brave, but my bones felt hollow, as if the calcium had been removed and all that remained of my skeleton was a hollow shell. Pizza box in hand, I stepped out of the Jeep. Bernie trotted around and stood beside me.

We could have been posing for a picture of Ma and Pa Kettle. Just two old married folks standing in a windy parking lot. Facing down the mob.

Frankie Valerio's driver got out of the car. I recognized him at once. That stocky build, wavy black hair, and beefy palms could only belong to one person. Eddie Sawyer. I thought he was in jail up in Richmond. He must have had a good lawyer. Duh. Of course. The mob wouldn't keep a bad one on the payroll.

Eddie had worn similar charcoal gray slacks and a navy polo shirt to dinner at my house last New Year's Eve. But the gun was a new fashion accessory.

Were all of Bernie's co-workers in the mob?

Why had I thought I was brave enough to carry this off? My eyes glistened with tears. If that wasn't bad enough, my knees trembled, my palms sweated, and my stomach churned.

Eddie pointed his gun in our direction. "Throw down your weapon, Cashour."

I was about to yell back that I didn't believe in weapons, when Bernie tossed a gunmetal gray pistol on the sand-swept pavement. My mouth went dry.

This was deadly serious. These people carried guns. They shot people who crossed them. My no-good husband carried a gun.

I craned my neck to look up at the stranger who had masqueraded as my husband for ten years. Something inside me snapped. "Since when did you start carrying a gun?"

His eyebrows arched high under his camouflage cap brim. Sad brown eyes peered intently at me through his oversized glasses. I got the message. He'd been carrying a gun for as long as he'd been married to me.

Ten long, lying years.

God, what a naive little fool I'd been.

"You got the merchandise?" Eddie asked.

That remark was directed at me. I hoped I was up for the acting performance of my lifetime. With both hands, I lifted the heavy foil package above my head. "Right here."

From inside the car, Valerio spoke, his voice low and guttural and indecipherable. I squinted into the gloomy depths of the sedan. No sign of a blond-haired kid. God. Where was Tyson? Was he tied up in the trunk? I had to get him away from these men.

Eddie cocked his head in my direction, his eyes and his gun trained on us. "Show me."

I tore the foil from the pizza box, handing the wadded wrapping to Bernie, who hovered at my elbow. Would he try to rip the picture frame from my hands? I imagined he wanted to use it to bargain for Arlene and her boys just as much as I needed it to save Tyson.

The image of a whole pizza adorned the box. My stomach knotted at the faint odor of pepperoni wafting up at me. I couldn't bear to think about food right now. I handed the empty box to Bernie. He tossed it on the ground. I held the stained glass frame over my heart, hoping I wouldn't be the next item discarded.

I locked my knees to keep them from trembling. Once I got Tyson we'd run out on the beach, far away from mobsters with guns. "Here's the frame. Let me see the boy."

I couldn't stop my mind from racing. Their faces weren't covered. In the movies, the bad guys always killed the folks that could identify them. I had no weapon of any kind. Just my wits and the knowledge that the cops should be combing the island for me.

With my skittering brain, my nervous stomach, and this empty glass frame, the odds of my long-term survival weren't that good. Where the hell were the cops when I needed them?

"For God's sakes, give him the picture frame, MaryBeth," Bernie urged.

Determination warred against common sense. People with courage weren't necessarily brave. But they were stubborn and so was I. My priority hadn't changed. Tyson's freedom was my immediate goal. "I want to see Tyson."

Eddie motioned us over with a flick of his wrist. Sunlight glinted off the gun in his hand. Oh, God. I was going to die. Right here in this deserted parking lot. My seemingly wooden feet shuffled toward the gun.

"Where's Tyson?" I peered at the tinted windows as wind whipped sand and salt spray around the empty parking lot. Overhead a solitary gull cried. The sun slid behind a cloud.

"How the hell should I know?" Eddie answered. "Hands in the air, both of you."

This wasn't the ending I'd envisioned. How could I achieve my goal if they were changing the story line? More to the point, how could I save Tyson if he was elsewhere? "You don't have him?"

Eddie shrugged, his gun leveled at Bernie's heart. "Why should I grab the kid when I can get the same results by telling you I grabbed the kid?"

Bernie peered intently at the tinted glass windows. His shoulders sagged. "You don't have Arlene and the boys either, do you?"

Eddie guffawed. "You fell for the oldest trick in the book. Some G-man you are, Cashour."

Bernie and I exchanged glances. We'd both been fooled by their threats, but I wouldn't change a thing I'd done. Tyson was safe, and that was what mattered most to me. My new priority was to save my own neck.

I wouldn't sit back and passively do everything I was told to do. I'd done enough of that for one lifetime. Bravado shot out of my mouth like a fiery cannonball. "You'll never get away with this. Sandy Shores is an island. The cops will catch you before you hit the causeway."

Eddie aimed the gun at my heart. "If you called the cops, you're dumber than I thought. I'll shoot you so fast you won't even realize you're dead. Where are the diamonds?"

"Rudd hid them in the picture frame," Bernie's voice rose as he spoke.

"Show me," Eddie said.

Bernie took the frame from me and with some difficulty opened it. I could have shown him how to do it, but that would have spoiled the surprise. Bernie's befuddled expression at the lack of diamonds pretty much said it all.

"What's this?" Eddie asked, jabbing his gun into Bernie's broad chest.

"I don't know." Bernie shook the frame and peered into the empty tube again.

A trickle of laughter bubbled up my throat. I fought the urge to laugh at the dumbfounded look on Bernie's face. He wasn't going to find a single diamond in that frame.

"She's been under constant surveillance except for your drive here," Eddie said. "She has to have them."

Eddie's aside to Bernie confused me. Was Bernie on my side or theirs? I couldn't tell, which made me glad I'd hidden the diamonds. The longer I dragged this out, the more chance I had of being rescued.

Bernie's face glowed bright red. "Mary-Beth?"

I took the picture frame back in my hands. It wouldn't stop a bullet, but I needed to hold onto something. "You people think I'm a dumb female, and maybe I am, but I've got more sense than to bring a fortune in gems out here. Let's make a deal. I want to live, and you want the diamonds. You with me so far?"

"This is a very bad idea, MaryBeth," Bernie warned. "Just give them the diamonds."

I clutched the frame to my chest. "I'm

tired of being played for a fool and taking orders from you. I make my own decisions now. Got it? Put that in your pipe and smoke it."

"We've got a problem, boss," Eddie said.

"The diamonds, MaryBeth. Where are they?" Bernie was using his no-nonsense voice, the voice he always used when he told me there was no point discussing this further because he'd already made up his mind. No way was I going back to that kind of intellectually stifling mindset. I'd rather die here in this parking lot.

I glared at Eddie and Bernie. Bernie could be pretending to go along with me to gain my cooperation. He could've been hiding out with the mob for the last six months for all I knew. Anger fueled my rash words. "When this is over, I expect you people to leave this island and never come here again. Is that understood?"

Frankie Valerio emerged from the car. His paunchy stomach hung over his belt. A passerby seeing his striped golf shirt and pressed trousers might think he was on vacation. He was taller than Bernie, taller and meaner looking. The nasty glint in his eye caused a huge lump to form in my throat.

He flexed his fingers, then he took something from his pocket. A shiny metal object, which fit over his knuckles. In a lightning fast move, he double pumped his fisted hand into Bernie's gut.

Bernie dropped to the ground like a sack of potatoes.

The blood drained from my face. I swayed on my feet. How could I have forgotten for one second these people had already killed once for those diamonds?

Frankie ripped the picture frame right out of my hands and smashed it on the ground. Shards of colored glass scattered over the sandy pavement. I bit my lip, the pain bringing me startling clarity.

Would he hit me next?

His cruel smile chilled my blood. "Good. You're finally taking this seriously. I don't like hitting women, but I'll do whatever it takes to get my three million dollars' worth of diamonds back."

Bernie writhed on the ground, a thin line of blood trickling from his mouth. "Give him the diamonds, MaryBeth."

"Shut up." Frankie stepped on Bernie's glasses with a sickening crunch. He kicked Bernie in the ribs.

I clasped my trembling hands to my breastbone. No way would I survive a direct hit of his meaty fists. "I don't have them."

Bernie moaned. Whether in pain or frustration I didn't know.

I glanced down at Frankie's foot as he prepared to kick Bernie again. I was so scared I could barely think. Somehow I found my voice. "But I know where they are."

CHAPTER 29

Frankie waved his fist in my face. The sight of those brass knuckles made my knees go weak. My lungs froze in mid-inhale, but that was all right. I wouldn't need air if he punched me the way he hit Bernie.

He struck my shoulder with a glancing blow. "I don't have time for games. You double-cross me, and you're gonna wish you were dead."

Air whooshed out of my lungs from the impact. I staggered backward. My glasses slid down my nose, and I panicked. He was going to kill me and I'd never see it coming. I scrambled to right my glasses. Waves of pain emanated from my shoulder.

My brain reverted to fire mentality — stop, drop, and roll, but I was afraid to take my gaze off of Frankie and Eddie. I didn't want to find out how much pain I could endure. My shoulder throbbed like crazy.

Mac Rudd's bloated face swam into my

thoughts. He'd scammed them, and he was dead. I wanted to hit Frankie back, but survival was my main goal. My wits were the only weapon I had. I'd better start using them. I trembled visibly. MaryBeth-the-coward had already used up her allotment of bravery and courage for the year.

All I had left was fear.

Fear was a powerful motivator.

Eddie duct-taped Bernie's hands together behind his back, then tossed him in the back of Frankie's car. My hands were taped together, just like Bernie's. A wave of the gun, and I was tossed in the front seat.

"Which way?" Eddie asked, as if he were a cab driver and I was his paying fare.

I directed him along Ocean Drive to the mermaid sign. The sun came out from behind the clouds in blinding intensity. As we drove, I tried to let my fear work for me. If I could just start a chain of rational thoughts, perhaps they would lead some-where. Otherwise, I had nothing.

I chewed my lip for clarity. Time to take stock. I'd hidden the diamonds to bargain for Tyson's life. He wasn't at risk right now, I was. But once I dug up the buried gems, what would keep them from killing me? I had to be resourceful. The cops sure weren't rushing to my rescue.

Eddie turned into the parking lot of the Island Suites Hotel. I breathed a sigh of relief at the sight of cars in the parking lot. They couldn't shoot me in front of witnesses. Another car pulled in behind us and drove to the sheltered check-in area.

I pointed to the sand dune just off the road. "There. I buried the diamonds beneath the mermaid sign."

Frankie leveled his gun at Bernie's head. "If you're playing with me, he's dead."

A blast of wind buffeted the car. I saw a flash of color through the window. Along the exterior corridor of the hotel's second floor, a dark-haired maid pushed a white laundry cart. As I watched, she ducked into a numbered room.

Great. Not a soul outside to hear me yell for help. I might as well be back at the Blue Heron. So much for my hope of witnesses.

I couldn't give in to my fear. I had to believe I would get out of this mess.

If only I was allowed to get out of the vehicle. Once in the parking lot, someone might notice my hands were duct-taped together.

Where the hell were the cops?

Reality intruded. Once the mobsters had the diamonds, I was dead. I should've touched base with Detective Monroe before

I rushed out to rescue Tyson. Where was Detective Schorr? He was supposed to be watching me.

Oh, for a rewind button to start this lousy morning over.

"How you want to play this, boss?" Eddie asked.

Frankie reached over the seat and grabbed a hank of my hair. "Bring me the diamonds, bitch, or I'll blow his brains out right before your eyes."

Tears blurred my vision. Getting killed wasn't part of my plan. I was supposed to be rescued by now. Why the hell wasn't my brain working? My goal was to get out of the car, and it looked like that was going to happen.

I seized on that thought. To escape, I needed a plan. All I had was a queasy stomach, a two-timing husband, and the knowledge that Eddie had already killed once for these diamonds. I blinked back my tears. "I'll get the diamonds, but I can't dig them up with my hands taped behind my back."

Frankie cursed. "Cut her loose, Eddie." He yanked my hair again. "You give me a minute's trouble, and I'll chop your fingers off one by one. Then I'll start on your toes."

Eddie whipped a carpet knife out of his

pocket, pushed my face down in my lap so that my bound hands were exposed. The sharp blade sliced through skin and tape, but my hands were free. I stumbled from the car with cuffs of duct tape stuck on the fronts of my wrists. Eddie followed me.

My shoulder and wrists ached. I was sure I was going to throw up any minute the way my stomach kept jumping around. Think, MaryBeth. You're going to dig up the diamonds. Then what?

Then you're going to find something to throw at Eddie. That's when you're going to run away. With any luck, someone will come along, and Eddie won't shoot you in front of a witness. Bernie would have to fend for himself. I'd probably have to spend the rest of my life at the police station to keep from having my digits amputated, but at least I'd be alive.

Sand swirled through the parking lot. A northeaster. That's what the locals called a big blow like this. Grains of coarse sand gritted in my teeth as I staggered to the sign.

The mound of shells was nowhere to be seen. They wouldn't have moved unless someone took them, but they could be covered by blowing sand. Was all my scheming for naught? Anguish stilled my heart, froze my lungs. Time stalled, and my life flashed before my eyes.

Snapshots from the past overwhelmed my emotions. My mom on her deathbed. Bernie's red face as we argued before he disappeared. My father's beaming face as he pushed me in the tree swing.

No.

I couldn't give up. I would find those diamonds. And something solid to throw at Eddie.

I fell to my knees and pawed through the sand like a hound on a scent. Blood from my wrists trickled down my hands. My thoughts were stuck on oh-God, oh-God, oh-God.

I crawled farther behind the sign. Eddie's dark shadow covered me. His gun was tucked out of sight from a casual observer, but it was clearly visible to me on the ground. "I can't find the diamonds," I said, allowing fear to coat my words. "I put them right here."

"Find them or sleep with the sharks tonight," Eddie snarled. "Your choice."

"What's taking so long?" Frankie called from the car.

"MaryBeth, don't do anything stupid," Bernie yelled.

Stupid was all I had left as both hands fisted over the seashells, the diamonds, and one of Jolene's giant glue gobs. "Found 'em!" Triumphantly, I stood in the strong wind, bracing my legs to keep from being blown over, and showed my finds to Eddie.

As my left hand opened and the diamonds sparkled in the sunlight, Eddie plucked a glittering teardrop diamond off my palm. He made the mistake of looking back at Frankie and nodding. I fired off both fists full of projectiles at Eddie's unprotected face. The giant glue gob whammed him right between the eyes like a fat bullet. As my right arm came down, I simultaneously stripped the gun from his hand and kicked him hard in the groin.

I heard a ruckus coming from the car. I hoped Bernie wasn't dead, but he'd made his bed. I picked up the gun and ran into the road right in front of Detective Monroe and about twenty other cops.

Ten minutes later, Eddie and Frankie were cuffed and in police custody. Bernie was also handcuffed with his hands in front, but he sat on the curb. I glared down at him, so full of emotion I didn't trust myself to speak.

As a paramedic examined his vital signs, Bernie glanced up at me. He must have mistaken my silence for sympathy. "That's my girl."

I inched away from him. "I'm not your girl anymore."

Bernie managed a half-smile. "I knew if I told you not to do something stupid, you would."

"You're lucky I'm so contrary these days. The old me would have listened to you."

"We need to talk, MaryBeth."

"I don't have anything to say to you."

"You're still my wife."

"Really? My husband is dead, and I have the papers to prove it. As I recall, you have another wife and kids who want you. I don't. Goodbye."

Bernie glared at me. "Who the hell are you, and what have you done with my sweet, compliant MaryBeth?"

CHAPTER 30

"Don't yell at me!" I hated Bernie for what he'd put me through. I massaged my aching shoulder and spat sand from my mouth. If only it were that easy to be rid of my husband.

I glanced down at my clothes, surprised to see that I wasn't covered in blood. My bold kelly green twinset taunted me with its brightness. The feel-good color might as well have been poison ivy green for all the misery I'd been through today.

Sand caked in my eyelashes, fouled my glasses. I could taste salt on my lips. A migraine pounded behind one throbbing temple. My teeth chattered with cold. But one fact was crystal clear. I was alive.

And my dead husband wanted things to be like they'd been before he disappeared. Fat chance.

If Frankie hadn't already hit Bernie, I would've smacked him. Hard. He believed he could just waltz back into my life and pick up where he'd left off. No way in hell.

The paramedics loaded Bernie onto a stretcher. He caught my hand and cradled it tenderly, just like he'd done a million times before. Back in the day when I thought he was my faithful and loving husband. I shuddered and tried to pull away.

"This isn't settled, hon." His insistent yet patronizing tone irritated the crap out of me.

Anger welled up, harsh and ugly. I voiced my pent-up rage, something the old Mary-Beth wouldn't have done because she didn't like to make waves. Conversely, I wanted to make so many big waves that Bernie would drown in them.

"Damn you, Bernie Cashour. You can't expect everything to be like it was before you died."

The male paramedic lost track of Bernie's pulse as he stared at me. I glared at him until he looked away. I didn't have time to explain Bernie's resurrection to every Tom, Dick, and Harry.

Bernie's fingers tightened around my hand. "Now, hon, don't be that way."

I considered cutting my hand off to get away from him. I wanted to go lock myself in my house with a dozen molten chocolate cupcakes. I wanted to burrow under every blanket I owned because I was so damned cold, I could barely think straight. But I was not stupid enough to buy Bernie's lines.

He was a jerk. A lying, thieving bigamist. I wanted him out of my life. I didn't care if he had broken ribs or ruptured internal organs. He had to deal with reality right now, because I couldn't stand being around him.

As the stretcher moved toward the ambulance, Bernie kept his tight grip on my hand. "I'm not giving up on us. Valerio threatened to kill us both if I didn't give him the diamonds. At the time, I didn't know Rudd had hidden them in the stained glass frame he gave me. I figured if I faked my death, Valerio would leave you alone."

"I don't believe you. Stop lying to me. Your plan sucked, Bernie. Valerio came down here after me. He didn't care who he killed as long as he got his diamonds. Your cowardice made a bad situation worse. I'll never forgive you for what you put me through."

"I love you, MaryBeth." Sincerity dripped from Bernie's words. "I never stopped loving you."

I squashed a tiny flicker of sympathy. Liars lied. I tuned back into my anger. He'd cheated on me and stolen from me — for years. "What happened to your loyalty and integrity? You didn't cherish or protect me. You left me hanging out to dry, Bernie."

"You're wrong, hon. I protected you. When I heard Rudd was looking for you, I came down here to watch out for you."

Outrage boiled through me, giving me the strength of five women. I wrenched my hand free and flexed my stiff fingers. Then I leaned closer. "Leave me alone. I don't ever want to see you again. You abandoned me. You broke my heart. Go back to your other wife and kids."

Bernie's jaw gaped as if he couldn't believe what he was hearing. "Hon, give me another chance."

I shook my head and backed up. "You don't get it. I'm hiring a lawyer and divorcing your sorry ass."

He turtled his head up to look at me. "We can have it all again, hon. It'll be better this time, I swear."

I shook my head dismissively. "I won't let you con me again. Tell me this, if you were so selfless, why were you openly living with another woman and her sons?"

Confusion flickered across Bernie's heavily whiskered face. "Those boys need me."

Bingo. I was right not to trust him. "Then

by all means, stay with Arlene and her boys. You're not getting me back. I won't live a lie again."

"It wasn't like that." He blinked rapidly. "Let me explain."

I leaned down into his face. "Don't presume to tell me what it was like. I wasted ten years of my life on you. I've built a new life down here, and I don't want you in it. Is that clear?"

The paramedics prepared to lift the stretcher.

Bernie lunged for me again. "Don't leave me, hon." His voice wavered.

Be tough, I told myself as I stepped away from him. Don't believe his alligator tears. "There is no *us* anymore. My mom had a saying that fits this situation. Fool me once shame on you, fool me twice shame on me. I won't make the same mistake twice."

The paramedics hoisted Bernie up in the ambulance. As they closed the doors, I heard Bernie telling the paramedic, "She'll come around."

I turned and walked smack into Detective Shanelle Monroe. She steadied me with a hand to my good shoulder. Concern shone in her brown eyes. She asked, "I have paperwork for you back at the station. All finished here?"

The siren wailed on the departing ambulance. I watched it leave the parking lot, relieved that I could finally close the book on a miserable chapter of my life. "Yeah. I'm through."

CHAPTER 31

"Where were you people?" I wrapped the blanket tightly around me. My hands wouldn't stop trembling. A cup of steaming coffee sat in front of me on the table at the busy police station, but I was too over-wrought to hold it.

Detective Monroe looked up from her report and frowned at me. "We were on our way when a call came in about a fire down at the marina. We split up, and I drove directly to your shop. You weren't there. I thought I told you to stay put."

"I planned on staying put. Then they called and said they had one of my art students. They said they'd kill him if I didn't bring them the frame. I wasn't too worried about my safety because I figured Detective Schorr would be right behind me. Where is he?"

"Someone bashed Schorr on the head. We found him in the bamboo thicket at the edge of your parking lot. He's already been transported over to the hospital for observation."

Fear for him furrowed my brow. "Is he all right?"

"Takes more than a bump on the head to keep Schorr down. Something tells me he'll be dating a solid string of nurses for the next little while."

I had no doubt that Detective Hottie would score with the nurses. "I bet Bernie hit him. Eddie Sawyer and Frankie Valerio were waiting for us at the Blue Heron. What's the truth about Bernie? Is he a fed or is he mob?"

"We're still checking into that. His cover was buried pretty deep if he's a fed, but even if he was a fed, he could've changed sides."

I rubbed my gritty face. "God. I'm so tired of lies. I want this to be over."

"It's almost over. What inspiration drove you to hide the diamonds?"

"It wasn't so much inspiration as opportunity." I shivered at the memory. "I was sick to my stomach and couldn't leave the diamonds in my Jeep with Bernie. I realized if I handed over the diamonds, they'd have no reason to keep me alive. I wanted to live."

"You did good. By your quick thinking,

we got Cashour and the diamond thieves. And you may have caught an extra break. There's a sizeable reward posted for these diamonds."

"A reward? I can scarcely fathom it. I'm so glad to be alive. How does this all tie together? I know Mac Rudd stole the diamonds from Valerio. Who killed Rudd?"

"Sawyer. He trailed Rudd down here, not knowing you were the reason Rudd was here. They agreed to meet at the fishing pier late at night. When Rudd didn't fork over the diamonds, Sawyer found out Rudd hid the diamonds in a picture frame in Bernie's office. With Bernie supposedly dead, all Sawyer needed to do was to track you down. He shot Rudd and tossed him in the ocean. But Sawyer didn't consider the tides when he got rid of Rudd. He didn't wash out to sea."

Mac Rudd's dead body rolled in my thoughts. "No, he didn't. After today, I don't have any trouble picturing Sawyer as a thug, but back in Maryland, I had no idea. He sure conned me."

"That was his job. How did Valerio and Sawyer find you?"

I groaned. "I found them. I called Valerio to ask questions about Bernie when we first suspected he might be alive. Valerio asked for my address, and I gave it to him. That wasn't too smart, was it?"

"What wasn't smart was you not staying put this morning. These people are ruthless. You were very lucky we came along when we did."

I tried a sip of my coffee. "How did you find me?"

"It's an island. Once we realized the marina fire was a diversion, we started sweeping the main roads."

"I'll bet Bernie set that fire."

"He well could've. We'll get his statement at the hospital later today."

"Is he going to jail?"

"He'll be detained until we learn the truth of his involvement. Meanwhile, we can hold him on assault charges. Believe me, there will be a full investigation on his disappearance and resurrection. He won't be bothering you anytime soon."

I took another sip of my coffee. Warmth filled me, warmth and determination. "I don't want him to bother me again for any reason. I'd like to file a restraining order and anything else you can think of to keep him away from me."

Monroe beamed. "Not a problem."

CHAPTER 32

John Curtis finally got his wish. Since I didn't finish up at the police station until a little after three, I had nothing prepared for my craft students. Hence, today's class would consist of painting plastic sharks.

That is, if any kids showed up. I couldn't blame their parents if they kept their kids away. The cops had been right about my being connected to Mac Rudd's murder. All of the recent crime on the island was a direct result of my having moved to Sandy Shores.

But I'd helped to bring the criminals to justice this morning, so maybe I wouldn't be blackballed. Like an actor with a show-must-go-on motto, I didn't want to let the kids down. And I could tell them that the scary man wouldn't be bothering them anymore.

Damn Bernie for terrorizing the kids.

I wasn't going to ruin everything by thinking of him. Craft time was about the children enjoying creativity. So I should do all I could to make this experience pleasant and welcoming.

With the shop being shut up all day, the air seemed stale. I turned on the freestanding countertop fans and enjoyed the breeze for a moment. Then I lugged out a bin of sharks. I shivered at the sight of their jagged teeth. A real mob boss had offered to let me sleep with the sharks tonight.

Putting that thought aside, I laid out old newspapers on the table. Where was the red paint? I rummaged in drawers until I found some. A bottle of red paint went between each set of chairs. A paint brush went at every seat.

I wiggled my sore shoulder. The paramedics thought it was bruised, so I'd taken some ibuprofen and promised to get it X-rayed later.

I was lucky to be alive, luckier still to have a decent life, one that didn't involve the criminal underworld. Hopefully this would be my one encounter with the darker side of life. From here on in, I would definitely walk the straight and narrow path.

It felt like I was forgetting something. What was missing? It was too quiet in here.

Music. I needed music.

I perused the CD rack. I didn't feel like barking dogs, didn't want glorious heavenly choirs proclaiming alleluia. I needed David and Goliath music. Something that reflected that little, insignificant me had survived against all odds.

The "Little Drummer Boy" wasn't exactly right, but it suited my mood. One person. One person who only knew how to do one thing well. And it had been enough for salvation.

I painted a test shark. Gentle drumming filled the airwaves. What was my one thing? What did I have to offer someone? Why had I survived my encounter with the mob but Mac Rudd had died?

Somehow I didn't think stubbornness counted. Or knee-knocking fear. I had both of those in spades. But I also had — faith.

I believed help would come, if I kept making chances for myself. I hung onto my wits, and I didn't let fear rule my thoughts. Of course it helped that I didn't have a bullet between the eyes or lodged in my heart. That would have greatly altered my survival chances.

The door opened. I whirled to see who was brave enough to spend an hour with me. John Curtis flashed me a huge smile over the platter of chocolate cupcakes he carried. His eyes lit on the sharks and his gap-toothed smile grew wider.

"Cool. Christmas sharks!" He set the platter down on the back counter and raced to the shark bin. Withdrawing handfuls of sharks, he sat down and immediately began painting.

Daytona skipped in holding baby Gwen. "Hey, Mary Christmas! See who I brought? It's my day to hold the baby."

Daisy Pearl came in on Daytona's heels with another tray of refreshments. I saw a pitcher of lemonade and a carafe of coffee amidst the cups.

"What's all this?" I asked as I lifted the coffee carafe off the tray.

Daisy Pearl set the tray on the back counter and immediately started filling cups with lemonade. "A celebration is in order. You've had quite the day, haven't you?"

Unexpectedly, my eyes misted. I couldn't pull off being strong if Daisy Pearl reminded me of what happened today. "Well, yeah."

"But you didn't want to disappoint the kids, did you?"

I shook my head to the time of the rum-pa-pum-pum. All of a sudden, I didn't feel so good. My stomach leapt into my throat. I wanted to bawl my eyes out. My chin started quivering.

Daisy Pearl took one look at me, then wrapped me in her arms. "It's all right, baby girl. You're safe now."

My breath came in ragged bursts. I breathed in the solid essence of this wonderful woman who had a big enough heart to raise twenty-four children. Thank God she had room for one more. "I was so scared," I mumbled into her ample chest.

Her hand soothed the back of my head. "You should've been, but you done good. I'm proud of how you handled yourself. All those bad men are in jail now."

"I'm sorry I brought these bad men down here to your island."

"You did no such thing. If you blame yourself for any of this, I'm going to string you up by your heels. Got that?"

"Yeah."

"Now, eat a cupcake. You'll feel better."

Daytona strolled by, humming to the baby in her arms. John Curtis smeared red paint all over his hands. He held one hand up as a pretend shark fin and chased his sister around the table.

Daisy Pearl snagged the baby from Daytona's arms and sat down with a cup of coffee. The Barbers came in next. Steven's dad looked inside, saw Daisy Pearl, then ushered his kids in.

"Won't you stay for a cupcake, Mr. Barber?" I asked.

"No, thanks. I wanted to make sure everything was okay in here."

I flashed him a grin that welled up from the tips of my toes. "Yeah. It's okay in here."

Steven and Claudia Barber helped themselves to cupcakes and Christmas sharks. Tyson came in next. My heart leapt at the sight of him, whole and healthy. Thank God Frankie hadn't grabbed the blond-haired boy. I motioned him into the room. "Come on in. We're having a party."

Tyson sat down next to Claudia, which earned him a fierce scowl from Jolene, who entered next. I explained about the Christmas shark crafts and the cupcakes while Jolene wandered around the room.

A few moments later, I noticed her sitting directly across from Tyson. On her plate were globs of glue dotted with shiny sequins and tiny shells. Her tenacity made me smile. Her glue globs had helped stun Eddie, so who was I to complain about her craft choices?

Maybe we could find a way to market the little missiles.

"Frosty the Snowman" came on next. The children sang along, and I caught Daisy Pearl's gaze and smiled. It was chaos in here, but it was healthy chaos. I loved being around the children, loved being a part of their lives.

Russ poked his head in the door. His sharp gaze flicked up and down my length after he assessed the pint-sized occupants of the room. "Am I invited to this party?"

He'd shed his pharmacy coat, and he looked like a regular guy, albeit one with a keen intensity about his whisker-darkened jaw. Was it wrong that my heart leapt at the sight of him? I didn't know what to do about that little problem. "Sure."

Gosh. There were so many things I wanted to say to Russ, like, "Whoops I found my dead husband, and he's alive." But I couldn't blurt out something personal like that in front of these kids. "How was your trip to the podiatrist this morning?"

"It took longer than I wanted. Seems there was some excitement on the island in my absence. I expect a full accounting."

"Later." I managed a wholesome smile. Not the one I wanted to flash him that said much more.

Friends and family. That's what life was about. I'd found both here in Sandy Shores.

"Look at my shark, Mary Christmas," John Curtis said.

I glanced at the shark swimming before

my eyes. It was indeed a unique rendition. He'd painted narrow racing stripes down the length of the shark. It looked like an aquatic candy cane, albeit one with bloody teeth and fins. A laugh bubbled out of my throat at the comical sight.

"Wow, John Curtis. I may have to hire you to make those for my shop."

Daisy Pearl pursed her lips. "Don't be putting fanciful ideas in this boy's head. I need him next door at Sweet Things."

"Oh, I'm sure there's plenty of John Curtis to go around."

John Curtis ran over to show Russ his shark, and I felt like the jolly, happy soul with a corncob pipe and two eyes made out of coal.

Unlike Frosty, I wasn't returning to the hills of snow. On Sandy Shores Island I'd found my true place in the sun.

ABOUT THE AUTHOR

A scientist by training, a romanticist at heart, **Maggie Toussaint** loves to solve puzzles. Whether it's the puzzle of a relationship or a whodunit, she tackles them with equal aplomb and wonder. Maggie's previous cozy mysteries are *In For a Penny* and *On the Nickel*. Her other published works are romantic suspense books, one of which won Best Romantic Suspense in the 2007 National Readers Choice Awards. She freelances for a weekly newspaper. Visit her at www.maggietoussaint.com.